THE BACCHANTES

Borgo Press Books by LÉON DAUDET

The Bacchantes: A Dionysian Scientific Romance
The Napus: The Great Plague of the Year 2227

THE
BACCHANTES

A DIONYSIAN
SCIENTIFIC ROMANCE

LÉON DAUDET

Translated by Brian Stableford

THE BORGO PRESS
MMXII

CLASSICS OF
FANTASTIC LITERATURE
NUMBER THREE

THE BACCHANTES

FIRST ENGLISH LANGUAGE EDITION

Published by Wildside Press LLC

www.wildsidebooks.com

THE BACCHANTES

CONTENTS

INTRODUCTION

Les Bacchantes, romain contemporain by Léon Daudet, here translated as *The Bacchantes*, was originally published in Paris by Ernest Flammarion in 1931. It was the third of four novels by the author venturing on to the terrain of the roman scientifique, following a satire on the medical profession (to which the author had been refused permanent entry after failing his internship), *Les Morticoles* [The Morticoles] (1894), and a story of catastrophe, including but not restricted to a future war, *Le Napus, fléau de l'an 2227* [*The Napus: The Great Plague of the Year 2227*] (1927). It was followed in 1934 by another future war story, *Ciel en feu* [Sky on Fire] (1934). The author also wrote several speculative short stories, four of which are included in the posthumous *Quinze Contes* [Fifteen Stories] (1948).[1]

Léon Daudet's literary career, like those of his mother Julia (née Allard), his Uncle Ernest and his younger brother Lucien, was inevitably overshadowed by the enormous reputation of his father, Alphonse Daudet (1840-1897), one of the great French writers of the nineteenth century. Alphonse Daudent made his initial reputation as a Naturalist of a considerably milder and more sentimental stripe than Émile Zola, Edmond Goncourt or Joris-Karl Huysmans, many of his works being autobiograph-ical, although he scored his greatest popular success with the more extravagant *Tartarin of Tarascon* (1872), whose protago-nist was established as a comic type-specimen of flamboyant

---

1. I hope to translate most, if not all, of this other material in the future.

but fake Provençal bravado, and featured in several sequels by popular demand.

Léon Daudet (1867-1942) might not have followed in his father's footsteps had he not taken umbrage when his quest to qualify as a physician ran into a snag, but fate apparently took him in hand, and he soon became very prolific as a novelist, journalist and critic. His first and second novels, *L'Astre noir* [The Black Star] and *Les Morticoles*, both published in 1894, sold well and provided his alterntive career with a solid basis. In 1891 he had married Jeanne Hugo, Victor Hugo's grand-daughter, and had thus been welcomed into the upper echelons of Republican society, but that ran into a hitch as well when the couple divorced in 1895. Again, Daudet's reaction to the hitch brooked no half-measures, and he appears to have turned against the entirety of Republican endeavor, and also to have adopted a rather reckless lifestyle, which generated a certain amount of scandal, including a notorious affair with the Opera singer Lucienne Breval.

In 1903 Daudet married again, this time to his cousin Marthe Allard, who was also a writer—she signed herself "Pamphille"—but that does not seem to have calmed him down entirely. She did, however, encourage his political sentiments. His stance became gradually more reactionary, reaching a climax of sorts when he helped to found and then became the editor and leader-writer of *L'Action française*, which became a source of strident anti-Republican propaganda. His campaigning briefly won him a seat in the Chamber as a député, where his eloquence obtained further exercise, but he never stopped writing, and continued to write a certain amount of fiction alongside his journalistic work and memoirs. He was always billed by his publishers, once the fact was established, as "Léon Goncourt de l'Académie Goncourt," but everyone knew that he had won that position by inheritance rather than by election, his father having been named in Goncourt's will but dying before the will was belat-edly proved and its provisions activated. Although his hatred of Germany prevented him from lending the same vocal support to Nazism that he lent to Mussolini's Fascism in the early 1930s he collaborated with the Vichy government in World War II until his death, which completed the job of demolishing the remnants of his personal reputation. In the meantime his gourmand appetite, coupled with his distaste for physical exercise, gradually inflicted a morbid obesity upon him.

Les Bacchantes was written shortly after Daudet's return to France from a two-year exile in Belgium, to which Daudet had fled to avoid a prison sentence (for defaming the driver of a taxi in which his son had mysteriously died in 1923). The story is, to some extent, provocative merely for the sake of being provocative, and can be read as an unrepentant but oddly nostalgic defense of his once-turbulent private life, but the manner of its provocation and defense is interesting in its originality and method. That method seeks to combine mythological allegory with distinctively modern imagery in order build a philosophical scheme that links all kinds of creativity, including scientific creativity, to the erotic impulse. In developning that thesis the novel shows an awareness of the ideas of Sigmund Freud—the narrative features one of the most flamboyant instances of deliberate Freudian symbolism ever given literary form—and those of Friedrich Nietzsche, specifically his contrast of "Apollinian" and "Dionysian" styles of creativity and his extravagant plea for the reconstitution of a synthesis of the two styles that had been found and then lost again in the heyday of Greek drama.

From the perspective of the historical development of speculative fiction, *Les Bacchantes* is interesting as a participant in a set of stories examining the hypothesis of a technological device that allows imges of the past to be recaptured and replayed. First introduced in Eugène Mouton's comedy "L'Historioscope" (1883; tr. as "the Historioscope"), such an instrument was occasionally used as a facilitating device in stories exploring the past, including John Taine's restoration of the Age of the Dinosaurs, *Before the Dawn* (1934), but obtained far more interesting consideration in a series of *contes philosophiques* investigating the possible social consequences of such a discovery, beginning with the intriguing Christan fantasy *The Vicarion* (1926) by Gardner Hunting and continuing with such deftly pointed analyses as T. L. Sherred's "E for Effort" (1947) and Isaac Asimov's "The Dead Past" (1956).

It is probably safe to say that no one other than Léon Daudet, on imagining such a device and asking himself "If I had a means of calling up images of the past, how would I make use of it?" would have come up with the answer deployed in *Les Bacchantes*, but that only adds to the originality, not merely of the story, but of the philosophical aspects that are tangentially treated therein. At least one of the machine's odder side-effects is probably included simply to facilitate the plot, but the general theory of transtemporal influences underpinning the hypothetical machine, although it is only vaguely sketched out, does have some interesting implications and corollaries worthy of further contemplation. There is, however, a sense in which the speculative element of the story is merely a technical convenience assising the author to embellish and activate its mythological recapitulation.

In order to introduce that aspect of the story it might be as well to summarize the strange career of its cenral mythological character, Dionysus. The author renders the name in question as Dyonisos—which is a variant spelling sufficiently common in nineteenth-century French texts, though rarely found elsewhere, to be regarded as an authentic variant rather than a mere misspelling—presumably as an affectation, but perhaps also to emphasize that his Dionysus is not quite the same as any other representation, including Nietzsche's, although it necessarily embodies all the essential features of the myth, as well as a few of its more eccentric embroideries.

Early Classical writers record that Dionysus was fathered by Zeus on Semele, the daughter of the king of Thebes, thus annoying Hera, who was famously jealous of her husband's infidelities. Hera persuaded Semele to demand that Zeus show himelf in his true majesty, which she tricked him into doing—and was, inevitably, struck dead by the revelation. Zeus, however, snatched the unborn Dionysus from her womb and implanted the fetus in his thigh, eventually removing it when it came to term, thus justifying Dionysus' frequent epithet, the "twice-born." Dionysus was also known as Bacchus, that alternative also being of Greek origin rather than merely a Roman equivalent, although the convenional spelling is Latinized (from Bakchos).

The infant demigod still required protection from Hera's wrath, and was hidden; accounts vary with regard to where and how, but it always among women or nymphs, some of whom served as his nurses. Dionysus apparently developed a talent early in life for driving people mad, whch he was forced to use on a frequent basis when he grew up and began traveling the world, in company with a strange entourage that included a group of bacchantes, or maenads, who had apparently started out as his nurses but were now his sexual partners; they were prone to frenzy and to tearing people apart. His entourage also included the satyr-like Silenus, who later achieved fame in the singular as a protagonist of the farcical "satyr-plays" that provided early comedy relief from theatrical tragedies, although some Classical accounts refer to sileni in the plural and have difficulty distinguishing them from satyrs or fauns, although they were generally imagined as older, fatter and generally more repulsive. While being harassed by Hera, Dionysus was allegedly aided by the mother-goddess Cybele, who had a similar retinue of male followers, the Corybantes, similarly famed for dancing and wild behavior.

Exactly how Dionysus the demigod was awarded his promoton of full godhood, as the god of wine, is unclear, but he appears to have been in an ambiguous position in many of the tales of his wanderings, which mostly involve hostility on the part of mortal kings, either by virtue of disputes relating to Semele's family or insults leveled at his supposedly-effeminate costume, and usually end with mass epidemics of madness and people being torn apart; the best-known of those stories is, inevitably, the one dramatized by Euripides in the tragedy *The*

Bacchae. His travels apparently took him to many remote parts of the world before he finally took up his permanent abode in Olympus.

Anthropologists tend to account for this "original" account of the mythical Dionysus by hypothesizing that he was originally a Thracian or Phrygian god whose worship spread into Greece and whose native properties had to be accommodated into the Greek traditions by means of mythical invention, along with explanations for the conflicts associated with the ideological invasion. There was, however, a drastic transformation of the idea and image of Dionysus when his name became associated with the Orphic Mysteries, a new cult that emerged in the sixth century B.C., whose beliefs and rites were kept secret. Scholarly opinions vary widely—as they usually do in the absence of any reliable information—as to what the Orphic Mysteries actually involved, and how important they were as inflences on the burgeoning philosophy of their era, but whatever view is taken, the citation of Dionysus and his hectic rites in association with the new cult by late Classical commentators, who were probably also working in an informational void dusted and cobwebbed with rumor, is not only odd but intriguingly paradoxical.

Orpheus was a Thracian minstrel famous for his musical acumen; his patron deity was Apollo, who was said to have taught him to play the lyre. He features in some of the best-known stories of Greek myth, including his participation in the voyage of the *Argo* and, most famously of all, his ill-fated descent into the realm of Hades in the attempt to recover his lost love Eurydice. Orpheus died by virtue of being torn to pieces by women, for reasons that remain unclear, although one of the explanations offered in that they were bacchantes annoyed by some insult to Dionysus. The Orphic cult that developed to honor him—even though he was never promoted to godhood—presumably had a heavy emphasis on music, and is thought by some anthropologists to have been a considerable influence on Pythagorean philosophy, whose theory of numerical wisdom is said to have been initially based on the observation of mathematical relationships in music. That association suggested to some scholars that the cult might have been inclined to thoughtful asceticism, but the reputation it developed in the latter part of the Classical Era was very different, alleging that its rites were Dionysiac—albeit involving a considerable revison of the history of Dionysus.

The "Orphic" version of Dionysus' life-story is mostly derived from Nonnus' forty-eight-book epic *Dionysiaca*, written in the late fourth or early fifth centuy A.D. The story told by Nonnus identifies Dionysus with another, previously obscure, god named Zagreus, supposedly fathered by Zeus on the Underworld goddess Perspehone, who was torn to pieces by Titans. In order to conflate the two, Zagreus/Dionysus was said to have subsequently reincarnated by Zeus via Semele (thus being twice-born in a literal manner). Persephone, the daughter of the fertility goddesss Demeter, was sometimes included in rites addressed to her mother, specifically those celebrated at Eleusis, in which Persephone was known as Kore [the Maiden], and which became famous as the Eleusian Mysteries. Converting Dionysus into the child of Persephone/Kore and involving him in the Orphic Mysteries thus forged a link of supposition between the two sets of rites, of a kind typical of attempts to compile all-embracing "secret histories" of mysticism and magic, enthusiasm for which does not seem to have wavered over the last three thousand years.

Whatever the Orphic cult might have amounted to in its Hellenic origins, subsequent "revivals" of it in the Roman Empire were, in essence, lifestyle fantasies akin to those used to dress up many orgiastic instutitions, typified in English history by the so-called Hellfire Clubs of the eighteenth century. It was, obviously, the supposed Dionysiac associations of the Orphic Mysteries that recommended them to Romans (and, later, to Frenchmen and Englishmen) desirous of ennobling their drunken and licentious revels with some kind of antique and quasi-mystical gloss, thus adding to their piquancy. If, therefore, there had been any echoes of the Orphic Mysteries in Pompeii in 79 A.D. other than merely decorative wall-decorations, they would undoubtedly have adopted the Dionysiac form.

The association of Dionysus with the Orphic mysteries forged an unlikely link between Dionysus and Apollo, two gods that would seem to have so little in common as to be intrinisically antagonistic—a thesis and antithesis crying out, as it were, for an explanatory synthesis. As to whether or not the odd couple in question played any significant role in inspiring Pythagorean philosophy (and thus, by extension, Platonic, neo-Platonic and Gnostic philosophy, and, by further extenson, the entire tradition of modern occultism) we can only speculate. Inevitably, people have—and no one in modern times took up that invitation more determinedly and elaborately than Friedrich Nietzsche, who reshaped the myth of Dionysus yet again, for his own imaginative purposes.

In *Die Geburt der Tragödie aus dem Geiste der Muzik* (1872; tr. as *The Birth of Tragedy* [from the Spirit of Music]) Nietsche proposed that there is a crucial dichomotmy between Apollinian and Dionysian modes of thought, the former superimposing an element of formal differentiation on sensory experience while the latter seeks to receiver its allegedly-ecstastic rawness. Life, according to Nietzsche, involves a perpetual struggle between the two tendencies, in which either may get the upper hand, either individually or culturally. In his view, Greek tragedy was the highest form of art becuae it contrived to fuse the two quests into a seamless synthesis, exposing its aficionados to the full range of the human condition. Nietzsche hypothesized that the Dionysian element was represented by the chorus, originally consisting, in this conjecture, of satyrs, and the Apollinian element by the actors, whose performance he views as a kind of dream vision, involving the ecstatic ritual dismembering of Dionysus by the Bacchantes. In Nietzche's proposed historical schema, however, this synthesis withered and died after the era of Aschylus and Sophocles, under the baleful influence of Euripides and Socrates, and the advent of rationality, whih suppressed the Dionysian element and detached the Apollinian from its dream compponent—a suppression that lasted into the modern era, when music, especially that of Richard Wagner, began once again to offer some hope for a redemption of the synthesis.

By 1886, when a new edition was issued, Nietzche had changed his mind about the book, and all-but-repudiated it argument in a new preface, but he subsequently went back, at least partially, on the recantation. In his later works his references to the Dionysian seem to refer to the synthesis or resynthesis of the Apollinian and the Dionysian rather than to the separate and antithetical Dionysian—perhaps understandably, since the latter was the element in need of recovery following the victory of narrow rationality and the primacy of "differentiative" experience over "raw" experience.

In *Les Bacchantes* Daudet is clearly following in Nietzsche's footsteps in his depiction of the Master's attempts to recover a new synthesis that will marry (or at least couple) the creative aspects of science with what he considers to be the ultimate source of all creativity. Having one been "killed" by jealousy of his talents, and then miraculously reborn, he still requires a dramatic resynthesis of his creativity, which is conceived, in an ecentrically elaborate fashion, in terms of Orphic/Dionysian initiation. Although the two painings by Gustave Courbet cited in the story (the second of which appears to be fictitious) do not include the famous image of "The Origin of the World" (1866) there is a sense in which Daudet clearly has the double import of that painting it in mind. Daudet's version of Dionysian impetus is not identifical to Nietzsche, and is calculatedly confused with other ideas, but he is clearly attempting to follow a similar trajectory, albeit in the context of a novel aimed at general readers rather than a critical and philosophical essay.

Needless to say, this is an eccentric quest, and there is no resn to be surprised by the fact that *Les Bacchantes* is a unique book, but it is interesting for that reason. It might be reckoned an awkwardly-flawed book, just as Léon Daudet might be reckoned an awkwardly-flawed man, but it is an intriguing book that is abundantly supplied witth a certain wry eloquence and keen vision, just as Léon Daudet was in the various facets of his career. It is, at any rate, well worth reading for any connoisseur of the unusual.

* * * * * * *

This translation is taken from a copy of the 1931 Flammarion edition. I have retained the author's eccedntric spelling of "Dyonisos" and a few other eccentricities of usage and improvisation. I have attempted to provide adequate explanatory footnotes for most of the esoteric motifs that he introduces into the story without any explanation of his own but I have not repeated information already given in the introduction when reference is made to Zagreus, Kore etc.

THE BACCHANTES

TO ARTHÈME FAYARD[2]

To his admirable spirit of enterprise
and assemblage,
who has done so much for French letters,
on the golden anniversary of our friendship, begun in
1881 at Louis-le-Grand,
and continued, without interruption, until today.
His old comrade,

LÉON DAUDET
August 1931

---

2. Arthème Fayard (1866-1936) followed his father into the publishing busineesss, taking over the family firm in 1894. He produced an edition of the collected works of Alphonse Daudet, and Léon Daudet's *Les Morticoles*, but was best known as a canny promoter of popular fiction, including the highly successful Fantômas series.

CHAPTER ONE
A CRUEL ACCIDENT

In the laboratory of his residence in Avenillon, known as the Villa Dyonisos, in the heart of the Blésois Beauce, half way between Blois and Châteaudun, the great physicist Romain Ségétan, the French Edison—and more—was bringing to completion, by means of calculations and experiments, his supreme discovery: the waves of time.

A little over fifty, widowed ten months earlier, he had abundant smooth hair, half gray and half chestnut, a clean-shaven Romanesque face with chiseled features, dark blue eyes, both meditative and ardent, and a neatly-arched mouth with thin lips. A member of the Academy of Sciences, a Grand Officier de la Légion d'honneur, with a host of foreign decorations, a doctor of medicine and science, he was independent, very rich and generous. He was devoid of arrogance but thought very little of humans in general and the poor dignities they afforded him. His love of knowledge did not entirely mask his sensual love of women, which enveloped him with an atmosphere of desire.

A paunch, due to a strong appetite and a sedentary existence, had not yet rendered him heavy. He loved good food, books, the body of Venus and the stars. He understood faith without feeling it, and matter without submitting to it. A rare energy, interrupted by abrupt weaknesses, formed the aggregation of his multiple and confused heredity, half-peasant and half-bourgeois. He only kept company with superior people. All women interested him, especially if they were unhappy, oppressed and beautiful. The distant amity of his peers helped, he was sure, to make his life worthwhile. His family was extinct, save for distant, stupid relatives of whom he was glad to have lost sight.

The laboratory occupied a wing of the Villa Dyonisos. It contained a special apparatus designed for the production, emission and reception of rays of all categories, electromagnetic and photographic apparatus, sky-maps, tables of measures and large-scale diagrams. The majority of the instruments had either been devised or improved by the Master, who invented as one breathes, with an extraordinary facility. It happened in the following manner: at night, before going to sleep, at about ten o'clock, for half an hour and without thinking about anything else, he evoked the equally-admirable face and body of his dead wife, his Lili. Then he allowed darkness and dreams to come. The next day, when he awoke, a bold and naked hypothesis or the idea of some fertile experiment had germinated in his mind, springing up like mushroom. The critical and scientific domains communicated in him without intermediaries. He did not know whether that interdependence was rare or frequent; he had been subject to it for several months with a particular intensity.

He had met Lili—Félicité Duvoir—at the age of thirty-five, on a ship that traveled regularly between Buenos Aires and Bordeaux. She was then twenty-one. She was blonde, youthful and as full of life as a Rubens. Forcibly recruited in Paris by pimps, professionals in the white slave trade, she had been their prisoner but had been saved by agents of the Sûreté Générale, who had discreetly thrown the pimps overboard by night during the journey—with no witnesses, of course.

Immediately, Ségétan fell madly in love with the pretty girl, breathlessly infatuated, and the narrow pleasures of the cabin, even though it was first-class and luxurious, only sharpened his desire. It was then that he conceived the notion of the waves of time and meditated the means of capturing them.

Lili had a nature no less strange than his own. She, who had already known so many men, adored him exclusively; she did not leave his side by night or by day, following him with her gaze while he worked, educating herself assiduously—in the beginning, she barely knew how to read and write, but had made extraordinary progresss at the end of a year. He hired teachers of orthography and syntax for her, one of history and geography, one of music and one of drawing. She was thus his mistress, his pupil and his child at the same time.

To avoid slanderous gossip, as soon as they were duly married, they retired to the country and lived, in Avenillon, an existence of work and affection. That had only come to an end with Lili's death, which occurred in the wake of a double pneumonia. Ségétan's grief was immense but brief, for he had had the refuge of the astonishing discovery that was about to turn the world upside-down, and of which every magical quality echoed the beauty and charm of the departed. Absent, she was no less influential on the reconstructive imagination of her constantly-haunted widower.

The latter was aided in his endeavor by two other scientists of vast scope: his neighbors, who had been attracted by his genius. One of them, Félix Dévonet, occupied himself simultaneously with physics, dermatology and entomology, and was trying to establish communication between humans and insects—a supposedly insoluble problem. The other, his former fellow student Doctor Bénalep, known as "M'sieu Bienallé,"[3] was seeking new remedies by associating the roots of different plants in the ground, which he then submitted to the action of rays.

The three men had in common the investigative spirit that, sometimes by the mathematical and quantitative route and sometimes by the biological and qualitative route, knocks on the door of the Unknown, opens it by a crack, and then, after a few moments, finds it slammed in its face. Married to a young and ravishing woman, as dark as her name of Mélanie, Dévonet was almost as sensitive as Ségétan to the corporeal beauty of the exquisite sex. As for Bénalep, like many Semites, he had

---

3. Approximately, "Mr. Well-Intentioned."

periods of desire, which he satisfied rather poorly, and periods of chastity, which he devoted to botanical research and works of erudition.

For twenty leagues around, from Salbris to Tours, from Sully-sur-Loire to Châteaudun and from Vendôme and Blois to Chartres, there was little talk of anything but the "three sorcerers" of Avenillon, who attracted to the region visitors from England, America, Sweden, journalists, photographers and illustrious colleagues, sometimes received at the Villa Dyonisos, without being admitted to the laboratory, sometimes politely sent away by the old and sharp-tongued housekeeper Marianne or the chauffeur Abrice, an intelligent and resourceful Jack-of-all-trades.

The waves of time! Ségétan envisaged them as combinations of long and short, sonorous and visual "vibrations" composing etheric figures or "entities," which gravitated in accordance with unknown laws, returning like comets on fixed dates, determinable in advance. "Everything is full of souls and demons," said the ancient philosopher. There were souls and demons of duration as well as space, and their detection and capture was merely an affair of ingenuity: an annex to, or, rather, a prolongation of, the discoveries of Branly and Marconi, adapted from the spatial to the temporal.

After much effort, exploration and experimentation, the indefatigable researcher had succeeded in collecting, in the vast plains of the Blaisois, with the aid of infinitely delicate apparatus, ensembles or groups of a singular nature, which surely did not belong to the present moment. To what were they related? Distinguishable therein, with regard to the sonorous, were clamors, appeals, gunshots and collapses, and with regard to the visual, the redness of conflagration. Their periodicity was biannual, it seemed, during thirty days of October and twenty of February. Imminent applications of complex calculation were glimpsed therein, for which the physicist requested the collaboration and assistance of Bénalep, who was more quantitatively advanced than him and who could represent diabetes as an equation.

The waves of time! The idea was so much in the air, it has to be said, that in Avenillon, as in Brancheville, a village two kilometers away, the farmers and the peasants were following current fashion in talking about it. It was thus that an old man from Brancheville, invited to listen to the mysterious sounds of battle between the two villages on one Autumn evening exclaimed, nodding his head: "That'll be the affair in Châteaudun in October 1870, coming back like that to remind us of it."

That was, for Ségétan, a flash of light. Châteaudun was twenty kilometers away from there, but he had long admitted a spatial deviation of temporal waves, due to the intersection and interference of the vibratory "entities" of whose existence he now conceived. Besides which, his apparatus gave him the same results, clearly auditory and vaguely visual, all the way to the gates of Châteaudun, as far as the small square that had been witness to the famous combat of Lipowski's *Franc-Tireurs*.[4] The zone of the phenomenon was approximately twenty kilometers long by one kilometer broad, during the fifteen times twenty-four hours when it was detectable in autumn and winter.

The waves of time! That was only the start. Immense perspectives opened up before the three friends, when they considered the subtle instrument—the Dyonisos—as big as a medium-sized pendulum-clock, thanks to which one could summon, on the invisible wings of time, some past event or other. One day, history would live again by virtue of the temporal waves,

---

4. The battle of Châteaudun in October 1870 was an unfortunate episode in the Franco-Prussian War. After taking the town without any significant resistance the Prussians left it under the guard of a small contingent of troops. A colonel of *Franc-Tireurs* [riflemen], Emanuel de Lipowski, backed up by National Guardsmen, took it back, apparently for no better reason than that he could (it had no strategic significance). When the irritated Germans came back, Lipowski refused to leave, and the subsequent bombardment, followed by a massacre, virtually obliterated the town and decimated its population. French military history records it as a typical instance of German atrocity rather than a not-altogether-atypical instance of lunatic French bravado.

with its enchantments, its wars, its invasions, its revolutionary movements, its unexpected aspects, and the divine element that it contains, as earthquakes and eclipses do. The population of phantasmal deaths, such as the murder of Julius Caesar and the crucifixion of Our Lord Jesus Christ, would fall, visible, impalpable and noisy, among the living. What a haunting!

That morning, which was in June, bright and gilded, the scientist had the impression of advancing in great strides. He drank in light. He looked around him at the various stages of his discovery, fixed in infinitely delicate adjustments, in multiple depictions of the appearances, schematic and premature, of "entities" thus evoked.

Suddenly, there was a loud noise outside: a hard and abrupt impact, accompanied by heart-rending screams and cries for help. The chauffeur Abrice came in like a gust of wind. "Monsieur! It's Père Calvat's automobile, with has just crashed into a tree. He must have been killed immediately, but Madame Tullie is only bruised."

Père Calvat—the farmer of Les Arges, the rich neighbor who kindly lent his fields and meadows to any experiment! Ségétan ran outside.

From a clutter of metal and body-work, which fortunately had not caught fire, peasants were taking out a corpse—that of the old man, whose chest had been staved in by the steering-wheel—and a terrified survivor, the beautiful Tullie. The scientist ordered that she should be taken, with all possible precaution, to his own bedroom at the Villa Dyonisos, where Marianne would undress her and help her into bed. At the same time, it was necessary to alert Bénalep, who was still a practicing physician.

The latter immediately showed his square, meditative face with the thick eyebrows, dominated by a dome-like forehead, his shirt with the flared collar, and his thickset body. Without wasting time in exclamations, he said: "Let's get to it."

They both went into the cool room, where the curtains were half-pulled and the shutters almost closed.

Tullie, who had just drunk a vulnerary potion, was lying down, semiconscious, her adorable and delicate face, pale and symmetrical, framed by her black hair on the white pillow. Bénalep observed her briefly and then pulled down the coverlet and lifted up the rustic chemise that Marianne had provided.

A body worthy of Courbet appeared, dazzling and charged with glory, from the points of the fine breasts to the slender arched feet. To her compact velvety flesh, reminiscent of silk and fresh fruit, the light added a rosy reflection. Blue veins ran over the tapering thighs and calves, Gallo-Roman in proportion, shaped for a little domestic labor and a great deal of love. The addition of breasts that were devoid of heaviness, cup-shaped and divergent, was in accord with the smooth roundness of her shoulders, and from the long spine to the fleshy buttocks there was a sprinkling of seeds of beauty. By way of injuries there was only one dark blue patch on her left arm and a more serious contusion on the hip on the same side.

"It would have been a pity...!" Bénalep murmured.

He made sure that no interior organ or limb had been seriously affected. He moved the arms and legs slowly, which drew a few moans from the goddess. He helped her to turn over.

Only then did she ask: "My husband...Guillaume?"

"He's very seriously injured," Bénalep replied.

"I want so much to see him."

"Impossible, Madame. You must wait a while. We'll do what has to be done."

She uttered a profound sigh; the two men did not know whether she had understood—but her delicate and profound nature appeared in her bright aquamarine eyes and in the breath, at first contained and then liberated, of her anguish and pain.

Ségétan, thrown by such a spectacle into a veritable ecstasy, noticed that she had the most harmonious neck, swollen and bowed, slender and oblique ears, and a fleshy mouth, drawn back on one side over her delightful teeth. It is said that a slight physical fault is sometimes attractive to a veritable amateur, but the total absence of any physical fault is even more attractive.

For the first time since her death, the image of Lili had disappeared.

Such a sudden form of love is always shared equally. While the physicist calculated the delights of possessing that pure marvel one day, Tullie, for her part, was thinking: "Widow or not, I shall belong to that man." That voluptuous thought, like a euphoric poison, inspired a kind of shame at such a moment.

"She needs at least a week in bed and complete rest," said the worthy doctor, who then affected a certain cynicism. "Try to use the time profitably, my dear Romain."

At that moment they were in the antechamber, and alone. "Dear Roman" did not think for a moment of denying it.

"I've exhausted the memory of Lili and my scientific lamp is growing dimmer. She'll brighten it at a stroke. But where have you had the farmer's body taken?"

"To his home at Les Arges. His son and his servants will make the funeral arrangements after the legal formalities. I warn you that Jean Calvat, the son from a previous marriage, is infatuated with his stepmother. He's a village Don Juan, and also a brute, capable of anything. You'd do well to watch out for him."

"Amorous...or lover?"

"That I don't know—but I'm assured that he prowls around at night under the beauty's window, and has been seen in the hayloft weeping and clenching his fist over her portrait. It's a bad sign."

Late in the afternoon, in fact, Jean Calvat, a handsome fellow of athletic proportions, lanky, robust and muscular, with the head of a young wolf, steel-hard and malign eyes, and bushy hair as shiny as fractured coal, came to demand news of his stepmother. His father's death seemed to weigh less upon his heart than her bruises. He asked Marianne whether he could see her and speak to her.

"Oh, there's no question of it. The doctor has given instructions not to let anyone into her room."

"Not even your employer?"

"Not even him...at least for the moment."

"That's all right—I'll come back."

"When he said that," Marianne said to Abrice, "he had a frightful expression."

"Bah!" said the chauffeur. "He can be tamed." He was a good-humored colossus with a hearty appetite, very intelligent and solely responsible for maintaining the laboratory equipment. The scientist paid him and his wife, the cook Caroline, princely wages. They were very devoted to him.

* * * * * * *

The tragic death of Père Calvat caused great emotion in the region. He was a country squire who did not mistreat his employees, treated everyone fairly and managed his estate, one of the finest in the region, with wisdom and skill. His marriage to Tullie Moneuse, who was known as "the Italian woman" because of her Neapolitan origin, had generated gossip, but not too much. "One more cuckold," had been the smiling judgment of the Loir-et-Cher, the Indre-et-Loire and the Eure-et-Loir. The new farmer's wife was amiable and cheerful. She won forgiveness with her gentility and sparkling beauty. She was called "a royal piece." As she was at least thirty-five years younger than her husband, it was added that, when the day came, mourning would suit her "jolly well."

The funeral procession set out from the farm at Arges at midday, beneath a sky heavy with storm-clouds. Behind the coffin, at the head, Jean Calvat marched alone, his detached, almost arrogant attitude contrasting with the soft expressions of the uncles, aunts and cousins, and the sincerely-afflicted expressions of the servants. All the inhabitants of the villages of Brancheville and Avenillon were there, and people had even come from Blois and Vendôme. The file of black-clad individuals going through the fields recalled Courbet's famous canvas,[5] for

5. *A Burial at Ornans*, 1849-50.

in the Blésois, as in Normandy, Artois or Auvergne, all funeral or nuptial processions resemble one another, the ceremonies of life and death being packaged in the same fashion, so much have our kings unified France.

In the church at Avenillon, where the ceremony was to take place, people thought, they would doubtless see "the three sorcerers." Bénalep had forbidden Marianne to let Tullie get up, even for the mass. She was reading her prayers in her bed.

The curé, Abbé Parroy, was a saintly man of about seventy, universally respected, as thin and gaunt as the Curé d'Ars,[6] and who, like him, lived in the supernatural in the midst of an unbelieving population. The devotion to science of his neighbors, Dévonet, Bénalep and Ségétan and their natural impiety did not astonish or frighten him. He called them "the big brains" and willingly argued with them: "You look at the tapestry; I look at what's behind it." He was interested in Ségétan's discoveries and the work of the other two, as a providential florescence whose source was unknown to those who benefited from it. He felt pity for sensuality and scorn for concupiscence, as two traps set by the Evil One. His speech was slow, difficult and measured, nourished by Holy Writ and rudimentary theology, for he was of rural stock, with a face both knotty and hollowed out: "the tree of faith," Ségétan said.

The church, ancient and spacious, with a projecting roof at the door, was packed. In the second row were the pews of the châtelains of Brancheville, the Duc d'Ignacio, Spanish by descent although born in Paris, and his wife, the blonde and rosy-featured Ariana, a former "star" of the screen, with a child-like face, burnt eyes and harmonious gestures. The Duc looked like a portrait by Zurbarán.[7] In his elongated, equine, clean-shaven face shone two eyes charged with passion, green or black according to the angle of the light. Then came the

6. The Curé d'Ars—a small village near Lyon—was Jean-Baptiste-Marie Vianney (1786-1859), a famous ascetic who was canonized in 1925.

7. The Spanish painter Francisco de Zurbarán (1598-1664) was best-known for his religious paintings, including numerous saints and martyrs.

Maire, Monsieur Taupin, a vague bourgeois, liberal and timid; Madame la Mairesse, who was said to look like a deck-chair attendant; Roman Ségétan, whose sharply-defined head seemed a projection of profane stained glass; and Dévonet, no less singular by virtue of his high forehead, the ridge of his nose and strong jaws, with his Mélanie.

The last-named was, quite naturally, the most charming and reserved of the village madonnas, and her kneeling was gentleness personified. A fiery soul dwelt within her, however, of a kind less extravagant but more calculated and redoubtable than Ariana's. She had recently perceived that she desired Ségétan, that she would like to be enclosed, if only once, but fundamentally, in his vigorous genius, to sweat with pleasure between his arms, to pour over him the bold foam of her mouth. She had hoped that she might succeed Lili in the creative images to which the father of the waves of time had recourse, but now an accident had put the beautiful Tullie into his bed. Patience, though: all hours chime, especially for those who keep their eyes fixed on the hand of destiny!

As those violent sentiments gripped Mélanie Dévonet, to the strains of the *Dies Irae*, a sudden tempestuous desire for Jean Calvat, standing with his arms folded, in mourning-dress, took possession of the supple Ariana. By night, between the sheets, her husband whipped up his blood with vivid extracts from her past, which she related to him in a repentant tone, or laughing in the dark like a crazed child. "Oh, that was good, you know...he took it like this, and this...." And she did not spare the rude words, pretending to mistake his Christian name, putting Ignacio outside himself by means of some of those shrill remarks with which women are able profoundly to dissimulate their faculty for enjoyment.

By virtue of a well-known sensual repercussion, the ex-star had awakened in herself the demon of irresistible desire. The latter had just settled on the supple and proud peasant, like a young Bacchus, who had succeeded his father, along with his stepmother, in the direction of the farm of Les Arges. She could see the film, designed solely for a few rich amateurs: herself, nude, pursued by him, nude, in the remotest room in the château; the refusal, to improve the surrender; the fondling, like a dance whose steps she would regulate; and, finally, the embrace and the double, simultaneous, synchronic ecstasy, knotting the flesh for the eternity of a second and making, of two lives combined in a gasp, the most exquisite mortal frisson.

When they emerged from the church, the pretty woman, as lively as an eel, went up to the young peasant, who was going to his mercy-seat in the sacristy, and brushed against his entire body—leg, hip, side, shoulder—while looking into his eyes. He had never given her a thought, although he had met her several times in the fields, in Branchevlle and in Avenillon, while his fiery imagination was flowing around his stepmother. Even so, from that contact and gaze he received a kind of electric shock, which was not disagreeable, and extracted a silly smile from him.

Can he be a virgin? thought Ariana, who had once debauched an adolescent of sixteen in Los Angeles. *There's something of the unripe fruit about him.* Turning round, she perceived the chauffeur Abrice a few paces away, watching her with mocking eyes. As a legitimate Sultana in the days of Solomon, she would have had his head cut off.

When, then would she have another opportunity to approach the magnificent twenty-year-old athlete with the stormy pupils?

* * * * * *

As soon as he was back at the Villa Dyonisos, Ségétan went into Tullie's room to give her an account of the ceremony. She was sitting up gracefully in bed, clad in a short blue silk tunic, open over her lace chemise, which swelled over her white bosom. He asked after her health, negligently taking a soft and slender hand, which he held in his own, and told her what had happened. He named a few individuals, emphasizing the fine bearing of Jean Calvat, whom everyone had admired.

She avoided the subject.

He ended up by asking her: "He's said to be infatuated with you, and extremely jealous. Is that true?"

"It's true. He scares me, and now that his father's dead, I'm wondering how to escape his persistence."

"You don't like him, then?"

"Not at all. He's much too savage and violent. He's only touched me four times in two years, but every time I thought he was going to strangle or stifle me."

"You let him do it?"

"I had to. What a scandal if I had cried out and called for help—and what a shock for my old husband!"

An old song came to the scientist's lips, which he hummed while caressing the young woman's forearm:

> I shall try to be a good wife,
> Old Robin is such a good husband.[8]

She smiled prettily. "That was my entire program."

"And what are your plans now?"

"To take care of the farm."

"With your stepson?"

"How can it be otherwise. He's inherited Les Arges, along with me."

"Will you let me help you? I have some experience of the land and the region."

She looked at him, astonished and emotional. "You, such a great man, concern yourself with an insignificant woman like me! You can't be thinking of it, Maître Ségétan! Why such a sacrifice?"

He drew closer to her, his face inflamed with desire, and his hand moved along that arm, so gentle and so pure, outside the blue silk, trembling.

"Because I want you, do you hear?"

---

8. The quotation is from *Le Roman de Lamartine* (1909) by Léon Séché.

She replied simply, offering him her lips and closing her eyes: "Me too...." But she added, in a whisper: "Oh no, not this time. My hip hurts too much...and not here.... Abrice...Marianne...."

The reasons were good. He obeyed. At the same instant, his repressed desire brought him a reflection concerning the waves of time, which he had never previously made. He fixed it in his rapid memory, while delightedly aspiring Tullie's little mouth, like the calyx of a flower, moist, warm and profound.

At that moment, someone knocked on the door.

"Come in," he said, getting up.

Marianne showed her rustic head. "It's Madame's stepson, asking, like this, whether Madame can see him...." She made a gesture signifying: *no way of avoiding it.*

Ségétan slipped into the neighboring dressing-room and left the door ajar. He was thus able to see without being seen. His heart was beating as it once had in the first days of his cohabitation with Lili, when he was afraid that she might rejoin the pimps.

The young man went to the bed, hesitantly, his limbs stiff.

"Bonjour, Tullie. How are you today? It seems a long time since I saw you, since my father's death. It was a beautiful funeral, you know."

"Bonjour, Jean. Yes, so I've been told. Sit down."

He brought up a chair, which Ségétan heard scraping the parquet. Then there was a silence, and a sight that came from the boy. In a strained voice, he articulated: "So now we're the two owners of Les Arges, you and me. When are you coming back? I'm all alone. I'm missing you...."

"The doctor is still forbidding me to get up."

"Oh yes, Bienallé—the *other one*'s friend. They both intend to keep you here. They want to subject you to their devilries, their waves. They've already killed six of our animals. If it goes on, all the livestock and people in Brancheville will disappear."

"Shut up, you great fool—you don't know what you're talking about."

At that moment, Ségétan inferred that the boy got up and

went to her, then leaned over her violently.

The bed-frame creaked and a "No, no, oh no, not that—get off, not that here!" emerged, in a breathless supplication, from the lips of the beautiful victim.

Then there was a hoarse: "Yes, yes, I want to, I want you again, and right away...."

"Oh, you're hurting me. Enough, oh, leave me alone!"

"No—I'll take you whether you like it or not, you hear me—in spite of him!"

"Oh, you're mad! Let me go, you're scaring me. Oh...oh! Help me! Help me! He's going to kill me!"

Ségétan emerged from hiding and threw himself upon the black manikin who was struggling over the white skin. On hearing and seeing him, Jean Calvat released his beautiful prey, who tried in vain to shove him away, for he was already between her fleshy, taut legs. His face, pale beneath his bristling brown hair, had something faun-like and murdererous about it. With two bounds, he extracted himself from the grip of the scientist, who was off balance, then reached the door and disappeared.

Tullie was weeping, her arms adrift on the tangled sheets, and the scientist consoled her, kissing her awkwardly, savoring the salt of her shiny tears. With a sigh, she said: "Close the door." And then, in an even lower tone: "Lock it."

All of that had happened rapidly, and the two lovers never knew whether the servants had heard the noise or seen Jean Calvat running away. That evening, however, a repentant letter arrived from the latter, in which he declared, in a baroque style, that he had acted in a moment of delirium and distress caused by the sudden death of his father, humbly begged his stepmother's pardon, and begged her to apologize to the master of the house for him. If Tullie demanded it, he would go away for a time, leaving the administration of the farm to her. In that case, he would ask the notary, before the testamentary dispositions made by the deceased were effected, for an advance on his inheritance of a few thousand francs.

* * * * * * *

The prolonged sojourn of Tullie Moneuse at the Villa Dyonisos caused a great deal of talk, but the mixture of admiration and dead inspired by the "big brains" confined the rustic suggestions to the ironic and jesting form handed down from folktales to our own day. Besides which, the Paris newspapers and local rags were full of a frontier incident that might set France and Germany at odds again, and the apprehension of such a catastrophe deflected minds from everything else. On the same day that Tullie was due to return to the farm at Les Arges, Ségétan was summoned to Paris by the Minister of War.

Immediately received by the minister, the latter made him party to the political anxieties that were sending an alarm to the technical services and the general staff, and asked him where he was with his work on the disruption of the engines of aircraft in flight by means of waves. The scientist replied that he had, indeed, studied the subject at one time, and carried out a few experiments, with results that were worse than uncertain. At that moment his attention had been distracted by the problem of waves of duration, which now absorbed him completely.

"I know," said the minister. "I've read several articles on that subject in the papers. It's doubtless of more interesting, but it's a less immediate interest. Would it not be possible for you, my dear Master, in view of the circumstances, to return to your previous love—the disruption of engines at a distance? You'd be doing your country a great service. Of course, we'd put all the necessary means and personnel at your disposal, with the most absolute secrecy guaranteed."

"I'd like to, Monsieur le Ministre, but the disruption of determined research in favor of other research is one of the most difficult mental exercises there is. The spirit of investigation, when it's involved in the genesis of some X—or, more precisely, an ensemble of Xs—adopts by the same token a certain method, a certain atmosphere, a certain color. To abandon them for another method, another atmosphere and another aspect is almost impossible."

The minister, who was not stupid, sighed. "I suspected as much. What can I say? Do your best, my dear Master. I hope that, once again, we'll avoid war—but the more often the pitcher goes to the well...."

As he climbed back into his automobile, the scientist only saw, with regard to the first problem—that of the aircraft—a closed horizon, but with regard to the second, the waves of time, an open horizon.

When he was about thirty, he had believed, as Ramon Lull[9] once had, in discovery determined by means of a skillful and balanced play of the mathematical and the qualitative; now he saw that as a chimera, analogous to that of the possession of free will. Linked to his wife by secret bonds, discovery was even more fugitive than womankind.

When he got back to Avenillon, his house, deprived of Tullie, seemed to him to be dreadfully empty. It was still light. He decided to go and ask Dévonet whether he could have supper at his house, a comfortable dwelling at the entrance to the village, not far from Bénalep's.

When he went in, the brunette Mélanie was alone, reading Baudelaire. She was wearing a quilted jacket in green silk, as depicted in a painting by Vermeer, a white skirt, and she was making silver slippers dance at the end of her slender feet. Although her figure was charming, and even utterly desirable, he had not thus far experienced the slightest excitement on contact with her, even though everything about him attracted the young woman.

He told her about his trip to Paris, his meeting with the minister, and the latter's proposal. She put on a semblance of

---

9. The thirteenth-century philosopher Ramon Lull (or Llull) set out a supposedly logical theory of philosophical and religious philosophy in his *Ars generalis ultima* (1305; also known as *Ars magna*) based on the rational organization of ideas stemming from a limited number of axioms. His method influenced Gottfried Leibniz and is sometimes claimed as the ultimate origin of information science.

listening, but was asking herself, all the time: *Why that Tullie, and not me?*

That caused her to interrupt him with a question. *"She*'s gone back to Arges, then?"

"Undoubtedly," her astonished interlocutor replied. "You know, she's a extraordinary person, a farmer's wife with hands as white as one ever sees. I suspect that she's the natural daughter of a Neapolitan aristocrat."

"How the devil did Père Calvat unearth her?"

"Pure hazard, she tells me. She had to settle some business at a bank in Blois. So had he. They met there and struck up a conversation. She was alone, with no money, melancholy, doubtless disillusioned with regard to love, friendship and everything else. She was beautiful. He desired her. It was a rather banal adventure, save for the disproportion of age and education."

"Today it's the stepson who's conquered her, if popular rumor can be trusted."

"It's possible, but she's worth more than that. She has an absolutely original nature. She never says anything banal, and although I believe she's as capable of lying as you are, she's often brutally frank. She also sings like a bird, and carries you away to the land of dreams that way."

The contained distress of the jealous Mélanie had reached its peak when her husband came back, carrying a basket full of wild strawberries.

When he learned that their guest would be dining with them, Dévonet's consular face expressed a frank pleasure. "Phone Bénalep and ask him to come, darling. We'll have chicken *à la crème*—and as I passed by, I saw a magnificent gâteau in the patissier's window."

Soon, the three sorcerers were united around a good and genuine country soup with herbs and a base of potato purée, the recipe for which Caroline, the cook at the Villa Dyonisos, had passed on to the Dévonets' housemaid. Two chilled bottles of Saint-Martin-le-Beau, from a good year, seemed to have come up from the cellar of their own accord, followed by two bottles of Bourgeuil, for the guests were thirsty.

Ségétan was famished. The prospect of meeting up the next day—in the proper sense of *meeting up*—with Tullie, alone at the farm of Les Arges, was putting him in a excellent humor, when Bénalep, tucking the corner of his embroidered napkin into his collar, said: "Some singular phenomena have been occurring here in the village, and also in Brancheville and five kilometers away in Quatrebois, for some time. Two young women and one older one, and then a farmer, recently showed me dermatitis of an unknown variety on their wrists and legs. I sent them to see Dévonet—didn't I, old man?—who was amazed. At Les Arges, livestock have died suddenly of an illness that the veterinarian declares to be inexplicable. No other outbreak in the region. But that's not all. The children in the schools in Avenillon and Brancheville have given evidence this year of a precocity that amazes their headmaster, to such a point that he's been obliged to triple the prizes and citations. In that regard he's counting on you, as usual, to buy the books."

"The dermatitis," Dévonet added, "was analogous to that provoked by solar radiation, but of a more exfoliated variety. I took a small sample from one of them, and I'm in the process of examining it. There's something else: the number of births, between here and Châteaudun, has doubled, and according to the gendarmerie's statistics, the number of homicides and brawls has doubled too. Some of the peasants are convinced that it's connected with your experiments and waves, but others make fun of then. Among the former, Père Calvat's son has been mentioned."

"That was bound to happen," said Ségétan, laughing. "But you, Félix, who are trying to understand insects, and you, Bénalep, who are marrying plants in the soil, pass, as I do, for spell-casters."

"To a certain extent," Bénalep remarked, "we're interfering with what are claimed to be the laws of nature—or the idea that people have of them—and the supposition of a disturbance due to that intervention isn't totally absurd. I've been told about lawsuits prompted by rockets converting hail into rain, which victims of disaster accuse of having diverting storms over their fields."

While he was speaking the chicken *à la crème* circulated, embellished with soft mushrooms, and the Bourgueil poured out its crimson flood. The conversation turned to the difficulty of discerning, calculating and detecting in the waves of time the epoch to which it was necessary to attribute them.

Ségétan, in a firm voice, said: "We're still at the astrological stage. The hour of astronomy will sound, and new forms of calculation, like quanta—or hyperquanta, if you prefer—will permit us to draw up tables, according to the frequency of their vibrations, of the ages of the waves and their periodicities. All of that won't come about without new distresses, excitations and unexpected intoxications leaking out for that vast guinea-pig, the human species. The railway has had its accidents, aviation too. The waves of duration will have theirs. Everything down here has a price; Abbé Parroy tells us so."

During dessert, as was his custom, Bénalep made a speech. He was a philosophical improviser comparable to a Chopin or a Paganini, who extracted ingenious and powerful themes from the circumstances and ambiance. Mélanie's presence visibly inspired him.

"The mind," he said, "actually has two forms, which inter-mingle or separate in the most mysterious fashion: words and numbers; or, more precisely, verbal roots and numbers. The former is applied to movement and action, the second to mecha-nism, whether theoretical, technical or terrestrial. The former is qualitative the latter quantitative. Hence there are two forms of civilization. Ancient Egypt and present-day America are quantitative civilizations, with a predominance of numbers and machines. Perhaps that's a trifle schematic, but it's food for thought."

The coffee and cigars were brought in.

"Tomorrow evening, if the weather's as fine and calm as today," Ségétan concluded, getting up from the table. "I invite you to a wave experiment behind the farm at Les Arges. I think there's what I call a 'station of yesteryear' there—or, if you prefer, an echo of temporal waves—which it will be interesting to capture, and, if possible, situate. Besides which, we'll have a full moon, and the spectacle will be charming. I'll invite the Duc d'Ignacio."

"And the beautiful Ariana?" asked Mélanie, sarcastically.

"Certainly."

"And the no-less-beautiful Tullie?"

"Of course. The temperature is exceptionally warm. I shall ask all of you to come in evening dress."

* * * * * * *

Having returned home, Romain Ségétan found a letter on his desk in long, free-flowing handwriting, like a Breton shower. It was a hymn from Tullie Moneuse, uncertain in its spelling, with a hint of meridional exaltation that warmed his heart, transmuting desire into tenderness. However impetuous his blood might be, he was not unaware of the delicate sentimental network by which the sacred fluid circles and thus irrigates the immense domain of the heart. Just as there are names and numbers in the mind, according to Bénalep, there are a thousand shades of emotion in the heart, and in the mental frisson that results therefrom.

> *My lover, my master,*
>
> *The sum of the days that I spent in your home, after the horrible accident that made me a widow and your mistress, extends before me like a bed of scented flowers. I only live to breathe its perfume. I would like to live alone here with these recent, immense memories— alone and waiting for you.*
>
> *Whether it will be possible for me to go back to work, to continue the deceased or his shade, in the*

measure of my strength, I don't know. At least I'm close to you, and from my window, overlooking the fields, I can see the bell-tower and the nearest house of Avenillon. Everything important to me is there.

Jean stayed here in the end. He hasn't said anything to me. He's extremely useful to me. He issues orders like a true leader—but his gaze is still worrying. Bah! I'm not scared any more, when I think of you, my conqueror and the conqueror of nature, who can recall the deeds of the dead at your whim!

I'm press myself against you, my Romain. I'm counting the minutes before I see you again—but that's not enough to have you, and in order for you to have your

Tullie

The scientist read and reread the letter. With that woman, he felt strongly that a new element had entered into his life, amplifying the force of conception but also creating disturbances, as if charged with latent drama. The carnal exchange had been so magnificent that absence and separation were also fecund, but accompanied by a suffering whose extent he could not measure.

Tullie had taken him into an enchanted realm, the unknown aspects of which he was considering with astonishment.

CHAPTER TWO
THE MODERN EVOCATION

The nocturnal temperature was exceptionally mild. The moon bathed the immense plain of Les Arges farm and the three villages of Avenillon, Brancheville and Quatrebois with silver, mercury and tin. In the group of buildings overlooking Père Calvat's domain a few windows were still faintly illuminated, for the rumor of an experiment had spread and the peasants were staying up late in the hope of seeing something.

At the "station of yesteryear"—which is to say, the location capable of receiving, engulfing itself in and guiding the waves of the past—ten armchairs had been installed, in which, along with the "three sorcerers," the Duc d'Ignacio, Abbé Parroy and Maire Taupin had taken places, along with the three young women, Tullie, Mélanie and Ariana, all clad, in accordance with Ségétan's wishes, in low-necked white dresses. Their skin, various in color—silvery in Tullie, amber in Mélanie and blue-tinted in Ariane—in combination with the uncertainty of the shadows and the quasi-supernatural fringe of light, formed an incantation that mingled Watteau, Fragonard, Baudelaire and Chopin, as the Duc d'Ignacio remarked. A born artist, he possessed a gallery of all beauty in his Château de Brancheville, before which he stood for hours, bathed in ocular voluptuousness, before going to find his wife, with whom he was passionately and depravedly in love.

Intimidated by the feminine trio about whom the entire country was talking, the Mairesse, Madame Taupin—the "deckchair attendant"—had not come, in spite of her curiosity. Hidden behind the wall of the farm, at a point where the stones were dislocated, Jean Calvat, drunk with jealousy, was watching the silhouettes of the men and women, the latter naturally being more visible. No movement of either group escaped him. He was watching them in the fashion of cheetah, full of virtual bounds and bloody images. Even so, he was constrained by the respect that science has imposed, for a century and a half, on simple individuals, and which could easily, at a given moment, confronted with the ravages of the chemistry of war, be transformed into hatred and fury.

The apparatus for evoking the temporal waves, the Dyonisos, was there, isolated on a porcelain stand. Only Ségétan and Dévonet knew its exact make-up and manipulation, and if the two of them had died suddenly, at that moment, their secret would have disappeared with them—but that is the way of things in matters of discovery. The great Auclair,[10] a medical genius such as appears only three or four times a century— five at the most—took with him the principle of the cure for tuberculosis and lupus, the avian pancreas. If Léon Vannier,[11] greater than Hahnemann and his successor and heir in the realm of infinitesimal therapeutics, were to fall victim—an ominous warning!—to some accident, the sky of curative medical treatment would be obscured for a long time. If Maeterlinck were stolen from humankind, human understanding would be subjected to an incalculable diminution. When Mistral passed over, it was not only the Provençal landscape, but the entire soul of his homeland, evoked in *Calendal*, which put on mourning.[12]

---

10. Probably Edmond Auclair, author of *The Tonic Supreme, A Unique and Scientific Treatise on Human Regeneration* (1918).

11. Léon Vannier (1880-1963) was the most famous homeopathic physician in Paris from 1905 onwards, the founder of the journal *L'Homéopathie française* in 1912 and author of numerous books on the subject.

12. The Occitan poet Frédéric Mistral (1830-1914) was a close friend of Alphonse Daudet for many years. *Calendau*, translated into French as *Calendal*, was published in 1867.

Not to mention the unknowns, charged with mystery like certain sites and strata, powerful in their innominate emanation, who intervene secretly in the destiny of others, like beneficent or malevolent angels.

Eve asks questions blithely. "Maître Ségétan," asked the supple Ariana, like a *belle de nuit*[13] in full bloom, whose secret fiber divined, without her being able to see him, the hidden presence of Jean Calvat, "can you tell us what makes you think that a passage of waves from the past will occur here tonight?"

"Simple induction, my dear lady, based on a few tiny symptoms. The roots of plants, observed by Bénalep here, have manifested a magnetic hyperexcitation in the last few days, which almost always indicates the approach of temporal waves. It is the same with the general direction of flight of certain birds. It might be the case that I've disturbed you for nothing, but that would astonish me."

At that moment, a slight quiver of the little bouquet of antennae on the Dyonisos apparatus attracted everyone's attention. Three white silhouettes of the women got up and came closer. Calvat, from his hiding-place, noticed that the movement brought Tullie very close to Ségétan, who was waiting with his arms folded.

"Is it coming?" asked Bénalep, as thickset as a small buffalo with a human head—a head in a flared collar.

"Patience!" Dévonet replied.

The Abbé and the Maire were sitting up straight, in an interrogative attitude. Someone—doubtless Ignacio—made the remark that the presence of a priest added to the evocatory aspect of the séance, to the exorcism of time, but the remark fell into the silence.

About an hour had passed in the vain hope of the phenomenon, amid the mute immobility of the moon, spaces and forces, when a crackling of Dyonisos was immediately followed by a religious song and a vast trampling of human and equine feet.

13. This name is applied to more than one kind of night-blooming flower, most commonly to the Central American *Epiphyllum oxypetalum.*

At the same time, a flock of banners, like orderly butterflies, appeared, whose colors could not be made out in the moonlight.

"Here we go," murmured Ségétan, like someone absorbed in an internal dream. "Those songs, still indistinct, are of a kind and in a style that's very old, which doesn't belong to the seventeenth or eighteenth century. We need, therefore, to look further; here come appeals, cries of a sort, cheers...one moment, my friends, while I tune the amplifier. Dévonet, pass me the you-know-what. Shh—it's a procession, very large, to judge by the first indications, which is taking place on the high road not far away. Its direction is toward Blois and Tours."

Now the stream of sounds was quite clear, although the visual images were not as yet, remaining in the midst of a ruddy aureole. The whinnying of horses was audible, and the shrill voices of women and children were discernible as well as male voices. It was obviously a procession, in the midst of a considerable and impassioned crowd of curiosity-seekers, come from all directions.

The impression was that of an ancient and natural episode, enveloped on all sides by the supernatural, whose revivification was inexplicable. There had once been a surge of enthusiasm and an extraordinary faith, which had launched crowds on to the roads, in a given direction, among endless acclamations. Was it a great pilgrimage, a crusade or a departure for war?

At any rate, the event had been important, for the noise, the tumult and the polychromatic butterflies lasted for an hour, without dying down, accompanied by a march that was more military now than religious, punctuated by various curt orders. The historical ambiance of the returned, if not reawakened, scene was both hectic and mystically smooth at the same time.

"What a host! What a host!"

"Fifty thousand men must have filed past already...."

"And it's still continuing."

"There's been a mistake—it's under Bonaparte, or someone like him...."

"Wouldn't it be more likely, in view of the locale, to be the preliminaries of the Battle of Poitiers?"[14]

The three young women expressed thus, in laughter and chatter, the various sentiments that were agitating them on that strange evening, in which the fires of the sky and the moon were contemplating the petty efforts of human beings to escape from their mortal shackles.

Gradually, the witnesses, except for Maire Taupin, were shaking off the constraints of etiquette. Ségétan had taken the admirable bare arm of the leaning Tullie into his own arm, and was caressing it. Ignacio was hugging the pliable Ariana to him. For want of anything better, Mélanie was squeezing the skillful hand of her husband, the collaborator of the man she secretly loved.

Abbé Parroy observed these nocturnal and evidently pagan couples in silence, wondering what dark power was acting upon them in that fashion. The formulae of exorcism came quite naturally to his lips, but at the same time, he could not help admiring the astonishing discovery of his parishioner—who, moreover, gave him five thousand francs a year for his good works.

The lights of Les Arges had gone out. Behind a section of wall, a vigorous young man, livid with hate and moonlight, felt a whirlwind of homicidal images invading his brain and his will.

From the day when his stepmother had first come to the farm, he had desired her passionately. Violent and direct in her sensibility, very limited in her education, but nevertheless superior to her condition, Tullie was in his eyes the symbol of everything down here that is beautiful, forbidden, inaccessible, distant and yet present: the ripe fruit of the Terrestrial Paradise, between Thirst and the Serpent. Every night, an ardent dream gave her to him, and the morning took her away again. The fatigue of field-work disappeared thanks to her smile, even if it was for another. Without being positively jealous of his aged father, he

---

14. The second of the three major English victories of the Hundred Years' War, fought on 19 September 1356 and won by an army under the command of Edward, the Black Prince.

had, beneath the grief of his accidental death, found the inadmissible contentment of telling himself that at least he would no longer be able to hold the beauty against him in his gnarled and ugly arms. "The ape's gone," a demonic voice had murmured to him, while he followed the coffin behind the *oremus* of the choir of children in red and white.

Abruptly, the haunted fellow took his courage in both hands, emerged from the shadows and advanced toward the circle of audition and desire, which the star of Diana limned in silver and black.

"Bonsoir, everyone," he said, in a firm voice.

Tullie shivered. So did Ariana, but for a different reason.

"Bonsoir, Jean—have you come to listen to the past?"

"Bonsoir, Monsieur Calvat...."

"Bonsoir, Calvat."

Maire Taupin said: "Bonsoir, boy."

The Abbé said: "Bonsoir, child." The young man sometimes confessed to him, took communion, and then did not even attend mass for months on end. The priest considered him as slightly cracked, but avoided lecturing him, having observed that it was more likely to drive him astray, and that he found repentance easy. He defined him as a wavering soul.

The sounds of the procession were beginning to weaken, as if passing through the mesh of a net. The butterflies had vanished, as had the red halo around the moon. The phenomenon was about to end. What was it, and when would it return? The twelve strokes of midnight were sounding solemnly in the three bell-towers of the three villages

"Will you work with me and help me solve the puzzle?" said Ségétan to Tullie, who nodded her head, with a shiver.

Jean Calvat drew his stepmother aide. "Work at what, at this hour? Rather confess that you're going to sleep together."

"That's my business," said Tullie, curtly. "Go back to the farm."

Ariana had heard the fragment of dialogue. She slid swiftly toward the unhappy child, took him by the arm as if in play and whispered to him: "Forget that minx. I'll console you. Come to the château tomorrow at five o'clock; my husband will be in Paris."

He looked at her without replying, his eyes soft, his hair moist with dew, his skin on fire. She understood that he would come, without fail.

* * * * * * *

Going into the room that had decided her true life, Tullie Moneuse was expecting anything but what happened. In fact, her master and lover had arranged on two tables a list of principal events for the three départements of Loir-et-Cher, Indre-et-Loire and Eure-et-Loir, arranged in categories such as *love, marriages, religion, wars, military ceremonies, conventions and treaties, accidents, foundations, customs*, etc. Being in continual communication with the archivists of the three départements, he thus had before his eyes the groups of the past wave-sequences capable of being evoked by the Dyonisos. On other slips of paper he had noted the dates of reappearance that he had bee able to discover, as for the battle of Châteaudun. It was, of course, only an approximate research, in view of the immensity of the range of possibilities.

This evening, he was feverish and almost joyful, for he had his preconceived idea, at least in broad lines, and he said to his mistress, who was awaiting his orders, as beautiful as a Muse, ready for the choice of love or research: "Look in the list of processions and military corteges, while I go to the laboratory to check my apparatus, as I do every time."

She was left alone in the lighted room, in front of the shuttered window that overlooked the fields, and from which, during her convalescence, she had gazed at the landscape. She had work to do, and she applied herself to it conscientiously, for it was a matter of satisfying her idol, her god, her all, of helping him in a small matter, of making contact, even if were only by a thousandth of a millimeter, with his immeasurable mind—in a word, collaborating with him.

In a matter of days, by virtue of the power of Eros, her imagination had developed, her intelligence had been refined—like those of the children in Avenillon's school, according to Bénalep. A host of thoughts, of which she had previously known nothing, had come to install themselves within her. She felt renewed, and her marriage to Calvat and the years that had followed it, appeared to her like a gray dream.

A slight sound of shutters opening cased her suddenly to raise her head. In a momentary flash, behind the lighted window, she perceived the tragically pale face of Jean Calvat. It gave the impression of a severed head, which still had its eyes open. The latter inspected the room and the reader swiftly, and then everything vanished.

The piercing cry of a nocturnal bird traversed the plain.

When Ségétan came back up, two hours later, he saw his mistress lying on the bed asleep, in the same position in which he had confessed his love to her for the first time. Dressed as she was in white, modestly extended, her neck inclined toward the wall—for she had fled the electricity—she had the appearance of a flowery vessel of Purity floating on the river of Innocence. Although she now knew almost everything that one can know, she had retained, miraculously, a refuge of virginity in her soul, and to the interrogator of nature that survival seemed adorable.

On the table, clearly evident, she had left a slip of paper bearing the words:

10 May 1429. Passage of the Maid along the road from Orléans to Blois, three kilometers from the latter town. General enthusiasm.

"That's what I thought," he murmured, and immediately entered into meditation: *Are these recurrences of synthetic bundles of hearing and vision through time, accompanied by corresponding mental effluvia, auras of the past, more-or-less transformed or transmuted collective emotions? Could one explain in that fashion the ups and downs of peoples and human individuals, replaced by the temporal waves in anterior baths of anger, pity, faith, incredulity, remorse and desire?*

His eye, avid for beauty, interrogated Tullie, fled into slumber, begging her to come to his aid by means of the slight rise of her semi-uncovered breast, by means of the subtle breath of her slightly parted lips.

The formidable words of De Quincey came back to him: "the Dream knows best."[15]

* * * * * * *

The sky was dark, traversed by a yellow and sad five o'clock sunlight. The air was heavy and stormy. Sitting in the sumptuous antechamber of the isolated Château de Brancheville, Ariana, in a light gold lamé silk dress, whose translucency allowed her figure to be divined in its entirety, was awaiting the arrival of Jean Calvat. She had put on perfume, manicured her small fingernails and put gilded sandals on her delicate feet. She was ready for a well-deserved amorous session, in which she would guide the country bumpkin. She had sent away the domestics for the evening and prepared a bottle of burgundy and champagne, infused with myrtle-leaves, in an ice-bucket. It was a rediscovered aphrodisiac recipe of Greek origin, in current use among the stars of South America.

Through the spy-hole set aslant in the window in the door, she saw Jean Calvat arrive, dressed as an urban gentleman by the best tailor in Blois. She let him ring the bell and wait for a long moment. Then she opened the door and said to him, tenderly, in her musical voice

"Bonjour. Come in, come in—we're alone, and we have the entire night before us."

He was terribly intimidated, rather awkward, with the commencement of a foolish chuckle. He had hurried; he was

15. From the explanatory notice to the "Dream-Fugue" (1847) included in De Quincey's *Colleced Writings* (1854).

hot and his rather strong odor pleased the pretty woman whose hand he shook forcefully. He had clean teeth, combed hair and his fingernails were neither too long nor too black—but what excited Ariana most were his ardent and suspicious eyes, the definite contours of his suntanned face, and the svelte insertion of the robust torso into his loins.

She invited him to refresh himself.

"Oof," he said. "In this temperature, that's not to be refused. What is there in this beautiful bottle?"

"A mixture of my own, of red wine and champagne, which I've had refreshed for you. The biscuits are at the side. To your health, Jean, and that of your beautiful friend...for I know her!"

A shadow passed over his face. "Let's not talk about that. I'm too unhappy about it."

"On the contrary, let's talk about it, because it's to cure you and console you that I've invited you here. Handsome as you are, you ought to seduce all women, Tullie and the rest, but the great rule is never to run after them. Let them come, let them come—pay court to me, ostensibly, or to Mélanie Dévonet, or someone else, and after a few days, you'll have news for me.... Well, do you like my mixture?"

"Excellent. Can I have a refill? Aren't you drinking?"

"Yes, you'll see—pass me your glass. You don't waste time, do you? Now, let's go see the paintings, and I'll let you compare...."

"Compare what?"

Without answering, she took him by the tips of his fingers and led him to the great staircase, and from there to the room that served as an art gallery. One of the two principal pieces was a Courbet, representing the marvelous awakening of a splendid nude woman while her female companion was still asleep. The second was one of Fragonard's famous frolics, in which a hairy young man, seemingly exhausted, lay next to the rosy round-ness of his rude playmate, who was placing a crown of roses on is head. Here and there, Venus reigned, with her natural immod-esty, her enjambments, her haggard eyes, her admirable pleats and the dull rumor of her veins, in which fiery blood circulated. The standing partner in the Courbet was brandishing a multi-colored parakeet, while the recumbent partner replied in color by means of scattered tawny hair: two hymns to satisfied flesh and pleasure.

Jean of the fields looked at them with a hallucinated expression, into which the mixed wine inserted its disturbance. Ariana had started up an electric gramophone, which was playing a languorous tango. She unfastened her cloudy dress with a single gesture; it fell at her feet in a wave of pink and gold.

She had something of the Courbet and the Fragonard about her, mingling the firm breasts of the Île de France with the tender plumpness of the eighteenth century, all veiled with amber down. Advancing ceremoniously toward the "Jean-Jacques" she coveted, she invited him to follow her harmonious movements, as if on the side of an amphora. He had retained his dark garments, and was reminiscent of a Goya by virtue of the contrast of the dark brown fabric and the cright flesh. He had not even understood that he was supposed to undress completely.

That comic element, multiplied by a vast looking-glass with three shutters, disposed at an angle in front of the Courbet, cut through Ariana's scheme; she shouted over the tango: "Get rid of all that!"

Only then did she perceive that, while awkwardly following the rhythm, he was weeping.

She stopped. The gramophone fell silent.

"What's the matter, you little fool? Tell me, you big oaf, what's grieving you?"

He sat down on a sofa, ready for anything but amorous despair, but his big head between his wet hands and said, sobbing: "I'm thinking about Tullie. Oh, my God, my God! My Tullie!"

I've given him too much to drink, thought the star.

Before Ignacio she had already seen that number played on another social stage by a passionate Venezuelan, who got drunk. It was only a matter of time—but pleasure, in these conditions, became hard work. She hesitated over throwing him out. Then she took pity on him, and something maternal that she had never suspected quivered within her.

Without getting dressed again, she sat down with him, drew him toward her and received his warm tears on her golden Hesperidean breasts. They ran dry. That tenderness, full of delights of which he thought nothing, stirred up Jean's desolation, which had become a fountain intercut with sighs and hoarse appeals to the absent woman.

Remembering her former profession, Ariana, beneath her womanly resentment, admired the natural staging of the failed sexual enlightenment: their two silhouettes those of Titania caressing an entire donkey in jacket and trousers, instead of the Shakespearean head.

Now the boy talked, and abundantly, his tongue loosened by the myrtle and the wine—and what he said did not lack interest, in spite of the mingled syntax of the farm, the tavern and the grape-harvest.

"Madame, pardon me for what you will think of me and for responding with timidity to your generosity and advances. All your frolicsome deportment, which at any other time I would have wanted to satisfy, has raised up in me a pure and chaste soul, the misfortune of my life. For Tullie, excuse me, Madame, it's with my soul that I love her and not only my senses. Oh, that Ségétan who has taken her from me! I hate him, and I'll end up killing him. When I saw you like that, dancing, when you were like the painting, perfumed, all in bare skin, as if one were in fairyland, it turned me upside-down, and I thought that you were Tullie and that you were coming to me to take me. But no, Madame, you're not Tullie, and that's what made me weep and cry."

"Yes, child, yes! Come on, it's all right. Calm down. Let me get dressed. Lie down there and go to sleep. We'll dine quietly, in tranquility. You won't drink too much wine this time"—she pronounced it "thish time" to amuse him—"and after that we'll go to bye-byes at Les Arges before my own Ségétan comes back to me."

As she finished her sentence, a mighty burst of thunder, soon followed by a gigantic flash of lightning, shook and lit up the Château de Brancheville.

"Ah, the storm! Stay here. I'll go shut the electricity meter."

Exhausted by so much emotion, the poor boy had fallen asleep abruptly like a baby, lying on his back, and the regularity of his face and the abandonment of his torso brought back the antique and natural beauty that had seduced Ariana. She thus found herself, with respect to him, a little like Courbet's awakened woman, less the cockatoo. Besides which, Lesbos was not her scene. She had only landed there once, without enthusiasm, at the express request of Ignacio.

A second thunderclap, as violent as the first, made the house tremble again. That "Trafalgar" seemed as true as in the studio. Ariana, who liked atmospheric electricity, its discharges and relaxations, put on a light mantle of orange silk and went to stand at a window in her bedroom, from which the entire plain was visible. The yellow wheat-fields, the clumps of trees, the green fields of clover and the reddening vines were exhaling their various colors under the leaden skull-cap of the immense sky. At four points on the horizon lightning described zigzags of fire, in the midst of a veritable bombardment. The church bells began to sound the traditional tocsin. Sheaves of hail-preventing rockets could be heard departing here and there. A few hoarse cockerels were crowing obstinately in the direction of Les Arges farm.

The young woman thoughts about all sorts of things, in a fragmentary and disconnected fashion: about her bizarre eroto-maniac husband, idle and curious, inconceivably frivolous, who lived in a kind of theatrical drama; about her confused past, bristling with the faces of rich, satiated, drunken, maniacal men, men's arms, men's fingers, of which she retained the memory, like tattoos, the digital imprints superimposed; about herself, who, among her excesses, was searching for something that she had not found.

The manner in which that handsome little rustic who was

sleeping back there had twice pronounced the word "soul" had made an impact on her. Was his violent attachment to Tullie, which rendered him impotent for anyone else, a corollary of the soul, about which everyone spoke and no one ever saw? Ariana had once appeared in a German film, *The Surprises of the Soul*, which had had scant success but in which one witnessed the metempsychosis of the same "psyche" through several female bodies. Was there any truth in that, or was it a mere invention of the half-mad Boches, who put their nightmares into theory?

She had had a Freudian physician like that, Professor Murmel, who had nearly driven her crazy interrogating her avidly about her past and her dreams. He had seemed as naïve as the concierges who interpret the dreaming of cats as a bad omen—and everything, in Murmel's eyes, was sexual. The recent adventure with Calvat, however, and many other episodes in her eventful life proved to the former star that the business in question, between the legs, if it counted for a great deal in certain cases, was not everything.

Brroom, booboom, patapaboom...brrooom, boom!

She started. The points of illumination were joining up. The principal convoy of celestial artillery was passing directly over the château, and the lightning flashes were overlapping in such a fashion that they no longer formed anything but a single sheet of permanent white fire. Then the cataracts of the sky opened, and the lances of a diluvian rain, a broken necklace of watery diamonds and pearls, vertically unleashed, were furiously precipitated upon the ground. A moist mist invaded the land, a giant silken sheet that traversed the long, straight celestial jewelry display in a tumult of gurgles and splashes, mingled with the sound of bells. It was an aerial symphony, in which the fire growled, clapped and roared, in which the water shone and streamed, and in which the electricity danced like a demon, breaking and then recomposing the bewildering puzzle of the horizon.

How long did that last, with its intermittences and reprises? Ariana was not sure. When the watery mist that was hiding

Les Arges dissipated, in the midst of a vast drainage and pale outbursts fading into the distance, she picked up a set of Zeiss binoculars, a costly masterpiece of German optics, and directed them toward Calvat's farm. In the frame of a window with a stone lintel she distinctly perceived Tullie, dressed in black, admirable in her pallor, figure and attitude, deep in reflection, like her.

She's living, she thought, *in the permanent storm of Romain—a woman who, without that encounter, would only have been pretty flesh, rapidly corroded by the sun and exhausted by working the fields. Everything that surrounds us is astonishing, and what happens within us is no less so. Abbé Parroy, with his Providence, might be right.*

This time—"thish time," as a drunk would have said—there was a rainbow, the most tranquil and the best explained of celestial phenomena, simultaneously bourgeois and poetic: a good, solid, classic rainbow, whose parabola went from Blois to Quatrebois, with all its bands firmly in place. The suave odorous humidity that follows storms was in the air.

"Oh well!" Ariana murmured, to herself, "I'll go and wake my comical lover, with the strains of the *Pastorale*."

She let her observatory, keeping her mantle on her shivering shoulders, and went down to the gallery.

Calvat was still asleep in the same position, with an expression of dolorous gravity, as manifested, we are assured, by those marked by destiny. The noise of the thunder and the glare of the lightning had not woken him up. She considered him at length. He was a little crazy, that was sure, but there was a sort of elevated scrupulousness in him, which she had not yet observed in any other man. Behind his baroque and florid evening-school language, there was a singular and indefinable aspiration. In a zigzag of thought comparable to a lightning-flash, she told herself that the rescue of such a poor child would have been a more interesting project than the seeking of pleasure for pleasure's sake and esthetic voluptuousness.

To the strains of the *Pastorale* the peasant did indeed awake, and rubbed his eyes. Where was he? What was he doing? What had happened? A blush reddened his face, like that of a young god. He remembered.

"Let's not talk about all that foolishness," said Ariana. "There's been a terrible storm, which you didn't even hear. It's given me a appetite. If you like, we'll go and have a snack. Straighten your collar and give yourself a lick of the comb while I set the table."

They had become comrades, like two castaways on a desert island, with a good deal of esteem for one another. It was, with a difference of time and characters, the situation of Renaud in Armide's abode—a Renaud of a Beauceron farm, an Armide of the cinema.[16]

"You can do anything," said Jean, admiringly, as she sliced the pâté.

"It's necessary, in our profession...."

"What profession?"

"The cinema, of course. Didn't you know that I was once a star? Tullie never mentioned it to you?"

"Never, Madame—but then, when we were together, we only spoke about Papa and us."

The boy's widened eyes were sufficient evidence of his admiring surprise. So he had before him, for himself alone, one of those famous people that one sees on the screen, without ever meeting them on the street! She had danced with him, drunk with him—more than that; if he had wanted it, she would have given herself to him! Now she was eating with him, and he wondered if he might be acting on camera, if he were playing a part in one of the films that were shown in Sully-sur-Loire, Blois, Tours and Chartres. Everything about her seemed prodigious to him, including the way she made the salad, pouring

---

16. Renaud and Armide (Rinaldo and Armida in the original) are characters in Torquato Tasso's chivalric romance *La Gerusalemme Liberata* (1580), whose French translation was a standard school text in nineteenth-century France. Armide is an enchantress who sets out to seduce the knight Renaud cynically, but is won over by his nobility and falls in love wih him.

golden oil with her long ringed fingers.

A question was burning his lips, and he ended up articulating it: "When will he be back, your husband?"

"Soon. Ordinarily, he's not jealous, but there are days when he is. So I'll show you a place where you can hide by night when you want to see me again, to ask my advice, and imitate the cry of a bird or the mew of a cat, as you please. Then I'll come to find you—but you mustn't tell anyone about it, not even Abbé Parroy. You promise?"

"I swear."

The romantic side of the adventure amused him, and something told him that he would have need of this pretty woman some day, who was so good and kind to him.

When the meal was finished they went out together and she took him to a secluded redoubt three hundred meters away, locked with a key, built into the wall of the grounds, opening internally to the property and externally into a clump of trees. To that single, spacious and elegantly furnished room, where there was electricity, a telephone, a small bookcase, a large divan and an alcove forming a dressing-room, Ariana retired when she felt the need to be alone—which happened often. No one, including Ignacio, was to disturb her there; it was an absolute rule.

"There are only two keys to this place. Here's one. Keep the second. Unlock the exterior door."

He obeyed. All went well. The disposition of the little wood and its dense undergrowth was such that one could, even in broad daylight, go in and out without being seen—all the more so after nightfall. The beauty and the rustic were no longer merely friends; they were now accomplices.

They separated.

Ariana went back to the château alone. In the distance, the guard-dogs were barking. She cleared the plates and cutlery from the table, checked the doors and went to bed. An hour later, the servants came back, arguing in low voices. After reading for a while, she became drowsy.

She was more completely detached from her husband, in spite of his generosity and passion for her, than she had ever been. She heard him come back in and approach her bed; she sensed that he was looking at her tenderly, but did not open her eyes. Finally, he put out the electric light and withdrew on tiptoe.

The next morning he came to find her and gave her a wad of thousand-franc banknotes, for the running of the house. He had withdrawn a million the day before from the bank where it was deposited, for rumors of war were continuing to circulate, and he was afraid, with good reason, of the deceptiveness of the so-called moratorium. The artistic aristocrat was both a spend-thrift and skilled in business affairs.

Not without pride, he said to his wife: "Can you imagine that yesterday, on the train, I ran into Ségétan, who asked my advice about the matter of his interests, in the present harsh circumstances. I wouldn't be astonished if he had the intention of buying and making good use of Les Arges farm, or if he married the beautiful Tullie. He's a very extraordinary indi-vidual, and, in spite of his dyonisiac theories, science is every-thing to him."

"Don't you believe it! Women count for a great deal to him, physically speaking, and he has a way of looking at you, under the stars, and of taking hold of the arms or shoulders of one or other of them, that is unmistakable."

"Is he paying court to you?" asked Ignacio, already enticed and drawing the lovely star toward him with a feverish hand.

She pulled away.

"One can't call that paying court. He burns you with his incessant desire, which he carries around like a pocket torch. One senses that he's madly in love with Tullie, and yet capable of slipping into you in five seconds, if the fancy takes him."

"He must be as crazy as you are, the old satyr. You know his thesis: woman's beauty is the mother of discovery. Abbé Parroy says that he's a pagan; personally, I think he's a Platonist. But he's never asked you to show yourself to him like the woman with the parakeet?"

"Not yet, but if you want me to suggest the idea to him...."

The man's face changed, and he made a movement. She ran away toward the staircase. He pursued her. She reached her bedroom, plunged into it and drew the bolt. He shook the door like a great ape, begging and threatening, but, still preoccupied by the image of Calvat, she remained mute and insensitive. After a few minutes, she heard footsteps drawing away.

It was then that she wondered, with a certain anxiety, whether the experiments with the waves of the past might not be throwing everyone's minds into confusion, and whether Jean, who saw the scientist as a caster of spells, might not be right.

There are seductive monsters. Was the Master of Masters one of them?

* * * * * *

Some time after that, Ségétan, who had gone out for a walk in order to meditate—walking was a fecund source of inspiration for him—perceived the delightful silhouette of a woman coming toward him around the corner of the Quatrebois road, across the sunlit plain. It was Mélanie Dévonet.

On seeing him, the latter shivered. Her delicate bronzed face with the expressive eyes was framed by a flexible straw hat in the style of Marie-Antoinettte, ornamented by a large cherry-red ribbon.

"Bonjour, my dear. You find me in the midst of meditating on a remark made by Dévonet on the variations in the periodicity of our waves. There is, as we 'big brains' say a 'snag.' Happy are you, O stimulants and fertilizers of the masculine mind, who have no preoccupations of that sort."

She smiled sadly, which added depth to the exquisite oval of her pretty face. "What do you know? Our 'snags' are of another kind than yours, but they exist."

"Tell me one of them, for example."

"You."

"Oh, damn it!" said Ségétan, pretending not to understand. "You're worried about the gossip that's circulating about me in Loir-et-Cher—but it's of no importance. I'm not going to stand for election to parliament, or the Senate."

"I don't care about gossip. It's your person alone that's important to me—which I hide from my husband, your friend."

As she said that, they continued to walk side by side, without looking at one another—but various incomplete images of the delightfuil young woman who had made that point-blank declaration, in broad and blinding daylight, gave him the desire to indulge in Marivaudage.[17]

A few paces further on, on the edge of a field, was one of those abandoned huts carpeted with a bed of straw in which grape-gatherers sleep during the September heat. The door was missing, replaced by two simple planks of wood placed side by side. With a common accord, the two strollers headed toward that shelter. The surrounding countryside was hot, desrted as far as the eye could see.

"I know you, Mélanie," Ségétan said. "I've known you for years, since your marriage—but even so, I don't *know* you." He emphasized the verb the second time.

"Is Tullie no longer sufficient for you?" She articulated the question impertinently, and then, without any further pleading—for she knew him—she added: "You shall know me, fair sir. Wait outside a moment, until I call you."

She went into the cool, dark hut with the gilded floor. He waited, his throat dry, his eyes avid and speckled with round flames, attentive to the modifications that his present "aura" was bringing to Dévonet's question, either to simplify or confuse it. The wife was, therefore, about to come to her husband's aid, by

---

17. "Marivaudage," named for the early eighteenth-century playwright and novelist Pierre de Marivaux, refers to a mode of conduct and narration in which characters explain their thinking at length, with all its subtle nuances, to one another and to the spectator or reader. As the reader will observe, the desire experienced by Romain is quickly suppressed, although the author is, as usual, not slow to step in on his behalf.

virtue of an unexpected detour. The seeker's heart was beating strongly—which was a good sign.

A faint, clear voice said: "Come in!"

He went in.

There was an odor of straw and warm wood. In the sudden gloom, on the litter of sparkling woodchips, the most accomplished Tanagra[18] in the world presented to his quivering admiration, without any modesty, pure breasts, firm and strawberry-red, a rounded abdomen, and legs completely different from Tullie's, of another but equally elegant perfection.

Every accomplished female body—as he had observed and taken note—is a distinct work of art, a special creation, in its morophology and coloration, whose intoxicating essence will touch or exalt some part of the intellect. To the mathematician, the biologist, the poet, the dramaturge and the physicians, definite types of Eve, the sight, contact possession and ambiance of whom serve the cause or the end, correspond to the word or the number, the quality or the quantity. Thus is explained, by the harmony and uncanny splendor of its women, the power of the sculpture, the philosophy, the lyricism, the architecture and the dramaturgy of Periclean Greece. Thus is explained, by the beauty, the surge, the melting grace and voluptuousness of the female body of the sixteenth century, the genius of Shakespeare, Webster, Montaigne, Rabelais, Ronsard and Amyot.

These reflections, which had been rolling around Ségétan's brain for a long time, became precise at each new bound of a sensuality that overflowed the cup of his life.

At that moment, dazzled by the Mélanian flesh, as he had been just now in the sunlight, he was interiorly inundated by a major accord between beauty and truth, beauty being eternal, truth linked to the century, in that which concerns the earth.

The young woman turned round very slowly, in order to present two profiles to him successively, the face and the loins

18. Tanagra is a town in Greece noted in antiquity for the production of terracotta figurines, mostly depicting human figures in naturalstic costumes, which took its name.

thus corresponding to the four aspects of maternal ideas and the syntax that translates them. A bronze reflection rose from the straw, alloyed with the amber of her skin.

A moral and intellectual wellbeing took possession of the intoxicated spectator, to the detriment of his virile faculties. Although Tullie's body united all the powers in him, Mélanie's, for some unknown reason, divided them: one, the physical, was weakened; the other, the immaterial, was moved.

The beauty perceived that, having the experience of her husband, who was also drawn by love to scientific penetration, imitating the master.

"Are you satisfied, Master? Have I been useful to you?" she said—and picked up her clothes, with an agile dip, like a ballerina preparing for an entrechat or a swimmer about to dive.

"I'm delighted," Ségétan replied. "So much so that you've disarmed me...which is perfectly grotesque."

"In you, nothing can be grotesque. Anyway, it's so hot today that we'd be stuck together like postage-stamps. And that straw would be prickly! My feet are hankering for my stockings.

It did not take five minutes for her to get dressed again.

"Dévonet has had a narrow escape," said the scientist, by way of conclusion—and that statement brought a charming burst of laughter from her, child-like and caressing, but which could not match Tullie's broken laughter at the supreme moment.

When he got home, Romain Ségétan received from the hands of his beautiful mistress a letter that bore the postmark Napoli.

My dear,

> *The experiments in Avenillon are the only topic of conversation here. My young husband, who is, as you know, a highly-reputed American archaeologist and physicist, has to go to Paris soon to acquire electrical machines for the production of high-tension currents. He is taking me with him; it will be our real honeymoon voyage. We're leaving by car in ten days. Tell me the*

date on which your friend of childhood and youth can come to disturb you, in the company of her husband.

Entirely yours, and so looking forward to seeing you again,

Donabella

"I'm quite familiar with the remarkable work of Hatchinson," Ségétan said, "but how is it that your friend knows about me?"

"We correspond regularly. I was so happy and proud that when I told her about the death of Père Calvat I made her party to the profound change in my life. When shall we invite them here, then?"

"I'm planning, a fortnight from now, to gather thirty colleagues—French, English, German, Italian and Belgian—for a major séance of temporal waves, which, according to my calculations, will pass over us like a comet at a certain day and hour. Ignacio and Ariana will give them lunch in Brancheville. We can invite Hatchinson and his wife for the day before, and they can stay here, at Dyonisos for two or three days as they please."

CHAPTER THREE
DYONISOS' FIRST ARROW

The Villa Dyonisos at Avenillon had, as they say, put on its Sunday best. The American scientist Hatchison was expected, coming from Paris by automobile with his young wife Donabella. It was noon; the sky was clear and cloudless, a light blue akin to that of the Île-de-France. Old Marianne was finishing setting the table in the spacious and bright dining-room. Tullie was rereading the menu and deciding on the seating. She had invited Bénalep, the Dévonets and the Ignacios. With the travelers, they would be nine, in conformity with the gastronomic axiom "no fewer than the Graces, no more than the Muses."

The Dévonets arrived first, Mélanie in the full radiance of her gentility and beauty. Then it was Bénalep's turn, broad and massive, like a Hebrew Silenus. At that moment, a superb vehicle drew up at the door from which descended a tall, thin fellow of indeterminate age, a "stuffed shirt," as Dévonet put it, accompanied by a vertritable nymph, blonde and slim, with frank eyes, who immediately threw herself into Tullie's arms.

That was Donabella from Naples, Tullie's childhood friend, whom she had not seen for several years. The new arrival was clad in pink, heightened by a single golden nenuphar water-lily, as vaporous as a butterfly in the harbor of Rio de Janeiro; her greeter was in jet black, like a living statue enveloped in silky darkness—and their sincere joy described the scintillating spirals of Baudelaire's Lola de Valence.[19] That was the judgment

19. Baudelaire wrote a quartrain inspired by a painting of the Spaish

of Ignacio, who disembarked at the same time, accompanied by Ariana, dressed in pale green.

Ségétan, as natural as an element at rest, with his face a mixture of Napoléon and Dante, welcomed his American colleague cordially and his svelte companion gallantly. Meanwhile, Abrice took his fellow Pietro to the garage; in order to show off his erudition he had made the Fascist salute.

"Oh, my dear, how glad I am to see you again!" said Tullie.

Immediately, they switched into Italian, the words of which were outlined by brilliant fissures against a grave background of sun and shadow. If English is reminiscent of birdsong, with its mocking and dreamlike inclusions, Italian is the most distinct of languages, the most delimited by a pure and sonorous succession, while Spaish is sculpted in a sort of red dusk. The two young women—Donabella was four years younger than Tullie—thus exchanged, in a few seconds, an essence of memories that made them laugh and gave them the appearance of little girls playing around the Château de l'Oeuf.[20]

The American told his host how proud he was to be in his home, and assured him that in the United States he was known as the Edison of France—but that compliment scarcely flattered Ségétan, who considered the famous inventor of Menlo Park to be an ingenious mechanic.

They sat down at table, the host having Donabella to his right and Ariana to his left. Tullie, who played hostess like a legitimate spouse—but without benefit of Maire or Curé—had Bénalep to her right and Hatchinson to her left.

"Tullie and I have put together a simple menu," said the Master of the Waves, "but which ought to please you: hors

dancer in question by Édouard Manet in 1862, intending it to be inscribed on the painting's frame; it was eventually printed on a supplementary card. The fourth line refers to "the unexpected beauty of a pink and black gem," which is why it is relevant here, although Donabella is obviously much better-looking than the rather frumpy Lola.

20. The most ancient citadel in Naples, Castrum Ovi in Latin, Castel dell'Ovo in Italian, Egg Castle in English.

d'oeuvre with melon and port; salmon trout; braised leg of beef with olives; chicken Soubise; fricassee of cultivated mushrooms; lettuce salad; ice-cream medley; Loir-et-Cher fruits. As wines—for I presume, my dear Hatchinson, that you're not a prohibitionist in France"—the physicist shook his head—"I'll offer you a Château-Yquem, a Lur Saluces, with a hint of licorice, but a good year, and a negligible *vin de pays*. The driveshaft of the meal will be a Beaune Hôpital from the Maison Bouchard—which says it all."

"This evening, Madame and Monsieur," Bénalep declared in his turn, "I invite you and everyone else here present to be my guests. My old bachelor's cooking can't match Caroline's, but I'll personally make you a cheese soup and a classic cassoulet and offer you an authentic raspberry liqueur that an Alsatian colleague sent me. Finally, you'll make the acquaintance of my digitalis coffee—by which I mean associated with foxgloves in the soil, cultivated in Indochina according to my principles, and which, putting no strain on the heart, enjoys special therapeutic qualities."

This proposal delighted those who were aware of Bénalep's culinary skills as well as the newcomers. An ambiance of good cheer and lofty intellectualism was established. The name of the Blésois villa led to that of the magical apparatus that evoked the past, and also to the topic of the famous Villa of the Dyonisiac Mysteries discovered fairly recently in Pompeii, with its incomparable Hellenic frescoes, dating from the era of Greek greatness five centuries before Christ.[21]

---

21. The villa in question, and its so-called "Initiation Chamber," came to light during the excavations supervised by Amedeo Maiuri, begun in 1924. The actual sequence of ten images contained in the latter (which can be seen on-line) differs somewhat, especially in the later phases, from the descriptions given in the novel, and readily lends itself to other interpretations than the Dionysian one. There are, however, other frescoes in in the villa that are recruited to the series of images decribed in the novel, whose sequence is a composite. The villa appears to date from c50 B.C. rather than the era of the original Orphic Mysteries, as would be expected in Pompeii.

"I've heard mention of that," said Ségétan. "It appears that it's admirable in its artistry, and extremely curious from the viewpoint of the cult of Bacchus."

"That too is a genuine wave of time," said Hatchison, with a strong accent, comical in its effect, "I'm no poet, merely a petty electric cook who aspires to do well, but when I went into that painted room for the first time with Donabella, I experienced a kind of frisson that nothing had ever given me before."

"What does it represent?" asked Dévonet.

"Nobody really knows," Donabella replied, interrupting her husband, who was obviously searching for words. "It appears, so they say, to be a matter of the initiation of a Bacchante. She's a young and beautiful woman who is seen at first facing forward, covered by a veil, and at the end from behind, without the veil; who is alerted by a kind of plump angel reading a book; who takes part in a symbolic meal; who kneels in front of a large indistinct blob; and who is then whipped by another woman who is said to be the daughter of Bacchus. The god himself can also be seen, lying down, with one foot bare, and Silenus presenting a young man with a magic mirror, in which the past is perceptible."[22] She turned toward her neighbor at the table. "I beg your pardon, illustrious Master—the wave of the past."

"Oh, that must be interesting!" exclaimed Ariana. "Why hasn't anyone thought of making a film of that revelation?"

"I went to Pompeii once," said Ignacio, "but no one told me about that villa. Where is it situated?"

"Outside the city, in the fields; it's a countryside that's very similar to Provence. From there one can see Vesuvius smoking his pipe. As the place is separate, few visitors go there—that's why all those to whom one asks about the Villa of the Mysteries reply 'I don't know.' They know the others—Diomedes, the tragic poet, the philosopher, the evil place—but not that one."

While saying that, Hatchinson was devouring large forkfuls of the tender braised beef on a bed of very numerous pitted

22. This is pure conjecture; it is impossible actually to make out what the mirror shows.

olives, expertly prepared, neither salty nor bitter, and washing them down with mouthfuls of cool wine.

Ségétan had listened to these jabbered explanations with a extreme attention and concentration in his blue yes. The myth of Bacchus and the mysteries of Eleusis linked to his name had always intrigued him, as a kind of prefiguration of Christianity, of which they were an exact opposite, insofar as the emotional pleasures of the body are opposed to the ecstatic joys of the soul. He was, however, neither a believer nor an unbeliever. When talking to Abbé Parroy one day, he had said: "For you and those like you life is a gift from God; it's up to humans to give it a meaning. For me, life is a condition of nature, commanded in all its fundamentals by nature, which is the only God."

"You and Tullie absolutely must come to see that," Donabella said to him, turning an enthusiastic, child-like face toward him, open to life, through which all the scattered ardors of spring were passing.

Ariana, his other neighbor at the table, whispered in his ear: "I'll go with you. Doubtless you'll extract some new discovery from it."

"The resurrection of Greek antiquity, for instance," said Ignacio, jokingly, having overheard.

Then they talked about other things, notably the threat of war hanging over Europe and the possibility of disrupting engines in mid-flight. Over the table, Dévonet exclaimed: "Romain, you know they're counting to you to discover that marvelous trick. One newspaper has even identified you, indiscreetly, in so many words."

"The proverb assures us," the Master said, "that one can't be at the forge and the mill at the same time. But you all know the rule of modern physics: problem posed, problem solved."

* * * * * * *

While these remarks of a dyonisiac and scientific nature were being exchanged, the cook Caroline, the faithful Abrice,

Jean Calvat, the Dévonets' and Bénalep's maidservants and Sylvain, the Ignacio's valet, as well as a farmhand from Arges were surrounding Pietro in the servant's parlor and questioning him about his "bosses." He explained to them, with expressive gestures, in a mixture of French and Italian, that they were duly married—"That's not the case here," Caroline put in—that the *donna* was very kind and very generous and the Yankee rather uptight.

"Do you think he'll soon be cuckolded?"

As the Italian did not understand, Abrice put his index finger of each hand to ether side of his head, thus simulating two projecting horns.

Pietro laughed, and made an evasive gesture. "Possibly. My... *non seguro.*"

"You'd gladly do your '*bella donna*' a favor, eh, joker?"

Such baseness sickened Jean Calvat, but he still hoped to learn, by hanging around with the servants, something dishonorable about Ségétan that would aliment his hatred. The latter, however, by reason of his science, was the only person almost respected "below stairs," although Bénalep passed for an old fool and Dévonet for a sponger and a humbug, hanging on to the Master's coat-tails and trying to palm his Mélanie off on him in exchange for ready money.

""While I was doing theirs," Caroline declared, proudly, "I did us a third chicken Soubise—on the quiet, of course—so that we can lick our fingers. By the way, Sylvain, it promises to be quite a banquet at your place tomorrow! How many places are you setting so far?"

"Thirty," replied the individual in question, in a world-weary tone. He had a long wrinkled child-like face with the hilum of a haricot bean. "We've sent to Blois for three servers, legs of mutton, gateaux and little sausages from the Rue de la Foulerie...."

"The best in the region," certified Abrice, a connoisseur.

"...puff-pastry and rillons from Guet's in Amboise, an enormous Balthazar...."

"Is your dairy-cow, the beautiful Ariana, going to dance during dessert?"

Again it was the colossal Abrice who spoke thus. Calvat blushed to his ears; fortunately for him, no one noticed.

Pietro enquired, in his jargon, what all those people would be doing there.

"Witnessing experiments with waves, my little Mararoni," the chauffeur replied, swallowing a cake fresh out of the oven in one go. "Don't you know that my Master, Romain Ségétan, is the ace of aces, the king of Sorcerers, and that he makes events come back with a little machine about *this* big—events that happened three hundred years ago, and more. All the scientists in the world are drooling over it, including your American."

At this point Calvat thought he ought to intervene. "And even though it causes skin diseases that neither Bienallé nor Dévonet can cure, in the poor farmhands hereabouts."

"Shut up," the chauffeur retorted, gnawing a chicken leg. "You don't understand anything. A man like my master marches at the head of humankind. He was in the paper the other day, in the headline. If his invention gives rise to petty inconveniences, or even serious problems, so be it—but you have to see the goal."

"What goal?"

"Progress of course. You're nothing but a peasant, and peasants don't know anything. The day when an airplane in mid-flight comes crashing down to earth, because some doodad has cut off its whistle, war will then be impossible, you see, and you won't have to get your throat cut for people you don't know and affairs you don't care about."

To the entire domestic staff, the argument seemed peremptory, but Calvat shrugged his shoulders. Abbé Parroy had explained to him that the only true progress was an internal improvement procured by the moral effort of the individual, and not some external improvement, mechanical or otherwise, that has nothing to do with the soul. In his jealous eyes, Ségétan was nothing but a villain with a laboratory, of whom it was important to rid humankind, and it was to that conclusion that all his tremulous thoughts were directed.

* * * * * * *

As they left the table, Hatchinson, buoyed up by the good cheer and the wines, took the master of the house to one side. There was contained laughter within his "stuffed shirt."

"The large indistinct blob in the Villa of Mysteries that my wife mentioned to you...."

"What blob?"

"The one before which the initiate kneels...."

"Oh yes. So?"

"It's a phallus...yes, all in all, a pudendum."

Meanwhile, leaving the men in the smoking-room, Ariana, Mélanie and Tullie went into the cool drawing-room, the bay window of which overlooked the verdant garden, and in which there was a piano. They clustered around the lithe Donabella, who was sprawling on a sofa upholstered in the same pink color as her vaporous dress. They replied to her questions regarding the Master, his great discovery, his working methods and his habits; he had fascinated her in an hour of conversation and silence, and she was incapable of interesting herself in anything else.

"He's not human," Ariana affirmed. "He's a sort of demigod— isn't that right, Tullie?"

"Certainly—and the closer one is to him, the more one admires him, the more one sees that his thought knows no limits. He's like the sea, like the clouds, like the sun."

"Does he burn in the same fashion?"

"Very nearly."

Mélanie, thinking of the hut on the road to Quatrebois, smiled secretly—but she joined in the chorus wholeheartedly, for her silence would have been noticed."

"He has an atmosphere about him, you understand, Madame, and when that atmosphere penetrates you, it transforms you. It's like another form of oxygen. One is enlivened."

The pretty Neapolitan woman mimed that intellectual volup-tuousness—whose spur gave her a physical sensation—with the palpitation of her translucent nostrils. From then on, she was inseminated by the curiosity about the person of the male thus glorified, which is the human form of bestial desire, the equivalent of odor on the animal level. To numb herself, she talked about other things and told lively stories, in the style of Boccaccio, taken from Campanian folklore, some of whose meanings she did not grasp, and which displayed her innocence. The sound of laughter attracted the gentlemen, who arrived with reeking cigars in their lips to investigate the cause of the gaiety. They were brought up to date.

"You have no shame," said Hatchinson, affectionately, "bringing such childish tales into the sanctuary of the highest science!"

"No, I have no shame."

"Nor have we!" said the feminine chorus.

Bénalep seemed ecstatic. He fluttered his hairy and slender hands, which contrasted with is corporeal masses, repeating: "What a charming decameron! Nevertheless, a little music is required before our dimwits arrive. Tomorrow, in fact, will be the men's day, of discussions, speeches, numbers and every-thing ugly. Come on, Tullie, give us a song."

"I've just got up from the table, sorcerer, and since I became a farmer's wife I've given up singing."

"Impossible," Donabella protested. "It's in your nature."

Ségétan insisted: "Go on, my dear...."

"Well, I won't make you beg. So much the worse for the croaks!"

She launched into a popular song from Cap Misène, with a very simple, elementary accompaniment but a marvelously clear gravity, like the dawn over a misfortune. The birds chirping in the grounds fell silent, vanquished by the competi-tion. The voice, classical in its register, rose up like a skylark, then descended like a swallow in stormy weather, and the audi-ence, stirred, saw that flower of jet black and white skin, those superb arms, that upright neck, fill up with liquid sound.

An inexplicable twinge of jealousy nipped the semi-recumbent blonde, who was recalling her happy childhood in the land of song. She took out the golden nenuphar that was etiolating at her waist and threw it at the surprised Ségétan, who caught it in mid-air. Not knowing what to do with the flower, he put it down on the piano, with an amusing awkwardness.

While those moist strains were resonating, drawn from the forceful double springs of visual and sonorous beauty, an unhappy man was eating himself away in a thicket fifty meters away. The *other*, the accursed, had stolen that angelic voice from him, as he had stolen the incomparable body, covertly glimpsed at Les Arges through the cracks and the keyholes of the dressing-room and bedroom. Once again the young man, drunk on ardent and desolate images, swore to punish the thief.

At four o'clock in the afternoon, as the heat descended, the inhabitants of Dyonisos proposed an automobile excursion to their guests. A single vehicle would suffice. In fact, Dévonet had important work in progress, and Bénalep had to see to his meal, his soup and cassoulet. The Ignacios, husband and wife, wanted to preside personally over the preparations for the next day's feast. Thus, Ségétan, Tullie,, Mélanie and the two Hatchinsons climbed into the spacious limousine.

"What would you like to see?" the scientist asked his guests. "A little of Touraine a little of Sologne, Vendôme, Châteaudun?"

"Oh, a little of Touraine," Donabella requested. "So much is said about the châteaux of the Loire...."

The Master of the Waves pulled a face. He had a horror of that classic journey, so good for cars: Chambord, as sad as giant Savoy gateau in the midst of its skimpy woods; Chenonceaux, like a hump-backed bridge in the stifling heat of a flat, burning plain; Chaumont, a great formless building devoid of shape and interest, with its ridiculous drawbridge; Ussé, plastered and almost crushed against its wall. He would have given a good deal, he declared, not to have to live in one, among a hundred servitudes and clutter of all sorts. A historic château was like a yacht; one was its prisoner. It was necessary to play host to people one did not know, with shiny and runny noses, who debauched the servants, broke the furniture and spread nasty gossip afterwards.

Hatchinson and his wife listened in astonishment, wondering whether he was being paradoxical, forcing themselves to laugh with Tullie and Mélanie, who were accustomed to such outbursts.

"In brief," he concluded, "Since you insist, we'll show you Chambord and Chaumont from a distance. Then we'll go watch the sunset from the heights overlooking the Loire upriver of Amboise, the residence of king François I, where Leonardo da Vinci died."

"Oh, Leonardo da Vinci!" said the American, manifesting a great interest. "The man who painted *La Gioconda* and studied flying machines?"

"The very same. He probably knew as much as we do, and more, but dared not say so. All seekers are like that. I myself am a long way ahead, with my waves of time, at least in the mind—but I keep my advanced reflections secret, certain that they wouldn't be understood. Already, some of my colleagues are insinuating that I might be a trickster."

The last remark astonished Hatchinson, as well as the ironic tone in which it had been made. What a strange fellow this Frenchman was!

During this conversation, the automobile had ploughed ahead, and they arrived within sight of Chambord, which seemed small and cramped to Hatchinson, and at which Donabella, forewarned, barely glanced. Before Chaumont and its pile, she made a moue—which suited her—and said: "It's nothing at all...."

Amboise interested them more, because of François I, whose renown, although limited to beddings and the pox, had even reached as far as New York, Chicago and Boston. Ségétan got down in the Rue Nationale to make sure at the patisserie that the six puff-pastries would be ready for the next day's banquet, and at the pork-butchers to confirm the order for rillons and extra rillettes. From the old and curious little city with the ancient wooden dwellings, solidly embedded in the rocky ground—earthscrapers rather than skyscrapers—they went back up toward the forests and plains that adorn the "garden of France."

The pagoda of Chanteloup surprised the travelers considerably. "Yes, it's interesting," the Master remarked, without saying any more. "We'll doubtless have another opportunity to talk about it."

The excursion had been timed in such a fashion that they arrived at the edge of the historic woods ("Stop, great king—you are betrayed!") for the August sunset over the sumptuous hills of the Loire. No madman emerged from the thicket to throw himself in front of the automobile, though, as had once happened to the royal carriage. The five passengers got out of the car and took a few steps in silence, before the vague violets and yellows of the crops, bathed in the redness of molten gold.

The two men marched in front, talking about their work. The three women followed, ecstatic.

"One can't imagine anything as marvelous!" Donabella repeated. She took a few steps to one side in order to pick a wild flower intended to replace her water-lily. Romain, who had heard, turned round and ran after her, to whisper in her ear: "There's something even more marvelous."

"What's that?"

"I'll tell you this evening."

That little mystery intrigued the Neapolitan woman to the highest degree. Since her arrival at the villa—which is to say, since that morning—she had experienced an indefinable sentiment, like a malaise foreshadowing a delight. Its origin was in this large Frenchman, who carried a world in his head with a great deal of simplicity, and whose blue gaze penetrated the body all the way to the soul.

Within the young woman there was the same reserve of frissons and voluptuous transports as in Tullie—a reserve that had remained intact on contact with her American, as it had remained intact in Tullie on contact with Père Calvat. It was that, which exists to a greater or lesser degree in many women, as an accumulation of unshared sensations, to which Ségétan had set fire.

* * * * * * *

In spite of the unctuous cheese soup and the cassoulet with breadcrumbs on top, soft and smooth within, and the raspberry liqueur, the meal at Bénalep's house was morose, either because keen and curt impressions, repeated and not expressed, were restraining some of them, or because the moral exchanges of the busy hours had created imponderable disparities and mute quarrels.

The latter, like the mute attractions, are numerous when several people are gathered together, if they are of different sexes and charged with contrary or conjoined destinies. That is what creates the charm of solitude, the anguish of absence and the surprise of presence. All mixed-sex society is a mixture of latent discords and harmonies.

They left the table. Seated next to Donabella, the Master had not looked at her and hardly addressed a word to her. As they were taking coffee in Bénalep's study, also overlooking the silent countryside, she took him by the arm—a muscular, solid, determined arm—with a respectful familiarity and led him on to the doorstep beneath the stars.

"May I ask you a question?"

"At your orders."

"Well then, what's more marvelous than today's sunset?"

"You haven't guessed?"

"No...not guessed."

"It's the body of a woman, my dear Madame...yours, for example."

She uttered a slight "Oh!" half-shocked and half-delighted, fluttered her eyelids and stood up straight, as if she had received, on her left side, between the heart and the rib, a little arrow: the arrow of Dyonisos, initiatory and commanding.

In a low voice, Ségétan added: "So why did you throw your

water-lily at me?"

* * * * * * *

Everyone went home early, through the narrow streets of the sleeping village, the Dévonets in one direction, Romain, Tullie and their Neapolitans in the other. During the journey they met no one, save for the furtive shadow of a man, which disappeared immediately.

They were due to meet again at the following day's banquet, at the Château de Brancheville at one o'clock in the afternoon. They would sit down at table at one-thirty, in order to give the guests time to arrive, the majority by automobile, a few by rail.

Having wished their guests goodnight, the Master and his lover went to their room, which was adjacent to Dnabella's dressing-room. Hatchinson was lodged on the same landing in the opposite wing of the villa. The newly-weds kept their distance, according to the American custom, for it there is no more manifest "bad form" than meeting up in the same room and the same bed on a daily basis.

The two childhood friends embraced wholeheartedly, congratulating one another on the day, their excursion and their reunion. Shortly afterwards, the American was heard cautiously putting his boots and indoor shoes outside his door.

Once she was alone, Donabella tried to put her ideas—or, rather, her impressions—in order. It seemed to her that she had lived as much in the last few hours as in the whole of her previous life. Something considerable had overtaken her, accompanied by an immense and mute disturbance, which a few words had brought into focus: "It's the body of a woman, my dear Madame...."

Mine, or someone else's?

She knew that she was beautiful. Everyone had already told her so. When she was a girl, and then a woman, strangers and residents alike had turned round in the streets of Naples when she passed by. She had had numerous suitors and half a dozen seducers who had embraced, caressed and pawed her as they had embraced, caressed, flattered and pawed her friend Tullie. Among Latin peoples, that is of no great consequence, and, if one could believe Bobby Hatchinson, it was of no great consequence among the Anglo-Saxons either. Such encounters are the *hors-d'oeuvre* and premises of amorous life.

Without inspiring the slightest love in her, Hatchinson had pleased her. He was rich, intelligent in his profession, and honest, capable of enthusiasm, of humor, rather suspicious, very susceptible and rancorous. Her in-laws were far away; Donabella's father and two brothers lived in Rome; her mother was dead. She and the American had married joyfully, and were sumptuously installed in a large house overlooking the bay, in open country. Bobby had organized a magnificent and complete laboratory, provided with the latest inventions in waves and electromagnetism, and measuring devices of every sort, which foreign scientists came to visit. The couple entertained a great deal.

In sum, she was happy. But she knew, divined or foresaw that she lacked something: that special gasp of the heart, that generalized warmth which she had experienced in her first exchange of glances with the blue gaze of the magician.

After having undressed slowly, the blonde went into her dressing-room, like a cat, without making a noise. Behind the wall, she heard a feeble murmur of voices, which she recognized, with a little attention, as those of her hosts—but it remained distant and indistinct. Then she took a portable microphone of her husband's invention from her suitcase, which multipled sound by a factor of twenty for the listener, without the sound being perceptible to anyone else.

What she heard was of the keenest, most urgent and most burning interest, for it was about her.

The Master said: "She's a child, but of a form that one divines to be delightful, and an innocence of mind that is only explicable on seeing her lanky husband."

"Admit that you liked her."

"Very much, and right away. She gave me a blonde version of the sensual and intellectual shock that you gave me in brunette. If I weren't holding myself back...."

"I can guess the rest. You'd go join her immediately. But I warn you that the other—the American fellow, Père Pudendum—is already suspicious. When you went to say a few words to Dona on the terrace a little while ago, he never took his eyes off you. A little patience, damn it, Monsieur le Magicien. Do you know what I was thinking during lunch?"

"No—my attention was attracted by the two new...."

"Of a trip to Naples that we'll make—the entire colony of Avenillon, the Dévonets, Bénalep, the two of us and the Ignacios. There we'll meet up with Dona and her husband again. You can excite your imagination with her, while Ariana, Mélanie and I occupy the physicist, as best we can. I'll see my beautiful vigorous city again, and that bay, which has no resemblance to any other...."

"Except, a little, to that of Marseilles...."

"If you say so. Vesuvius, which, like you, gives everything that surrounds it a particular tremor.... We'll visit the redoubtable enchanted villa of the cult of Bacchus, the frescoes whose description—confess it—makes the mouth water. Finally, while you hold me tight, and I hold you tight, you'll be there, in the heartland of the past, in the midst of cosmic upheaval, and in the midst of antiquity—and since the waves of time obey you, what will you not evoke in such a place?"

Tullie fell silent, and the noise of love-making, and then of sighs, gave the blonde next door a kind of gooseflesh in which there was no infusion of dread. She left her night attire incomplete and ran to her bed, feeling guilty, still shivering between the cool silken sheets.

She had a dream: in a beautiful twilit landscape, a compound of Castellamare and Touraine, before a château bearing some resemblance to Chambord, she found herself alone with Ségétan. He had a profoundly sad expression and was dressed in black, like a widower. They sat down on a bench. He undressed her slowly; she let him do it, and saw his large impressive head, laden with discoveries like a bomb with explosives, at close range. Suddenly, though, when she no longer had anything on, in the dying light and the evening breeze, but a light silk undergarment, she perceived with terror that it was not *him* at all, but a very different man, an unknown man, who was holding her in his arms.

* * * * * *

Hatchinson did not get much sleep that night. Something—he did not know what—was tormenting him. Finally, he thought he had found it: was his host's miraculous invention genuine and authentic, or might it be a very skillful deception, half-voluntary and half-unconscious, similar to those practiced by spiritualists? The few words that the French thaumaturge had pronounced in the car, his allusion to those who considered him to be a trickster, had troubled him. He had not understood very much of the explanation—deliberately confused in any case—of the so-called Dyonisos apparatus. The Master—as he was claimed to be—was not reassuring, nor were his entourage: the clown who wanted to talk about insects and the physician who cultivated digitalis coffee. Very bizarre, too, was his fashion of paying court to the women, looking them in the eyes and covering them with compliments—scarcely compatible with the dignity and restraint habitual to scientists, demanded by respectable institutions, academies and conferences.

Hatchinson was American, and the people in question, who believe themselves to be infinitely superior by reason of their constant activity and the rapidity of their architectural, mechanical and other constructions, are, in fact, quite childish. They have adopted primary axioms that the European elites rejected a long time ago: that science is always benevolent; that democracy is the expression of the popular will; that a studious man is always chaste, or, at any rate, very conventional; that wine and alcohol are the source of all evil, finance and the stock exchange the source of all good; the myth of the self-made man, that everyone can succeed by means of work—Franklin retouched by Edison. But their greatest poet, and one of the greatest ever to appear on earth, Edgar Poe, was a drunk, and those abstainers have invented the cocktail, epilepsy in a glass, an iced perversion of the sense of taste.

Donabella's husband belonged to that vast transatlantic infancy, full of overweening conceit and nudging bonhomie, which is ambitious to replace culture—the true culture, handed down from the depths of the ages and the Greek and Latin texts—with a philosophy and a politics of facts for facts' sake, and that of surprise, of giant endeavors built on sand that will crumble tomorrow.

Hatchinson had married Donabella for love, but he had not found in the nuptial bed the satisfactions, indeterminate in any case, that he had expected—merely a slender statue of indifferent, resigned blandness, falling asleep every evening, unanimated by his contact.

That she might be animated by contact with someone else was something he had not imagined before the day that had just ended, when the throwing of the water-lily had filled him with astonishment.

CHAPTER FOUR
THE HAUNTED SITES

"Our parishioner is lucky," said Abbé Parroy, looking at the immense and radiant orb in the pale blue sky. "Today's the 'festival of the angels.' But how shall we see the phenomenon in broad daylight, in such weather?"

"Now, now," replied his housekeeper, a robust daughter of Knocke-sur-Mer, who had a Flanders accent, "the angels have nothing to do with these devilries. Is Monsieur l'Abbé going to the banquet? It appears that it's being held in the room of nudes and postures at the Château de Brancheville."

"No, my child, I don't have a place there. I'm only to witness the experiments in the afternoon. The entire village will be there, and also those of Quatrebois and Evinances. If the heart moves you...."

But Gertrude's only response was to make the sign of the cross and disappear, grumbling.

The warm splendor of the Blésois day had permitted the banquet-tent to be set up on the terrace at Brancheville, more spacious than the art gallery, where some of the paintings might have alarmed the guests. The latter disembarked, as anticipated, in two batches, by automobile and train. A charabanc with fifteen places awaited them at the station. The arrivals were greeted by the Duc d'Ignacio and Ségétan, assisted by Ariana and Tullie.

There were, for France, professors of the Faculté, the Collège de France, academicians of uncertain age and certain science, who were joined by two Germans, two Englishmen, an Italian, a Japanese and a Swede, the flower of world physics and mathematical philosophy—all of them desirous of getting an idea of Ségétan's discovery, the revelation of which filled the world. Two of them, the German Doppelwein and the Frenchman Pierretin, were considered to be the only ones capable of understanding one another, so inaccessible was the summit of their quantitative conceptions of life and motion. The former, the Boche, had the ruddy head of a split melon, cheerful but with two eyes sparkling with malice, sheltered by two bushy eyebrows. The second bore a false resemblance to Victor Hugo, crowned with hair even more unruly that that of the author of the *Contemplations*, and his bright eyes, staring into nowhere, seemed lost in a great dream.

They were all hungry, some after three and a half hours in an automobile, others after two and a half hours on a train, which had hollowed out their stomachs. No journalists had been invited, in order to avoid stupidities and erroneous interpretations. Except for Tullie, Donabella, Ariana and Mélanie, there was only one woman, the mairesse Madame Taupin.

After the ceremony of the cloakroom, when everyone had already taken their places at table according to the instructions of the staff, the prefect of Loir-et-Cher, Monsieur Dugerbier, arrived, and timidly slipped into the seat to the left of Ariana, who was presiding opposite Romain, with Pierretin to her right. Hatchinson found himself a long way from Donabella, who, as if under a spell, never took her eyes off the Master.

As soon as the ice had been broken under the influence of a generous port, accompanied by robust cantaloupes covered in warts, two currents became manifest: the incredulous and the skeptics, reserved even on subjects far removed from the waves of duration; and the convinced in advance, persuaded at a distance, with open attitudes and encouraging tones. The later had more appetite and drank more steadily than the former.

The Japanese looked anxiously at the perfumed rillons set on his plate, as well as the small sausages from Blois. By contrast,

Doppelwein swallowed a plateful without drawing breath, with a visible contentment, and made a sign to the waiter to fetch him a second helping. The bread, come from the Chaussée Saint-Victor, where it is particularly exquisite and renowned, and the so-called hill wine—but what hills!—had a considerable success. Professor Urpar of the Collège de France, for whom the waves of space had no secrets, cut thick squares of bread and crusts, like a peasant, which he engulfed with delight. It was also him who, on seeing a peacock's thigh on his plate—Ariana had put Juno's bird on the menu—grabbed it in both hands and devoured it enthusiastically, like a relativistic lion famished by quanta.

With her neighbor Bénalep, Mélanie Dévonet, a malicious observer, successively examined all those laborious physiognomies, bleak because they were unaccustomed to laughter and the pleasant parts of the imagination. Opposite her, she had the philosopher of quantity Abramson, the knowledgeable but pretentious author of *The Highways of the Mind*, who only admitted one rigor, that of numbers and geometrical diagrams, although there is another rigor, that of words and speech, and the actions that flow therefrom. Abramson, who though that Ségétan was too much of a fantasist, tainted by animism, had a large convex forehead, a cold gaze, which never settled on anyone or anything, and an air of priceless satisfaction. Everything about him said: "I am Abramson, the one and only, presently passing through the world. Look at me!"

Jean Calvat, after a night of insomnia, had requested to help with the service, in the capacity of a liaison between the "extras" brought in from Blois and the ordinary domestic staff of the château. As he had alternating bouts of pride and humility, that proposition had not astonished anyone. In fact, his jealousy, excited by Ségétan's great day, had suggested to him that he might kill the latter with a knife-thrust at the very height of his glory, as one cuts the throat of a pig—an exercise often practiced at Les Arges, which had excited him greatly as a child.

It happened that Hatchinson, also animated by rather malevolent thoughts in regard to his host, and with an analogous motive, had asked the young obsessive for a table-knife. When the latter brought it to him, their eyes met, and Hatchinson was able to read the homicidal intent in Calvat's eyes.

Well-gorged, the Ségétanians felt close to fervor, and the a-Ségétanians and anti-Ségétanians, who were less numerous, felt their doubt and hostility decreasing. They had reached dessert, ice-creams and the delicate tarts for which Blois is also renowned. Ségétan rose to his feet. His handsome and plump face exhaled a sort of attractive and communicative serenity. Naturally eloquent, thanks to the habit of conversing with himself, Dévonet and Bénalep, he only had a few notes in front of him, but he knew exactly what he wanted to say and preferred to semi-improvise his lecture.

Insensibly, Jean Calvat, who had a sharpened blade in his pocket at the ready, in a cork sheath, drew nearer to him, in such a way that he could reach his carotid with a single bound, irremediably.

A great silence fell, and the waiters listened religiously, like all the guests, with their white napkins over their arms.

"My dear colleagues, my generous friend the Duc d'Ignacio and I have invited you today to witness an experiment with the waves of the past to which, a year and a half ago, I called the attention of the Académie des Science, and which have already given rise to a great deal of controversy. You have here, at this table, my two principal collaborators, Doctors Bénalep and Dévonet, who have been good enough, to the detriment of their own very interesting research, to devote precious time to mine. I should like to thank them publicly.

"Everyone is familiar with the phenomenon of the mirage, by which places and appearances can be transported over great distances. This is a matter of veritable mirages, not in space but in time, due to bundles of waves of a particular nature, which I call waves of duration. They appeared to me at first, it is true, indistinctly, by virtue of parasites of a special kind, which I had noticed in sequences of short waves, which are, as you know, propagated simultaneously in two different fashions, some following the sun and others passing through the upper atmosphere at an altitude of about a hundred kilometers.

"Thanks to Dr. Dévonet's calculations, which we shall place at your disposal, we have been able to observe a kind of periodicity in the anomalies and changes of the upper atmosphere, which have permitted us to discern, along with to the now-familiar waves of space, those of duration, whose vibrations are produced in a very different plane. With these mathematical data, we have succeeded in constructing an apparatus of great sensitivity, called Dyonisos, which permits us to detect the waves in question and also render them visible and sonorous."

Herer the speaker paused momentarily, and his steady, strong, clear voice, emanating from his mouth, shaped like a classically-drawn bow, ceased to act upon his audience, violently interested not only by the man but his ambiance. Hatchinson watched Calvat, who appeared to be hesitating to carry out his murderous project, so interested was he in the demonstration.

Perhaps I'm mistaken, after all, thought Donabella's husband, *and have fallen prey myself to the strange atmosphere of this strange place.*

Ségétan continued: "The mechanism of that apparatus is extremely simple, and Dr. Dévonet will demonstrate it to you, because we designed it together. What I want to talk about here, in a few words, is the new conception of the terrestrial envelope of vast systems of undulatory vibrations, interpenetrating without being confused, that gravitates with us. The laws of their reappearance, their disappearance and their persistence are still unknown to us. Nevertheless, for a given region—this one—we have already been able to draw up a few tables, very rudimentary as yet, of presence and absence, according to the Baconian method. We have thus arrived at the establishment of zones of predilection for the waves of duration: of positively haunted sites. The plains that surround us are part of these privileged enclaves, comparable to certain areas of the skin particularly accessible to sensorial hyperesthesia, which are well-known to physicians. Thus, in the physical aspect, the phenomena can be observed.

"There remains a mental aspect, which we can, as yet, only glimpse and offer conjectures. Will astrology and its sidereal influences, which have recently been supposed to belong to he domain of chimeras, appear tomorrow to be sagacious anticipations of the impregnation of human being by these patterns of waves originating in the depths of space or the depths of time? Do the waves in question only enter into our cognizance, or into our destiny too? The characteristic of life in general is to be fecund, and the characteristic of human being is the fecundation of the mind and the body, the mind by concepts and the body by glandular reserves of desire—but that is not my domain, and I apologize for venturing into it."

Ségétan raised his champagne glass. "My dear colleagues, I drink"—he turned to Abramson, who had litened to all of that phlegmatically—"to the 'highways of the mind.'"

Unanimous applause greeted that toast, pronounced with confidence.

At that moment, the sound of a falling body was heard. It was Jean Calvat who had collapsed.

There was a moment of general alarm. Ariana and Dévonet, and then Tullie, were beside the poor boy in an instant. His stiffness, his convulsed eyes and a few bubbles of foam on his mouth left no doubt as to the cause.

"It's nothing, Messieurs," said Dévonet. "A simple faint. It'll be over in a few minutes."

With a entirely scientific indifference, the guests got up from the table and went into the smoking-room or the drawing-rooms for coffee and liqueurs.

During the meal, the sky, as happens on the banks of the Loire, had changed completely. From royal blue it had passed to the color of lead, uniformly distributed, and there was the threat of a storm, which would have rendered the manifestation of the waves of duration very difficult.

"Not impossible, Messieurs, for I repeat that they filter

through those of space, as, in our reflection, a thought of one order traverses a train of thought of another order—but the rain of a storm will blur your vision and we ought to hope that it will not develop. If our probabilities are exact, the phenomenon will occur in an hour or an hour and a half. Between now and then, those who wish to visit our friend the Duc d'Ignacio's admirable art gallery have only to go up to the first floor."

"I'm curious to see," Ariana whispered to Tullie, "how many of these fellows are interested in the paintings. Look, there's Doppelwein setting off with Urpar—but Pierretin, of course, is staying here to pay court to us."

In fact, touchingly, the false Victor Hugo, as infatuated with atoms as the other was with words, approached, cup in hand, and offered a rococo compliment to the "four flowers blooming in the arid fields of science." With that, a clumsy movement caused him to spill his coffee on an Aubusson of inestimable value.

Already, Ariana, gripped by hectic laughter, was declaring that "it was nothing." The young peasant's adventure had filled her with dread and remorse. She also experienced a vague scruple for having tempted him as she had. But how could she have guessed that he was afflicted by that terrible evil?

Joined by the stiff and frosty Hatchinson, Doppelwein and Urpar climbed the superb staircase decorated with delicately-woven tapestries.

"Vell, my dear colleague," said the German to the Frenchman, "are you gonvinced?"

"I'll wait and see," replied the swallower of bread and gnawer of drumsticks. "The thing's not implausible, for something happened to me...." He paused on a step and seized one of the button on his interlocutor's jacket—a gesture obsolete for two or three generations, which amazed Hatchinson. "I was with my wife at Piriac, the promontory of Tristan and Yseult...."

"Ja, ja, Wagner, *ja."*

"Wagner and also Bédier. We were looking at the sea, which was billowing, grey and steely. You've seen it like that."

"*Ja, ja, gewiss.*"

"Yes," Hatchison thought he ought to add.

"Suddenly, over the waves, a village appeared, as distinctly as I see you, probably Moroccan, certainly in the Arabic style, with a characteristic mosque and persons fro another time—I mean Orientals of another epoch; I've been in Africa and I know what it's like—who were walking back and forth. I said to my late wife: 'That's not an ordinary mirage. Look at it carefully, and tell me afterwards what you've seen.' The phenomenon lasted for about five minutes, increasingly distinct and impressive. Then it disappeared like a mist. Then my wife said to me: 'It's an image of the past; it's like a mirage lined with an apparition.'"

"Prodigious! *Wunderbar! Ungeheuer!*"

While talking, the two men had arrived in the art gallery, and without paying the slightest heed to the masterpieces brought together by their host, continued their confabulation, with which Hatchinson joined in.

"I'm a skeptic. Master Ségétan appears to me to have an imagination suggestive of such people as the Fakirs that we see in India, who extend a rope and climb up it."

"But my dear colleague," Urpar objected, "before the waves of the past he made numerous discoveries, universally checked and admired. The Minister of War said to us after a recent session of the Académie des Sciences, that they were counting on him alone for the disruption of engines at a distance, in case of war."

Doppelwein, who was working on the same problem himself, pricked up his ears, but his silence seemed suspect to Urpar, who nudged Hatchison's elbow. The latter did not understand, and launched into the mathematical considerations of the givens of the problem. An invisible spectator would have admired the three scientists, stirring their Xs laden with massacres, counter-massacres and super-massacres, in front of the ardent and voluptuous paintings of Courbet, Titian and other assemblers of female beauty.

At that moment, Abramson appeared, of whom it was said that in matters of nudity, he had never known anything but that of numbers. He had a triangular face in the form of an equation himself.

"Ah, Messieurs, I see that you've come to bathe your *mirettes* with the Duc d'Ignacio's paintings."

"What are *mirettes*?" said Hatchinson, nonplussed.

Dopplewein burst out laughing. "It's arcot for eyes. Ah, Monsieur Philosopher, you expect us to sbeak Parisian!"

"That little one wouldn't do me any harm," Abramson continued, tipsily coveting a variant of the famous woman with the parakeet, but lying on her back with her breasts jutting out, who was brandishing a bunch of roses and yellow flowers similar to narcissi. "What tits, damn it!"

"It's disgusting, filthy," muttered Urpar, who, not having had the time or the inclination, in the course of his long life, to make love more than a dozen times to his late wife, and in only in great haste, considered art in general, and paintings of nudes in particular, to be a simple morass of insanities and obscenities.

The author of *The Highways of the Mind*, who had heard the remark, shrugged his shoulders and went to look at himself in the full-length mirror in which Ariana habitually reflected herself, and then collapsed into an armchair and immediately fell asleep. A few minutes later he was snoring, while the three learned colleagues continued to quibble about waves.

The purr of automobiles was heard. It was several chatelains of the region, attracted by Ségétan's renown, in spite of his reputation for concubinage, that the latter had invited to his experiments, some of whom had brought their better halves. The Master received them ceremoniously, without making any introductions, and invited the ladies to sit down.

The latter were half-disapproving and half-intimidated in confrontation with the gracious feminine quartet, who were quite untroubled by the irruption. Orangeade circulated, and the change in the weather was an agreeable topic of conversation.

Tullie got to her feet in order to obtain news of Calvat. On the way, she met Dévonet, who said to her: "The seizure didn't last. He's on his feet and has recovered his composure—but it's serious. It's epilepsy. Poor lad! He's never had a attack before?"

"Never, so far as I know."

"What about his father?"

"He was eccentric too, though less bizarre than him—but I never saw him have a fit."

The well-articulated voice of the Master announced: "My dear colleagues, Messieurs, it's time, if you'd care to come on to the balcony.... The weather seems favorable, and I hope that we'll have a useful session."

Seats had been disposed on the terrace, in sufficient number for the spectators. The academicians, including Pierretin and Urpar, were in the front row, along with Préfet Dugerbier and Maire Taupin.

The arrival of Abbé Parroy in his threadbare soutane, with his mystical eyes brightening his wrinkled and craggy face, made a certain impression. "It appears zat he pelieves in the Tevil," Doppelwein whispered in his neighbor's ear. The latter shrugged his shoulders.

Behind the walls the conversations of the people of the three villages, who had flocked to the demonstration, could be heard. The leaden sky formed a kind of somber screen, on which the scientific evocation would appear in great detail. The atmosphere was still heavy, as if filled with redoubtable secrets.

Donabella's heart was beating forcefully, as if at the approach of some great event or important person. Tullie's did likewise, and Mélanie's too. Scarcely had Dévonet set the Dyonisos on its stand than a slight quiver was perceptible, and then a sort of distant concert, played on a harp.

At the same time, in the direction opposite to Les Arges, on the darkened horizon, a vast and beautiful château in the style of Louis XV appeared, and beside it, a delicately-shape pagoda, which immediately transported the imagination of everyone in the audience to China.

Then there emerged, from nothingness, or the ether, or time, individuals in courtly costumes, the women graciously bare-shouldered, the men in culottes and silk stockings, who were meeting, grouping together, conversing, separating, going from one group to another as if in the interval of a ball or a soirée. Suddenly, they all turned in the same direction, and a carriage was seen arriving, followed by another, and yet another. Valets in powdered wigs held the horses, while postillions took out two small valises, which they handed ceremoniously to a person of distinction who had come running.

Ségétan's voice rose above the sound of the harp. "This, my dear colleagues, is the residence of Chanteloup, thirty-five kilometers away, belonging to the Duc de Choiseul, Minister of Foreign Affairs to King Louis XV. You're witnessing the arrival of the Paris mail. It's evening, and amusement is about to give way to important business. For want of fireworks, however...."

He did not finish. Kites climbed into the sky, from which colored lanterns were suspended, in blue, red and yellow, brightly lit. The harp fell silent.

Gradually, the image dissipated, as a dream might do, here by effacement and there by gradual fragmentation, increasingly lacunary.

The spectators of that extraordinary scene, people with critical minds and reliable senses, were divided once again into the convinced, filled with an admiration mingled with amazement, and the doubtful, suspecting an implausible deception, in view of the circumstances, the destruction of Chanteloup and Ségétan's reputation. Again, the former far outnumbered the latter, and manifested an enthusiasm that passed from the physicists to the men of the world, and on to the servants, relegated to the background. Doppelwein's *wunderbars* mingled with the *épatants* of Urpar, Pierretin and the prefect. The former approached the Master and kissed him on his cheeks, which were as hard as marble, although the muscles of his temples were tremulous.

A dozen scientists followed that example, to the applause of Bénalep, as broad, gnarled and bushy as an oak tree, who expressed his enthusiasm in crude and paradoxical terms. "Oh, the swine, the rascal—when one thinks that one is the contemporary of such a giant, one feels positively sick! Romain, let your old Bienallé kiss you in his turn!"

The gentlemen and ladies of the châteaux, confronted by these extravagances on the part of illustrious professors, whose names were cited on a daily basis in their newspapers, and the unrestrained excitement and warm words, were slightly bewildered. Two or three better halves directed envious glances at Tullie, the farmer's wife, the woman of no account, the probable whore, who shared the bed of such a star—but the one that amused them most was the slender and lithe Donabella, expressing in Italian, French and English her unbridled enthusiasm for the Master.

One of those idiotic socialites, of whom there is no lack, approached the impassive Hatchinson, absorbed in searching for the "trick," and pointed impertinently to his wife. "Who is that excited young woman?"

"It's my wife," he replied, phlegmatically.

"Well, that'll make the Italian swallow a coin," said Abrice to Pietro. The latter shook his head and raised his eyes to the heavens.

Submissive to the amorous atmosphere, Pietro had designs on the Dévonets' housemaid, who was smitten herself with a farmhand from Les Arges, and who sent him packing humorously: "I'm not as warm as your motor, old man."

To escape the questions, the demands for explanation and all the dust of his gory flooding into his nose and ears, Ségétan had moved away slightly.

Ariana went over to him. "A great success, Master, wasn't it? But you're so blasé....I thought I noticed, however, that there's someone here—oh, not a Academician—whose approval is not a matter of indifference to you."

"Really, my dear? Who's that?"

"Her," the young woman said, pointing at Donabella, who was helping Tullie to hand out welcome refreshments. "I'm sure that she would inspire you, if...."

"Yes, but I don't really see how...for the dear little thing sleeps next door to our room, with her husband three paces away. Besides, she's leaving tomorrow. But I'll doubtless see her again."

"Nothing's more certain. Her American's jealous and scarcely leaves her side. Believe me, best seize the opportunity."

"Fine—but once again, how?"

"Follow me. There's a racket, no one's paying attention to us."

She drew him into the grounds, as if she were playing the coquette and playing tag with him. He followed her, massive and swift, with good muscles and joints.

When they were a little further away, he said: "So, you think I can take a woman as one quaffs a glass of port?"

"Very nearly. This is my private lodge. Here's the key. Go in. You'll find everything necessary for writing. In five minutes, I'll bring you the pretty woman, and in twenty minutes I'll come back to fetch you and take the two of you back to her cuckold."

Ségétan burst out laughing, while she drew away in haste, also laughing. He had heard talk about this "solitude," as they used to say in the eighteenth century, but he had never seen it. The furnishings pleased him, and, as he was hot, he put himself at ease, taking off his jacket and waistcoat and sprinkling his hair with eau de cologne.

As after every evocation of the past, he experienced a sensual need for a woman's skin—a sort of aura and frisson, in which desire was combined with thirst. Science, which came to him via Eros, at least in its creative aspect, momentarily left him via Eros—but it was necessary for the one he held in his arms to have thrown herself into them willingly, or better than willingly, completely carried away, and that he felt passion for her. The slightest reserve chilled him and, at the same time, deprived him of a beam of his intellectual radiance.

Scarcely had he finished his rapid ablution than the door opened and Donabella came in, her arms reaching out, her lips red, her bosom palpitating, intoxicating in her figure, her face and her movements, like a somnambulistic Venus. She came as if to a sacrifice, yielding to an irresistible attraction, and as soon as he touched her nacreous flesh, which illuminated the room, he sensed that she was melting, as if she were emerging from snow.

At that moment, a particularly strident whistle-blast resounded, and the angelic face of the blonde sinner expressed terror. While the demigod drew her to him, with a hoarse grunt of victory, and got ready to stone her like a fruit, she wriggled free and articulated: "My husband!"

And, transformed, revived and reawakened, with an astonishing faculty of physical and moral hypocrisy, she headed back to the terrace that she had only just left, at a pace that had become tranquil and conjugal again.

"You, old chap, will pay me back for that!" The handsome Romain, thus severed from the harmonious and smooth body that he had believed to be already in his embrace, pronounced his disappointment aloud.

He uttered a sigh of discontentment, closed the door again and waited. He thought that Ariana would come back. She did not, and it was him who, after a quarter of an hour, after the specified interval, came to rejoin the guests.

The latter were getting ready to leave, some in their automobiles, the other for the station. Ariana cast an ironic glance at him. Did she know, or not? In a corner of the drawing-room, to one side, Donabella, leaning on the blissful Hatchinson's arm, seemed the image of loving fidelity.

"Everyone's going, and I was looking for you," said Tullie, already anxious. "Perhaps you went to see Jean?"

"Good God, no. I needed air and a few minutes' rest. The best thing for the unfortunate Jean to do is to leave this place, where he'll no longer harvest anything but humiliation and suffering. Apart from that, were you content with the day?"

She turned her noble and gentle face toward him, ecstatically. "Better than content—delighted! All these illustrious men not knowing how to express their admiration, their enthusiasm!

That was worthy of you. It was splendid."

* * * * * * *

The communal dinner of the seven friends and lovers of Avenillon was held at the Villa Dyonisos, in the cheerful intimacy that follows the reception of people to whom one is indifferent. The Hatchinsons took part in it, not being due to leave until the next day. The Duc d'Ignacio had sent over the abundant tasty leftovers from the banquet, and each of the nine guests recounted what they had seen and heard, detailing the observations they had been able to make. They were astonished not to have seen Abramson anywhere, at any time, except at lunch.

"He must have been running after a housemaid," Bénalep suggested. "These mathematicians are so salacious."

"But he can't have been running for five hours along the highways of the housemaid and the mind."

Ségétan, Ariana and Donabella, who had the memory of a recent chase of the same order, in a garden of their acquaintance, smiled at such a supposition.

With a common accord, they avoided talking about Jean Calvat's fit, although the allusion was on the tip of their tongue. That restraint, by an association of subterranean ideas, led the Master to explain the mental effects of the waves, at which he had only hinted to his guests.

"They're of a very special kind, but which everyone, with some attention, can observe in themselves. The proximity of the waves of the past drives one to express what one would like to retain, inclining, in certain cases, to admission and confession."

"As opium and wine also do."

"In a more insinuating fashion. I've rarely taken opium, and never taken cocaine, peyotl, any convulsive narcotic, or absinthe. I've drunk a great deal of wine in my life and have always kept my scientific and other secrets—but after long sessions I've experienced spurs and temptations to offer confidences, to those whom one does not have one one's pillow, as

Alphonse Daudet puts it somewhere, and I've been obliged, in order to restrain myself, to redirect my interior conversation to some scientific or nonsensical theme."

"Damn!" said Ariana. "There, Master, is a revelation to prompt fear. A curse on waves that make us talk involuntarily!"

There was an awkward moment, when the irruption of Abrice distracted their minds from a hazardous zone. The chauffeur was distressed.

"Excuse me, Maame, and you, Master, but you need to know that Père Clope of Authy farm, has just died suddenly from the venomous bite of some unknown creature. He was walking back to Quatrebois after the séance, when he felt a sharp pain in his leg and which caused him to fall over. He thought at first that it was a snake, but he said he saw some kind of scarab running away. A kind of black blister formed immediately, and the poor fellow died as he was being carried to the farm."

On hearing that, Dévonet went pale, but did not breathe a word.

"It's unfortunate—a frightful accident—but no one can put the blame on us," observed Bénalep, deliberately inclined to optimism.

Abrice went back down to the kitchen. "They don't give a damn up there. Me, I find that selfishness sickening."

"Stay calm," said Caroline. "You're drunk. You'd do better to go to bed. You didn't even know Père Clope."

Marianne made the observation that men of science saw too much and in too many colors to get upset over an unknown peasant. "Monsieur doesn't have much heart, and when he can hurt someone he doesn't miss the opportunity."

"The Calvat boy, for example, whom he hasn't even asked about."

"He's his enemy and he knows it—and that he has only one idea, to screw the beautiful Tullie. He'd have to be a saint to get upset about that one."

"Me, I'm Italian," Pietro concluded. "But you lead an interesting life here. One would think that you were all a bit touched."

* * * * * * *

Everyone upstairs was tired. They separated at an early hour; but several incidents occurred, as if the material evocation of an episode of the eighteenth century had provoked mental perturbations among the witnesses.

Dévonet, when he got home with Mélanie after having seen Bénalep home, ran to his jars of insects. He perceived, as he had feared, the disappearance of an African scorpion of a particular ferocity, which he had named Jehovah. The animal had pierced a stopper of virgin wax, temporarily replacing a crystal stopper, and had escaped. That was evidently what had stung Père Clope. It was to be feared that the creature might sting others, if it did not die for lack of a sufficiently high temperature.

His wife reassured him. "It will surely die. I'm falling asleep. Come to bed quickly and don't think about it any more."

He grumbled. She had a desire to confess to him, recklessly, the desire she had for Ségétan, but she restrained herself, picked up a book and waited until he was asleep before joining him.

* * * * * * *

As they arrived at the château, Ignacio and Ariana saw the bean-like head of the plaintive Sylvian coming toward them.

"There's a man asleep in the gallery, Monsieur."

"A man asleep! And you didn't wake him up?"

"No, Monsieur, because he's a scientist from the banquet. I recognized him."

While Ariana burst out laughing, the Duc climbed the stairs at double-quick time, amid the noxious and musty odor of the cigars smoked by the guests. He opened the door, switched on the electric light, and made out the sprawling silhouette of Abramson. The philosopher woke up and stretched his limbs, amazed to find himelf in a room that he initially mistook for a hall in the Louvre.

Abruptly, memory returned to him.

"Excuse me, my dear colleague. I was extremely tired...."

"Not at all, my dear professor; it's me who should apologize for having disturbed your sleep."

"What time is it?"

"Ten o'clock in the evening. At ten forty-five there's an excellent train from Blois that will get you to Paris in about an hour—unless you prefer to stay overnight here."

"I don't have a nightshirt or a toothbrush."

"You can have both. Decide. Should I give the order to my chauffeur?"

The author of *The Highways of the Mind* hesitated at the crossroads. The fear of greater ridicule caused him to prefer the immediate departure. He took hasty leave of his host, without the subject of the afternoon session being raised.

"In sum," Ariana said to her husband, "he's come to Brancheville to sleep for from three o'clock in the afternoon until ten o'clock at night."

She had a strong desire to talk to him about Jean Calvat's fit and the slight remorse she felt on that subject, but she did not know whether he would be irritated or pleased, and the first would have been as unbearable as the second. As they separated for the night, he said to her in a tranquil tone: "What were you, Donabella and the Masteer doing running around after the banquet?"

"I went to show my little private cabin to the pretty little Italian, who wants to have one like it in Naples."

"Ségétan had his eye on her. I thought for a moment...."

"Oh, he's like that with all women. Goodnight, and until tomorrow!"

* * * * * * *

The Hatchinsons, who were due to leave early the following day, bid farewell to their hosts on the landing, and thanked them for their hospitality, arranging to meet them in Naples. Then the two husbands separated.

Half an hour later, the American scratched on the door of his blonde's bedroom, which was locked. She was following the new dialogue of Tullie and Ségétan with the microphone. She shivered, went to open the door and saw without pleasure the stuffed shirt who had come to exercise his rights with her. Entirely enveloped by the thought of the demigod, gripped by an insensate desire for him ignited by the sounds of love-making from the next room, she had conceived a physical horror of that body of varnished wood within the last twenty-four hours.

"Go to bed, Bobby. I'm not in the mood today."

"What's wrong, capricious child?"

She searched hastily for an excuse. "It's the way you whistled for me a while ago. I'm not a dog. I've already told you that I don't like it."

"It's my custom, and that of my friends. I've given you my money; it's only fair that you give me your skin, when I ask for it."

He had never spoken to her before with that rude frankness, and he pronounced the brutal pretention in a low voice, with a sort of disgusting human respect mingled with cynicism. At that moment, the young woman felt a new and unknown sentiment rising within her, which frightened her. Her teeth chattered; her tender flesh cried: "No, no, and no!"

Although he was furious and devoid of any natural politeness, Hatchinson read such resolution in the proud and angry gaze of his Italian wife that he turned on his heeel and went back to his room.

Then Donabella, thinking about the long months that probably awaited her, far from Ségétan, the impossibility of seeing him, and her unhappy destiny, lay down on her solitary bed and wept endlessly, bathing her silken pillow with her warm tears.

* * * * * *

That night was fertile in mental and material incidents of all kinds for ten kilometers around, some of which were known and others, more numerous, unknown.

The Mairesse, Madame Taupin, who was known as "the deck-chair attendant" and whose physical disgrace seemed to give her husband full marital security, suddenly confessed to the latter that she had slept with the sacristan five years before, in a grain-loft. The said sacristan had since died, which was a great relief to the worthy Taupin, thus saved from the duty of avenging his honor.

At the Château de la Piétonerie, on the far bank of the Loire, Baron Vauveron, the husband of one of the most devoted wives in the country, abruptly accused himself of having ravished a farm-girl, with whom he would have had a child, which he had had aborted, in accordance with convention, by an unlicensed veterinarian.

In the three villages, and even further afield, an abnormal amorous ardor augmented the departmental birth-statistics by a significant amount.

* * * * * * *

At about ten o'clock in the evening, Abbé Parroy, absorbed in reading Saint Augustine beside his pooor worm-eaten bed in the bare room of his presbytery, received a visit from Jean Calvat, who was quite calm and no longer seemed to be feeling the effects of the morning's scare. The boy's gaze seemed to have lost the fixity that had acted upon Ariana, to the point of suggesting the worst of stupidities to her.

The priest raised his head, took off his spectacles, and asked: "What can I do for you, my boy?"

"Monsieur le Curé, I've come to ask you what I need to do to escape the claws of the demon, because I've realized that there are times when the demon takes possession of me."

"I've already told you several times. You have to pray, confess and take communion."

"But it's at those times, Monsieur le Curé, that I'm absolutely incapable of praying. It's impossible for me, when I address myself to God, to hear the voice of the Providence that you say watches over all children, and it's as if my natural magnanimity were paralyzed by it."

The ecclesiastic was used to that grandiloquent gibberish, and he paid attention to the sentiments expressed, not the terms that expressed them. Calvat was exposing a well-known case of conscience, like a chessboard, the black squares being those of incredulity and the white those of eternal consolation.

"Well, when prayer doesn't come to your lips naturally, pick up your missal and read it mechanically, as you did at school: once, twice, three times. After six or seven readings, you'll sense what there is beneath the words, and you'll think about Our Lord, crucified for you, in order that you can converse with him. Do you know what the Lord says?"

"No, not in this case."

"That thou shalt not kill. I know that during lunch, before you fell ill, you wanted to kill Ségétan."

"That's true," said the young man, astonished by the divination. "I nearly did it. But what stopped me is that the wretch was about to show us something very curious, which might advance the science of the course of the ages and manifest progress."

"Why call him wretch?"

"Because he's taken Tullie from me by sorcery, because he's casting spells over the whole world, and because he's the devil's envoy."

These expressions, lyrical and bombastic, combined with the abbé's intermittent reflections on the subject of his illustrious parishioner and his three friends, Dévonet, Bénalep and Ignacio.

"But you know, my poor boy, that you wanted to take—or, as you say, steal—Tullie yourself, from your old papa, which isn't very nice."

"Monsieur le Curé, I love Tullie with my soul, and if that's a sin, it's not the same as his horrible one—the bandit Ségétan only addresses himself to women's bodies. The proof is that in the moments when I love Tullie the most, I no longer see her as she is, but as a celestial creature, almost an angel. Do you understand, Monsieur le Curé?"

The rustic's tone had grown progressively more heated, and in his eyes, no longer wandering but hardened and stabilized again, there were flames as shiny as a dagger.

The priest had before him—and was profoundly aware of it—one of those hybrid products of a time divided, in terms of its uncultured strata, between credulity with regard to science and incredulity with regard to the divine, and, for its cultivated strata, or those so-called, between devotion to a science with barbaric consequences and the denial of the divine. Doubtless this perverted petty peasant was sick, but his sickness was caused by the extreme disorder of his mind. The salvation of all these orphans of God, at the summit as in the depths of society, appeared to him to be an insurmountable task, the thought of which wore him out.

"Would you like me to confess you, and to take communion tomorrow?"

"No, I don't have any desire to do that, and anyway, I haven't any more to tell you. Forgive me for disturbing you."

The young man went out on tiptoe, with the supple stride of an athlete, as if he were fearful of waking someone.

CHAPTER FIVE
THE SECOND ARROW
OF DYONISOS

It was in the first fortnight of September, on a day of reverberant and torrid heat worse than August, that the so-called fête of the three villages—Avenillon, Brancheville and Quatrebois—fell, which attracted vigorous young men and girls in smart dresses from all over Blésois Beauce. The generosity of the Duc d'Ignacio and Ségétan permitted the three municipalities to organize, for the day and the evening, a great ball, with two brass bands and refreshments in profusion, and superb traditional fireworks.

By virtue of this magnificence, numerous outsiders came in their automobiles or horse-drawn carriages to the show of equine dressage and livestock, and so-called American attractions. There was even a booth featuring supposedly Moroccan dances, executed by a few pretty young women, who were not very primitive, guided and exploited by a Parisian impresario, as large as a sideboard and coiffed in a fez.

Ségétan, Bénalep, Tullie, Dévonet, Mélanie, Ignacio and Ariana strolled casually among that affluence of peasants, where they were saluted at every step, the first-named with a mixture of admiration and dread. The scientist of the Villa Dyonisos and the châtelain of Brancheville distributed money in profusion, paying for children and young people to take turns on the shooting-range, the coconut shy, lotteries and rides.

Here and there they encountered their servants—Marianne,

Caroline, Sylvain, Abrice and the rest—who were enjoying themselves in their own fashion, with a sort of comical disdain for those they called "the country bumpkins." They were very thirsty; Abrice had already drunk a respectable number of tankards of beer, and was waxing tender over the departure of Pietro, who had written to him from Rome to give him all his news. "Like the boss, I'm all for the Latins, Pietro's landed in clover. He's been swept away and raised up, with respect to his Hatchison and the Donna. Well, he doesn't hold back, and we're mates now, at a distance, it's true, but for life, until death."

"Let's go see the 'Moroccan dances,'" said Bénalep, who found all the bustle amusing, and who gave brief consultations to his rustic clients as he passed by.

The gramophone was playing some jazz number. It was supervised by one of the dancers, three-quarters nude in the Parisian fashion, with a beautiful sweat-pearled skin, plump and perfect breasts and a few pink ribbons around her torso, both faded and garish, as in a painting by Renoir. Mélanie remarked on the slenderness of her legs, devoid of stockings, of a voluptuous elegance. Next to her was a child of about ten, her son, who looked at her tenderly and helped her change the records. On the improvised stage the audience members were fidgeting around a rather disquieting travesty advertised on the program as "the beautiful Ottaro."

As he passed by, Ignacio undid the string that was retaining the "musician's" corsage, thus revealing the breast of a goddess terminated by a rounded buton reminiscent, in the dim light, of a mulberry. At the same time he slipped a hundred-franc bill into her hand, which was small with dirty fingernails, Then the little boy took the gentleman's arm and indicated the stage on which the ragged dancers were twirling, as if to say: "Pay attention to those, not this one." That childish protection was so touching that Ariana's hisband softened, and doubled the tip. The dancer looked up at him covertly and made him understand, with a slight movement of the head, that he could meet her in the wings. He did nothing, but was very amused when, at the exit, the robust "Alta Turca" boasted to him, in a low voice, in crude terms, of the exceptional qualities of the "royal piece."

Couples tangoed rhythmically on the compacted earth of the ballroom, which was decorated with tricolor flags. Jean Calvat, elegant, slim and calm, came to invite his stepmother Tullie, as beautiful as an ancient priestess in her white dress, to dance—but she refused, the death of Pere Calvat still being too recent, and she gave him to understand, in a few words, that it would be better for him to abstain too. He made no reply, and invited the beautiful Ariana, clad in a mauve veil as light as a butterfly, who lent herself to the handsome rustic's tremulous and awkward grip.

This time, he did not unclench his teeth or make her any confidence, but at a given movement he lifted her up and held her positively pressed against him. She was delightfully excited by it, and immediately thought about the little cabin out there on the edge of the grounds, where the Master had failed dismally with the beautiful Donabella.

Meanwhile, Romain had put his arm around the waist of a delightful peasant-woman from Brancheville, who was some thirty years old, with two children, and was whirling her around, without holding her tightly, in an old-style waltz, in the midst of the tangoing couples. He did not even know her name. From afar, people watched the quinquegenarian sorcerer, who did not disdain to pivot a respectable peasant woman in front of everyone, with wonder and irony.

"What's your name?"

"Adélaide, Monsieur."

"I couldn't resist the desire to approach you—but it can't be very amusing to dance with an old bear like me."

"Oh, I swear to you that it's ever so good! You're the man that everyone is talking about and all the women thinking of, more or less. But have no fear of getting closer, or holding me tight."

"Do you love your husband?"

"Not at all. He's dirty and a drunk, and he beats me. I only stay with him because of the children."

"Have you ever seen a laboratory? Would you like to visit mine one day?"

"But there's Tullie."

"She won't be there. Or if she is, she'll close her eyes."

"But the domestics...Marianne, the fat Abrice, Caroline."

"I'll send them away."

"People will see me going into your house."

"Do it after nightfall. Let me know a day in advance, when I take my walk and your husband's on the booze."

They had that conversation while twirling, his voice ardent, hers hesitant. Ségétan made sure in that fashion that his fluid was always as active and as fascinating, and the semi-swoon of the little peasant-woman in his arms procured him an incomparable intellectual delight, the most agreeable and fecund of trances. This one too, like Donabella, was naïve beneath the weight of her ignoble drunkard, no more ignoble than the American of varnished wood.

As he sat the weak-kneed woman with the odorous chestnut hair down again, he thought he heard once again the strident whistle-blast that had snatched the soft blonde bread from his mouth at the door of Ariana's cabin after the banquet—but it was the whistle of a horse-trainer.

"Oof! It's hot!" said the scientist, on returning to his wife and friends.

Bénalep laughed. "But you're twenty-five—you're extraordinary! My dear Tullie, this isn't the Master of the Waves, it's Don Juan—or, rather, Bath-au-pieu."[23]

"What vulgarity, M'sieu Bienallé!" Thus spoke Mélanie, mimicking the Blésois accent.

All seven continued the tour of the fairground, now completed by a jumble sale, where household objects of all sorts were on sale. Ségétan, as cheerful as a child, bought a batch of old ribbons, of various amusing colors, which he made the three young women put on. Then there were boxes of bonbons and

23. *Bath-au-pieu* is an argot term making vulgar reference to someone— male or female—who is "good in bed."

nougats, and, to cap it all, he gave Bénalep, with a flourish, the useful present of a gilded porcelain chamber-pot.

"The very image of ill-acquired fortune!" cried the delighted Silenus.

The heat was scarcely declining. Ignacio and Ariana went back to Brancheville. The three scientists and the two young women returned to the Villa Dyonisos, read the newspapers, chatted and relaxed until dinner, which consisted of a copious cold meal, permitting the servants to stay out as late as they wanted at the fête. When the guests had done it full honor, they returned to the local press.

"Here's something curious, damn it!" exclaimed Mélanie, whose alluring face with the large eyes became serious. She read: "*Châteaudun, tenth of September. Two local farmers died, a few hours apart, from the sting of an unknown insect, having developed an enormous black and purulent blister and a generalized intoxication. Conjectures as to the nature of the venom and the creature have been fruitless, both being unknown in our region.*"

"Well, what!" said Félix Dévenot, negligently. "It's Jehovah, my scorpion, continuing to do his thing. A superb specimen! I'll never console myself for having let him escape."

"The price of science! Humanity will see many others, when our successors make discoveries at will." Having said that, the Master plunged back into his reading, with a shrug of his shoulders.

Momentarily, he looked up at Tullie, sprawled beneath an electric lamp sheathed in pink, with a serious expression and a penetrating gaze. There had been talk about the enormous hayricks in the fields and the mingled odors of straw and roses, as intoxicating as that of freshly-mown grass, which emanated from them, and an Avenillan rose-garden nearby. An amorous fantasy crossed his mind.

He got up and said to Tullie, in a tone she knew well: "I'm stifling, darling; let's go take a walk." Then, after shaking hands with the Dévonets, husband and wife and Bénalep, he disappeared, followed by his brunette, already consenting.

Avoidng the fête, where the maroons announcing the fire-work display were exploding, they went around Les Arges farm, scarcely illuminated by a faint crescent moon, everyone being at the fairground, and went into the fields that extended as far as the eye could see, dotted with somber clumps of trees and giant phantasmal hayricks.

They thought they were alone. The song of crickets wore away the silence, as a file wears away iron, with an insistent whine. The air brought them, in heavy waves, the perfume of the hundreds of red roses cultivated a hundred meters away by a renowned horticulturalist, and the somber yellow warmth of the scraps of the cut and threshed wheat. The high conical tower of the assembled and heaped-up stalks formed, by virtue of its edges, a kind of tapered crib carpeted with glittering litter.

"I understand," she said. "Don't say another word."

He turned round and stepped aside while she undressed hastily, throwing her dress, slip, underclothes and transparent stockings on the ground, pell-mell. It was the movement of a rural bacchante, on whom the lunar half-light projected a pale, almost marmoreal radiance.

At that moment, a gunshot resounded, followed by a terrible groan, which ended in a croak.

The fireworks! Tullie thought, in a flash—but already Ségétan had collapsed, two paces way from her, as if struck dead, and from the depths of her terror she heard the sound of footsteps running away.

No longer remembering that she was naked, she threw herself on to her lover's body and saw his bloody face.

"He hasn't killed me," he murmured, "but I received the charge full in the eyes." Then, with his usual self-control, he added: "Get dressed, quickly."

"But who fired the shot? Who?"

"Jean, of course. I recognized his silhouette when he raised the gun."

Supported on one hand, he straightened up, getting to his

knees. With the other hand, he groped around and grasped the fabric—a skirt—that she was holding out to him. He wiped his face. He only had a slight wound, having received a scattered blast of hunting-shot at some distance —but he could no longer see. He was blind.

"Help, help! Murder! Help!" Tullie shouted in the darkness, in a heart-rending voice, formidably intermediary between nightmare and delirium, reinforced by dolor.

Soon, running footsteps were heard. People came running.

The amazement of the first witnesses was extreme when they recognized Ségétan, and they brought him to his feet, swaying, like a huge mannequin, while twenty skyrockets, departing at the same time, lit up the plain, the tragic hayrick and the beautiful farmer's wife from Les Arges, twisting her harmonious bare arms in front of the rick. In her anguish, she had forgotten her stockings and satin slippers, and, testifying to her distress, her small and delicate feet were blooded by the prickly straw.

Four solid fellows from Les Arges, moved by their employers' tears, wanted to carry the wounded scientist by the arms and legs, but he refused, and said, in a masculine voice: "Just guide me—and two of you run to inform Doctors Bénalep and Dévonet."

"But what happened?" they were asking one another. "Who fired the rifle-shot?"

"It was Jean Calvat, Calvat's son, my co-owner. The Master saw him taking aim, the wretch." Recovering her composure at a stroke, and drying her tears, Tullie denounced her stepson without the slightest hesitation.

"What, it was Jean! Oh, that's too much—the swine! We have to catch him and hang him."

"No, he has to be handed over to the gendarmes."

"To maim a man like that, who's the glory of the region!"

"The glory of the region! Rather say the glory of France! Perhaps he's gone mad, Calvat."

"He's a shit all the same! They'll cut off his head, mad or not, and it'll be a good thing!"

As they drew closer to the village, curious people surged forth from all directions, blue and red silhouettes in the glare of the fireworks, and the indignation grew. A few peasants, armed with pitchforks, were already dispersing in all directions in pursuit of the criminal. One of them discovered the rifle, still hot from the crime, under a bush. It was observed that both cartridges had been fired. The homicidal intention was certain.

In the meantime, when Ségétan had been taken home and laid on his bed, fully dressed, Maire Taupin arrived, with three rural policemen, from the fête, and then Bénalep, Dévonet and Mélanie, in great distress. The villa was in uproar. Abrice, who was howling for vengeance and stirring up the people of the neighborhood, was given orders to go to Blois immediately to inform the gendarmerie and the examining magistrate, summoning them to mount a search and catch the murderer.

Tullie, Mélanie and Marianne, serving as nurses under the direction of Bénalep and Dévonet, undressed the Master silently, put him to bed and bathed the wound on his face with infinite precaution. One eye, the right, was tumefied, black and closed. The other seemed in better condition, but was absolutely fixed, as if it were made of glass. The lead shot had mostly peppered the forehead, the lips, the upper one being lacerated, and the cheeks.

The two physicians exchanged a glance laden with anxiety. They could not yet assume the worst, and it was necessary to postpone a full examination until the next day, but for now, blindness, at least in one eye and perhaps complete, was to be feared.

The wounded man was under no illusion. He asked the women to leave, and when he was alone with his friends he said: "Will I remain blind? Don't leave me in suspense, I beg you, for doubt is the worst thing of all."

"My dear chap," Bénalep replied, paternally, "it's impossible for us to reply. Persently, you can't see anything—that's understood—but it might be that tomorrow, or in three days, you'll have recovered vision. It's also possible that you won't recover it until later."

"Or not at all," observed Ségétan, sardonically.

"Or only on one side. At the earliest opportunity, tomorrow, we'll telephone Pénétrot in Paris, asking him to come immediately with his instruments, and he'll give you a sure diagnosis... at least insofar as it's possible to be sure of anything."

"I have a severe pain in the depths of the left eye—a horrible pain. Give me a little morphine, Bénalep—two and a half centigrams—right away. Has the little bastard been arrested?"

"No, not yet. But it won't be long, I think. He's an epileptic and a madman. At any rate, he'll be locked up, and Tullie and you will have nothing more to fear." So saying, the old Silenus made the injection in his friend's muscular thigh.

"It's just that my eyes," the latter added, "are the most important thing to me. My vision, as you know, is narrowly linked to the faculty of investigation. Blind, I'll be good for nothing but dying."

"Don't be like that, my poor Romain. We'll get you out of this—you have Bénalep's word."

"And Dévonet's."

Marianne opened the door slightly, after having knocked timidly, to ask whether Monsieur could receive Monsieur le Maire, who had come to tell him something interesting, and Monsieur l'Abbé Parroy, who had just arrived.

"Send them in!"

The Abbé was distraught, the Maire comically solemn.

"Oh, my dear friend, my dear friend!" said the priest, and embraced the invalid with cautious effusion.

"I don't need your services yet, Man of God," said Ségétan, jokingly, "but I've had a narrow escape. Fortunately, your parishioner isn't a good shot."

"The wretch! The demented wretch!"

"And you, Monsieur le Maire—are you there? What have you to tell me?"

"That the key piece of evidence has been found, but not the man. He must have run off toward Quatrebois. The rifle is Père

Calvat's. It's a current model. I regret, my dear Master, for you and the commune, this exceedingly unfortunate incident."

The falseness of the term brought a wry smile to the patient's bandaged face. He murmured, as if to himself: "I can't see anything—anything at all."

The rapid passing of the vital tranquil confidence in the acquisition of light had changed his mental horizon in an instant. Nevertheless, he could see the superb hayrick, Tullie undressing, the starry sky. Had he contemplated those various beauties for the last time?

* * * * * * *

Meanwhile, the young murderer, crawling and bounding from thicket to copse and from hayrick to hayrick, like a cat, had reached the secret cabin at the Château de Brancheville. He was firmly convinced that he had killed Ségétan and he only had one idea: to escape the consequences of that murder; to flee, if he could, and disappear, or to commit suicide if he could not.

The fireworks had ended, along with the distant music of the fête. The search had not been organized yet. Jean Calvat unlocked the door with the key that Ariana had given him, went in, opened the window, and gave voice in the darkness to the sinister screech of the barn owl.

It happened that, at that moment, the "star" was taking the air on her balcony, thinking confusedly about the singular circumstances of her life. She shuddered. *It's him, without a doubt. What's happening?*

She was in her nightdress. She threw a light mantle of black taffeta over her shoulders and was just about to go downstairs when someone rang the bell at the château gate.

Breathless voices were audible; someone—doubtless Sylban—climbed the stairs and knocked on Ignacio's door. Five minutes later, the latter came into his wife's room.

"Something's happened. Young Calvat has shot Ségétan. The poor fellow's been taken to Dyonisos, dead or alive. Bénalep and Dévonet have been summoned. I'm going too. Will you come with me or join me there?"

"I have an atrocious headache. I've just taken some aspirin. If it gets better, I'll be with you in ten minutes. If not, send me news, for I'm terrible anxious too. Poor Ségétan!"

Her husband disappeared. She went to her cupboard and grabbed a wad of banknotes—money is always useful in a drama—and picked up the mantle again.

Within five minutes, Ariana was in the cabin.

"I couldn't stand it any longer," Calvat told her. "I've killed the monster. You've been very good to me. I didn't want to leave without saying goodbye."

"Where will you go, and how, you stupid child! Why did you do it?"

"Because he stole Tullie from me, because he's cast a spell on the farm and the region, and because he struck me down with the fit. You don't believe it, but he'll destroy you all, and I'll be damned if I'm not certain—yes, certain—of everything I've accused him of."

"You don't have any remorse?"

He uttered a somber and cruel laugh. "Remorse, no—joy. Whatever happens to me, I've got my own back. Adieu, Madame! My only chance is that Brancheville isn't surrounded yet. Then again, it's dark, and a lot of people are drunk, because of the fête."

"Do you have any money? You'll need that, in any case."

"No, I don't have any money. That would only slow me down. I'll do what the prisoners did in the German war and travel by night, without eating."

"Take these thirty thousand francs in memory of me. Never tell anyone I gave them to you."

"Oh, Madame, is it possible? But will I be able to I pay you back some day?"

"Don't worry about that. I have no need of it. Go—run! Adieu!"

He threw himself on his knees.

The image of the victim suddenly presenting itself to her eyes, Ariana pushed him away, with a movement full of horror and disgust, and disappeared.

He put the wad of bills in his jacket pocket, opened the wooden door slightly, and then, with a lithe bound, slid into the thicket. He crouched down there.

A short while afterwards, he heard the sound of voices some distance away. They were searching for him. He had his plan, formulated a long time ago, which Ariana's magnificent gift had just simplified unexpectedly: to wait for first light as best he could, to reach the railway branch-line between two stations, at a favorable location he knew, to jump aboard the four a.m. goods train, lie down in an empty wagon and thus to reach, if not Paris, a distant village in the direction of Paris.

In case, for whatever reason, he did not succeed in carrying out this initial plan, several days ago, he had hidden a bicycle, a change of clothes and a hat in the grass of a ditch lower down the Loire. By that means he counted on reaching either Orléans or Tours by road, and by the grace of God. At any rate, it was necessary to act quickly, before the alert was sounded to the police of the entire region.

Briefly, he had thought of taking refuge, once the shot was fired, with Abbé Parroy, who surely would not have refused him sanctuary. The presbytery dog knew him, and would not have barked, and the Flemish servant hated Ségétan, as he did—but a singular delicacy, which counterbalanced his ferocity, caused him to abandon that plan, for he would have put the worthy man in the situation of concealing a criminal, and, if there was an investigation, of perjuring himself.

The murder, in soothing his mind, had rendered him lucid and liberated him from all metal confusion, as well as any apprehension of a further fit. He was entering into a second life by a solemn door, red-stained by diabolical blood. Some other-than-providential power had furnished him, via the hand of an amorous pretty woman, with thirty banknotes, with the aid of which he expected to conquer the world.

For the moment, though, he said to himself, *it's as if I had nothing, since I can't use the money.* He imagined, with amusement, the frightened face of Baume, the grocer in Brancheville, if he were to go in calmly, after this drama, and ask him for change for a thousand francs!

The baying of hounds, not far away, reminded him that there had been a trial of police dogs two years earlier in Blois—but after one of them had become rabid and had bit its handler, that kind of sport had been abandoned. So much the better. The gendarmes knew the roads, but not the multiple shelters of the clumps of trees on the plain and the backs of the Loire. Calvat had a gift, precious in these circumstances. He could crawl and bound like a cat, and no one could catch up with him when he ran. Had someone picked up his rifle, which had been suspended, since his father's death, from a nail in the dining-room at Les Arges? A family, heirloom, what!

He was hungry. Having put in his pocket, at hazard, a hunk of bread and a slice of sausage, he nibbled both, while pricking up his ears. He recalled the arrival of the morning bread, the young woman as blonde as Ariana, but less beautiful than Ariana, who attended to the hot galettes and gilded loaves in the kitchen. How good that was, with milky coffee, and how adorable Tullie was, passing the butter to everyone with her beautiful arms! Only then did he imagine the grief felt by his stepmother, whom he had adored since the first time he had seen her, so polite and gentle among the peasants, so ignorant of matters of the land, but so avid to learn and make herself useful! Today, infatuated as she was with the monster, she must be cursing him and wishing him dead.

Jean had seen the dawn many times, in various seasons. Never had he awaited it with such impatience, as the prelude to his deliverance.

They'll all end up going to bed, and between the time when the peasants go back to the farms and the time when they wake up again on the day after the fête, I'll have a good three hours. As for the local police and the gendarme, they're not made of more solid matter than the others, and they must have only one desire by now—to go to bed.

His conjecture was sound. Having taken care to bring his watch and wnd it, he observed, by the concealed light of his pocket torch, that by two o'clock in the morning, the vain search had ceased. It was time to go.

The screech of a genuine night bird cut through the darkness. Just as long as Ariana didn't imagine that he was calling her back! But there was such a difference between that authentic cry and his that he smiled. He knew that the point on the railway that he had chosen was about five kilometers away. It was half past two. The goods train would come around the bend at Image, slowly, at ten past four.

He risked leaving his hiding-place, on all fours. The night had become absolutely calm and silent. Every hundred meters, large hayricks marked out the route that he knew by heart, to the branch-line train that it was necessary not to confuse with the main-line train. The crossing of each of those hundred meters, in the open, represented the worst of ordeals for the young peasant prey to fever. That caused him him to curse the memory of the man whose murder had condemned him to the torture all the more. From time to time, while making a muscular and mental effort, he murmured: "Oh, the bastard!" addressed to the scientist, who was asleep—but not, as he hoped, between four planks.

Thirst had gripped him since eating the sausage, and he had nothing to drink. That was something of which, in his homicidal rage, he had not thought. While wriggling like a snake between the trunks of phantasmal cones, he imagined a bubbling spring, a trickle of water, even a pond, where he could slake his thirst and refresh his burning temples—but the plain remained arid and dismal, and the clumps of trees, convenient for hiding, did not offer the slightest humidity presaging a spring, or even an infiltration. The total absence of birdsong was characteristic of that damnable dryness.

He arrived in that fashion, like a serpent, beneath the green-tinted celestial dome, at the gate of an old cemetery, defended by a worm-eaten barred gate against the improbable curiosity of passers-by. Automatically, he shoved it, begging it not to creak. The grating of a lock, the barking of a dog are so many risks for a man running away, his crime accomplished, seeking to escape punishment.

O miracle! Between two graves with effaced names, invaded by verdure, there was a pitcher full of fresh water, doubtless forgotten by some pious commemoratrix, wife, mother or daughter. The blood-stained fellow knew how to pour water down his throat without his lips touching the vessel, having had a brave Catalan by the name of Gomez under his orders at Les Arges, who had abducted a girl from Quatrebois. He seized the pitcher with a firm hand and emptied its contents into his mouth in an ample—but not too ample—jet. It was a paradise populated with cool angels that inundated his gullet, his pharynx, his esophageal tube and stomach. Those delights he absorbed completely, and until the last icy drop, he thanked heaven for such a gift.

It was then that dawn suddenly broke, as fresh as the redemptive water, fringed with a hint of pink that reddened almost immediately, and then a narrow colar of nacreous light. It was as beautiful as Tullie and he lent it Tullie's forms, in a sort of desperate amorous ecstasy.

The gate creaked. Jean shuddered. Who was coming here at this hour?

A little old lady appeared, who resembled Mairesse Taupin, the "deckchair attendant," but tiny and desolate, at this more than early hour. She had a shiny watering-can in her hand.

She came to the young man and whispered to him, in a shadowy voice: "Monsieur le Gardien, can you show me the way to the tomb of General Saint-Onyx-Grane?"

"I don't know, Madame."

"How can you not know? I've come from Arras, and I sent you notice of my visit last week." She added, with a pinched expression: "I'm the general's mother."

Damn it! thought Calvat. *Here's a witness who could ruin me.* He advanced toward the little skeleton, in hat and dress at four o'clock in the morning, looked her in the eyes, and said: "You haven't seen me, have you? If you ever tell anyone that you saw me in the Lès-Branchillon Cemetery today, I'll find you and kill you...."

Then, leaving the early riser to her amazement and fear, he continued on his way at top speed.

He was no more than three hundred meters from the little station of Chaussée Saint-Victor, through which the single-track railway passed, when he saw a sleeping gendarme leaning on the barrier, his rifle at his feet. The first rays of the rising sun lent that scarecrow of sparrows a gilded aureole, comparable to those of saints in books of hours. At Les Arges farm, there was a pious image of that sort, handed down from Calvat great-grandparents. Jean remembered it, on seeing the policeman.

He flattened himself against the last hayrick in the plain of the three villages, and wondered what to do. A metallic sound cut through the dawn. The four o'clock train was being signaled. Too late! Only the route to the Loire remained open, the bicycle and the disguise. Three kilometers in the open was nothing to him.

He set off, having made sure that he still had Ariana's beneficent banknotes in his pocket.

Rapid and light, as if in a dream, he reached the main road, and thought he was safe there—but his very haste had doomed him. In fact, a watchman, this time in civilian clothes, who was stationed behind a tree on the edge of the road from Paris to Tours, intrigued by the tall slim body launched like a slingshot, sounded several strident whistle-blasts.

Silhouettes appeared in all directions. The real manhunt began.

While accelerating his run in the direction of the river, Jean weighed up his last chance of escape. Three curtains of trees and a few houses separated him from his bicycle. He would only just have time to get astride it, abandoning his change of clothing, and ride off along the Loire, in the opposite direction to Blois. He knew a little ferry of which he could make use. If he got a start, he could cross the river with his machine and get to the other bank—where his pursuers, for lack of a bridge, would be incapable of catching up with him. Once he had shaken them off, he would reappraise the situation. His hope of escape was diminished by half, to be sure, but not completely lost.

The roar of a motorcycle heading toward him at top speed on a steep pebble-strewn slope caused him to make a right turn into some bushes, fortunately not thorny. He did not fall—unlike the gendarme pursuing him, who ran into a large stone and was thrown violently, along with his machine, against a small dry stone wall. There was a dull thud, consecutive to the lurch, and a frightful cry.

He must have been knocked out, Jean thought—but he did not even look round, and, galloping along a bumpy path through a wheat-field at top speed, he perceived the landmarks that he had carefully memorized, and arrived there flat out.

Leaping back on to the bicycle, he assumed that the comrades of the injured gendarme would attend to him first, which is what happened. He therefore thought he was safe when, to the stridulation of whistles and echoes, he saw a sort of colossus rise up in front of him, holding out an arm and shouting: "Halt!" He thought he recognized him as Ségétan's chauffeur—and it was, indeed, Abrice.

To fight was impossible. The countryside, as the unfortunate well knew, was guarded. There was nothing else to do but die. With a twitch of the handlebars he headed for the Loire, toward a gap in the levée, and plunged violently into the river, flying off the bike, with Tullie's sweet face in his eyes.

"The bastard's getting away!" shouted Abrice.

He took an automatic pistol from his pocket and fired in the direction of the drowning man—a cruel and unnecessary precaution, as the fellow could no longer get away.

An hour later, his body was found floating in the midst of water-weed and creepers close to the bank. The bicycle had disappeared, stuck in the mud or carried away by the current. The streaming corpse was pulled on to the bank. His face was still clam and resolute.

In his inside jacket pocket the captain of the gendarmerie found thirty thousand-franc banknotes. "It's really money—he must have stolen it, the bandit!" he concluded.

One of his subordinates appeared, kepi in hand.

"Well?"

"Dalin's not dead yet, Captain, but he has a fractured skull. We sent him to the hospital, dying. As for the motorbike, it's in pieces."

* * * * * * *

The news of the drama soon spread throughout the region, including the discovery of a large sum of money in the Calvat boy's pocket. Some said that it was the money from his inheritance, others, more malevolent, that it was Ségétan's, which Tullie had given him as the price of his attempted murder.

"Good riddance," said the Master, laconically, when he learned how his murderer had died. That was the general opinion, Jean being too different from others to have been liked, or even missed. It was also said that he was mad.

That was, at any rate, the appreciation transmitted to the examining magistrate in charge of the investigation, Monsieur Clépeside. He was a timorous magistrate, who sometimes went fearfully to court and sometimes concluded that a death was suicide in order to simplify the formalities and shorten the investigation. In every case he was given, he was in haste to reach a conclusion. His horror of the unknown, of enigmas, was great, and learning about the banknotes—soaked but still intact, although the numbers were indecipherable—put him in a bad mood.

"Oh," he said to his old, permanently coughing clerk Reniflon, "why did the cretin need to take that money with him to his death? What an annoyance! What a sinister annoyance!"

He was nervous of Ségétan's deposition—which was, however, indispensable. On entering the dark room in which the latter was confined to bed, consigned to obscurity on the orders of his Parisian colleague Pénétrot, his first words were to reassure the invalid.

"My dear Master, the death of the young villain puts an end to the judicial action, so it's just a matter of a simple formality and purely oral information, which I'll transmit to my clerk, who will write it down.

The scientist recounted, in the clearest and simplest fashion, how it had happened, and how he had only escaped death by a miracle, in view of the short range at which the shot had been fired. In his opinion, Calvat was a madman, inspired wth homicidal ideas by jealousy."

"That's surely true—there's no doubt about it. I'll transcribe that declaration word for word. I shall only ask you, finally, what it was that prompted his jealousy?"

"His stepmother, Madame Calvat-Moneuse, the widow of the well-known farmer, with whom he lived at Les Arges farm."

"And whom you have, Master, I believe, married...." added the eminent blunderer.

"I haven't married her yet, but I intend to do so when cured," replied Ségétan, coldly.

Clépeside knew about the rumor that the thirty banknotes had come from Tullie. In the course of her own deposition, he asked her whether it was true. She replied indignantly in the negative, and that it was an imbecilic and slanderous rumor— but that she had no idea where the money could have come from.

"With whom did the deceased keep company, except for you?"

"Peasants like himself."

"Was it his inheritance from his father?"

"There were no so-called liquid assets in the legacy. It was all in farmland, in the wealth of the sun, and the Calvat son and I were in joint ownership."

"Did he pay court to you?"

"Yes. Twice he threw himself upon me while his father was alive and I was obliged to fight him off...."

"And since old Calvat's death?"

"He remained placid, but I know that he hated my fiancé."

"But he supervised the recent meal at the Château de Brancheville, to which the scientists were invited?"

Tullie told him about the epileptic fit, which interested the judge considerably, because it provided a rational explanation for the murder attempt—but it did not explain the wad of thirty banknotes. He anticipated that the Court in Blois would demand an explanation of that.

In the meantime, a host of journalists had descended on the three villages. They had come from Paris, the South, the West, the North and the center of France, some as correspondents of English and American newspapers, and they were collecting the gossip of the country folk, because Ignacio, Bénalep and Dévonet had made the miake of shutting the door in their faces. Abrice, the hero of the latter part of the drama, pocketed five thousand-franc bills in a matter of days.

Then came the photographers who took pictures of the Villa Dyonisos, the Château de Brancheville, Les Arges farm, hayricks, the station, the valley and the levee of the Loire for the illustrated papers, along with portraits of Ségétan, Tullie, the gendarme who had crashed into the wall, Maire Taupin and the Mairesse. Abbé Parroy, tracked by the objective lens as he emerged from his presbytery, had to yield gracefully.

Tullie, of course, received no quarter, and her beautiful face and figure, so voluptuous, went overseas to excite the imagination of remote peoples, cowboys on the pampas and gangsters in Chicago.

* * * * * * *

Ariana, the former star, fearful of the evocation of her rather tumultuous past, shut herself up at Brancheville and did not see any reporters. Her husband had locked the art gallery and then left for Paris.

After a week, assuming that the tumult would have died down, he came home.

"Well, how's Ségétan?"

"He still can't see; he's somber and silent, and Tullie is crazy with anxiety."

"What about the case?"

"The investigation is over. The judge has gone back to Blois."

"The journalists?"

"Gone—the coast's clear."

"None too soon. How did Calvat's burial go?"

"There was no one there apart from the curé, who, in spite of the obvious suicide, took the body through the church and gave him absolution."

Ignacio did not approve of that. What would Monseigneur de Blois say, whose severity in such matters was well-known? That paradoxical decision summed up Abbé Parroy, for whom nothing existed outside the spiritual life, which interprets the actions of poor humans broadly.

Ariana expected one final question, which—was she under the influence of the evocative waves?—she had resolved to answer squarely. That was a new twist in the perilous trajectory that her life had followed, for she was playing heads or tails with her husband's intermittent erotic jealousy. She did not notice any alteration in his long equine face when he asked, as if he were certain: "Has the judge discovered the provenance of the thirty banknotes? The boy hadn't a sou, and the old man's inheritance hadn't been liquidated."

"It was me who gave him the money," said the star, in the most tranquil tone imaginable. "This is how it came about...."

And she recounted, without a pause, the scene in the cabin after the crime, and how she had been gripped by pity for the unfortunate epileptic.

"Who had just shot our great friend," the suspicious hidalgo interrupted, for the first time. "Was there only pity in your action, or were you obeying some stronger sentiment?"

She burst out laughing. "Amorous of that fellow—that laborer with dirty fingernails and callused hands! You can't think that, my poor friend! I realize, nevertheless, that that generosity to a murderer—the victim being the Master—might seem surprising to you. I thought the same myself, as soon as I had done it. I gave the matter some thought. I was acting as a 'star'—I wanted to complete the film. My profession got hold of me. You'd put too much money in my hands, and I like squandering it."

She was already sure, given her lord and master's expression, that the affair would turn out well, and she had anticipated the inevitable conclusion of the film—so she had put on for the occasion the same gold lamé silk dress that she had once worn for the temptation of the drowned man. Her husband and lover was already reaching out for her....

* * * * * *

As Ignacio had foreseen, Amédée-Jules, Monseigneur de Blois, summoned Abbé Parroy, Curé of Avenillon and Brancheville, to a meeting a few days after the scandalous burial. The priest put on his best soutane and set off for the bishop's residence on the morning of one of the most glorious days of September.

He liked to pray in the open air, before the blue sky, in which mystical and experienced eyes discerned legions of angels, only visible to pure hearts. "That's *my* 'Dyonisos,'" he was accustomed to say to the "big brains" when the latter teased him about the population of his other world.

The heritage of a pious old spinster, the bishop's residence, dating from the seventeenth century, had an aristocratic appearance. The abbé climbed the steps of the perron, had himself announced, and waited in the antechamber for the end of a conversation between the Monseigneur, a distinguished theologian and gourmand, and the Archbishopric's butcher, with whom he was exceedingly displeased. The thunderous bursts of a high-pitched and severe voice could be heard, dominating the wheedling voice of the unscrupulous supplier.

So much the better, the worthy curé said to himself. *He'll wear out his discontentment that way; there'll be less left for me.*

Finally, the crestfallen butcher emerged.

"Can you imagine, my dear Abbé," said the bishop, robust and majestic, indicating a seat to the thin priest, "that that animal has been stealing from me, as if in a wood. And his meat's not even the best quality! Yesterday, he sent me a veal-tongue that was as tough as a dog's! I don't know whether you're a lover of veal. It's excellent and healthy nourishment, and my cook, if I dare say so, has a knack with it."

Abbé Parroy, who would have eaten shoe-leather, and generally contented himself with poorly-seasoned vegetables, expressed his preference for choice veal as best he could. After a few remarks about tomatoes mixed with aubergines in the mot delicate proportions, the Prince of the Church, changing his tone, got to the subject of the visit.

"Well, Abbé, you've been stirring things up in your plain! I've been assailed with letters complaining that you've opened the church to the remains of a murderer, who had shot Professor Ségétan, caused the death of a gendarme, and then committed suicide. Is all that true?"

The curé explained, fortunately without mumbling, how things had transpired: the singular life of the scientist, and the character of Jean Calvat, definitely afflicted, in his opinion, by madness, whose confession he had often received.

The bishop listened indulgently, amused by certain details. He had a real veneration for the old country priest, whose piety was exemplary, and who resembled, morally and physically, the Curé d'Ars, with the difference that he loved and cultivated the Humanities. He was a distinguished Thomist himself, and devoted the time left to him by the administration of his diocese to the study of the *Summa*, his recreation being gastronomy.

"Tell me, Abbé"—he never said "Monsieur" to the members

of his clergy—"What do you think of the so-called 'three sorcerers,' that you have as parishioners?"

"That they're utter pagans, Monseigneur...great minds in a darkness of the soul. They have a vast breadth with respect to the terrestrial, but with regard to Heaven, they're idiots. If Ségétan remains blind, it will merely complete an absolute moral blindness."

"Nothing to be done with them? Do they sometimes attack you with regard to the divine principle, with regard to religion?"

"I've tried. They're not rebellious. They answer me politely, even with amity. From time to time, they accompany their ladies to mass. They donate generously to the religion, but that's all, absolutely all, and the word Hell amuses them. I also have in my parish a great nobleman of Spanish origin, the Duc d'Ignacio, married to a cinema actress, who gives me money for the poor but never comes to mass."

"Are the women pious? Do you think they might bring their husbands round one day?"

"That seems very improbable to me, Monseigneur."

The Bishop sighed, and his sigh ended up as a yawn, for lunch time was approaching. He had thought about inviting the curé to eat with him, but decided that the politeness in question might suggest approval of the religious funeral of the suicide-murderer, so he refrained.

CHAPTER SIX
IN THE NIGHT

Sly or sudden, human evils are great schools, and the Greeks saw that clearly who said: *"Pathemata, mathemata."*[24] But for those who do not have faith in the Crucified, those schools can turn out badly, for the first stage—that of revolt—is prolonged indefinitely through false resignation.

Ségétan, a complete scientist, gave himself the assignment, in his dark room, of discerning by its absence the role of light and color in a mind like his, and the means of remedying the deprivation of those two essential goods. He had been struck by Goethe's sublime definition. "Colors are the deeds and suffering of light."[25] Until now, the colors and the forms of the divine female body had been narrowly linked, in him, to the mechanism of research and discovery. What was going to happen, now that he only had their memory?

He began with the daily administration of hours of reading, alternately provided by Tullie and Mélanie, and hours of conversation, scientific and other, with Bénalep and Dévonet, or Ignacio and Ariana. Any other visit, except for those of the good Curé Parroy and Maire Taupin, was strictly forbidden. Dr. Pénétrot came from Paris twice a week to monitor changes. The

---

24. One learns by suffering.

25. In *Zer Farbenlehr* (1810; tr. as *The Theory of Colors*) Goethe tried to disprove Newton's theory of light, arguing that the spectrum is a compound phenomenon produced by the interaction of light and darkness, the latter being perceived as an independent entity rather than a mere absence.

rest of the time, the Master reflected, recollected and meditated.

He could not see anything at all; there was darkness—which is to say, a substantial fraction of death. In the first few days, his efforts to evoke, in that darkness, simultaneously inconsistent and absolute, the voluptuous and soft images of what he had experienced, remained utterly vain. He perceived, in a strange remoteness, a woman's arm, a leg, a gaze, that he had difficulty identifying, in reassembling, as the synthetic power of vision does in a flash. As for colors, there was no prospect. Everything that appeared to him was gray, and, at the same time, diminished in its relief.

He asked Tullie to come to him in the nude; he slowly felt her beautiful breasts, her neck, the curve of her hips, her buttocks, without any intellectual or sensory excitement, because the mental representation was lacking, because touch is like an invalid, procuring shreds, not a whole, and because only the whole gives birth to desire. A primary, and important, observation was therefore that the eye is an initial mind, synthetic in the same fashion as the mind, and, like him, created for desire, for the amorous fecundation of intelligence, either by form or by color. Touch communicates form poorly, partially, shabbily. It knows nothing of color.

The latter preoccupied him greatly, along with Goethe's remark. Why the "suffering" of light? Was there a suffering of the latter, then, as well as the suffering of its disappearance? He discussed that with Ignacio, who made long and pleasant visits, and who had revealed to him his complicated and twisted sensuality, corresponding to vast esthetic knowledge.

"Why that suffering?" The latter said. "But my dear master and friend, because color is a decomposition, a division of light, and everything composite that is divided suffers. Joy is in unity. The immense joy of the first Christians doubtless originated from the unification of their God as much as is incarnation. As for colors, each of them is a caricature of light. Green is the caricature of infnity. It's banal to say, of red, that it's blood, revolt, and also punishment, justice and victory. White is ecstasy, which comes via prayer or the skin."

"Let's not talk about black," said Ségétan. "It's desolation, nothingness. I've eestablished that today, alas."

"Undoubtedly, but by virtue of its opposition to white, it becomes a stimulant of voluptuousness. *Othello*, the master-piece of erotic jealousy, rests on the vignette contained in one of the earliest scenes: "An old black ram is tupping your white ewe."[26] Baudelaire drew his splendid works from the brown gleams of Jeanne Duval before the fire or under the lamp, or beneath the sun of Montmartre."

Meanwhile, Bénalep and Dévonet had conferred. They feared that their friend's blindness might be definitive, and that he might commit suicide in consequence, for the loss of the spirit of discovery would be a veritable Hell for him. They had heard talk of epidermal substitutes, frontal and otherwise, for loss of vision, and the work of a physician at the University of Bonn. They had written him a detailed joint letter explaining the case to him and asking for details of his electromagnetic and undulatory mechanism. They had not mentioned that step to their colleague Pénétrot, a professor of the Faculté and, as such, fanatically orthodox and conformist. The reply they received, without being exactly dilatory manifested a certain skepticism, resulting from failed experiments. Nevertheless, the Boche advised them to try and surrendered his formulae to his French colleagues. Dévonet undertook to study them from the mathematical viewpoint, Bénalep from the physiological view-point—for they had resolved to try everything for the salvation of their friend.

The first purchase they decided was, naturally, an electric gramophone of the latest model, with Jacques Hébertot disks, the best chosen, the best composed and the most original of all.[27] But those pieces of the music and songs that he loved, by

---

26. Iago to Brabantio in Act One, Scene One. Ignacio seems to be endorsing Goethe's theory in his summation of this and his other example.

27. Jacques Hébertot, who was born André David, was an important theater director, whose Théâtre des Champs-Élysées was a principal center

virtue of the contrast and vain excitement, plunged the glorious invalid into a dangerous melancholy, to such an extent that the trial was halted after a few days.

That veritable catastrophe had deprived Ségétan of his appetite, although he usually ate gluttonously and drank the same way. The physicians recommended Tullie not to push him to take nourishment or beverages, multipliers of carnal desire and imaginative labor, and, in consequence, of emotional regret for their diminution or dormancy. The young woman therefore waited for a mental relaxation to serve delicacies and Burgundy. That happened twelve days after the drama, in the following circumstances.

The Hatchinsons had learned from the press in Naples about the attempted murder of which their host in Avenillon had been the victim. The physicist had not been surprised by the occurrence, after what he had seen in the course of the banquet, but Donabella had been violent moved and had written a letter to her friend, who read it aloud to her husband.

My dear,

> *We have just learned, with horror, what has happened in the beautiful country where we spent such pleasant hours in your home. That a genius such as your husband, so noble and so good, so necessary to his country and to humankind, should be at the mercy of a poor madman, confounds reason. Bobby and I have reconstituted the frightful scene, knowing the locations and the people. So the Master is confined, for some time, to a dark room. We have complete confidence, however, that he will soon be cured, and that his convalescence will take place here—won't it?—in the Bay of Naples, where the force and splendor of the light combines with prodigious memories of the past,*

of musical performance in Paris in the early 1920s; after leaving in 1925 following financial disputes, he started a recording company.

to permit everything to be sensed and almost every-
thing to be understood. Needless to say, I look forward
to that moment with a tremor of joy.

My husband assures me that a German physician in
Bonn, whose name he has forgotten, can confer vision
by electrical means on certain areas of the epidermis
(is that the right term?) which thus become able to
substitute for a wounded or destroyed eye. You can
seek further information.

I don't want to keep you any longer, for I can
imagine your concern and your efforts. It's not only
your love but that of thousands of others that you're
safeguarding at present. It's you who are guiding the
sacred vessel through the reefs toward a safe haven.

America and Italy embrace Italy and France.

Donabella

"How well put that is," said Ségétan. "A mixture of naivety and vivacity, that little Neapolitan is astonishing...almost as astonishing as you."

As he spoke thus, a singular phenomenon occurred within him. He had just seen—in the true sense of the word *seen*—the gilded nenuphar water-lily that the young woman had thrown at him, and the pink silk of her dress. That gold and that pink had been, for him, as stimulating to his torpid desire as a glass of fresh water to a thirsty traveler in a desert.

He thought at first that the two temporal images, accompanied by a voluptuous frisson and an aura of discovery relative to the waves, would disappear and be abruptly stolen from him; but no, they remained present, helping him to recover, with delight, the charming face of Donabella, and then, by tacit renewal, as lawyers say, the boldly sensual visage of Mélanie—without her supple body, it is true—and the eyes and forehead, but nothing other than that, of Tullie, whose soft voice with the grave inflections was still singing in his ears. All of it was suspended from a little flower, negligently tossed through a beam of light by a pretty young woman from Naples!

That transformation had not escaped Tullie, and when he told her about it, she was able to reply: "I already knew."

Naturally, however, he had kept silent about Mélanie, so it was the sight of her, albeit incomplete, that remained longest in his memory, although he would have preferred that of Donabella and that of Tullie....

Having repeated mentally, several times over, the word "nenuphar," he perceived that the word alone did not stir up anything, and that it was Donabella's name, accompanied by a round and gilded throwing action, that gave him the irreplaceable commotion of desire.

The word is the parent of the action, but the feminine proper noun is the parent of masculine lust, and that is why it is so important that a beautiful woman has a forename befitting her form, her color and her beauty.

That evening, Tullie, a diviner in medicine as in everything else, brought a bottle of Chambertin and ordered Caroline to prepare a chicken with mushrooms in the so-called Franchard style, of which her lover was very fond.

As they finished the meal, feebly illuminated by a candle masked by a pink shade, Abbé Parroy was announced.

"Send him in! Bonsoir, Abbé...I can't see you and I can't imagine you, but I can hear you. My morale is a little better. What news have you brought?"

"Very unexpected, but rather troubling—Monseigneur de Blois, having great sympahthy for your accident, wants to pay you a visit."

"Oh, damn! He'll try to bring me to the good Lord. It's his profession, after all, even his duty. Well, let him come—the day after tomorrow, for tomorrow I'll be talking medicine with the other two sorcerers. Will you be there, Abbé?"

"No, I'll yield my place to my superior...in the ecclesiastical hierarchy."

Ségétan laughed, for the first time—a brief laugh, which did not animate the expression and was, in sum, rather sinister. He asked about the weather (fine and stormy), the grape harvest (reasonably good), and the spiritual condition of the neighborhood.

"Very sympathetic to you, and to your friends, who are looking after you so well. There's no more talk about the thirty thousand francs, which remain a mystery. Oh, by the way, there have been three further deaths, here and in Châteaudun, due to the mysterious homicidal insect. The Entomological Society has been alerted."

The Master reported this information to Dévonet. "Has it got wings, then, your scorpion Jehovah? How has it covered so much ground in so little time?"

"It's hitching lifts, the little devil—that's one of its characteristics—in carts, trains, automobiles, airplanes, traveling rugs... anything inanimate and in motion. It only attacks living things. It's a true eccentric."

The ravages of his former favorite were, for Mélanie's husband, as if nonexistent. Besides which, he had abandoned his insects in order to delve into the problem of epidermal vision. He blindfolded his semi-naked wife and scanned her back and face, according to the prescriptions sent from Bonn, with an electro-wave detected indicating the cutaneous areas or points capable of replacing vision. Out of love for Ségétan, Mélanie consented to these fatiguing and mostly fruitless sessions, sometimes witnessed by the dry-mouthed Silenus Bénalep, whose was verifying the procedures.

More days were passing and the scientist was becoming more depressed. Readings of his favorite authors—Montaigne, Shakespeare, Rabelais, Molière—delivered in a nuanced voice by Tullie or in a grave voice by Mélanie, and the conversations of his friends, gave him the impression of a rain of ashes in his darkness. He found it hard to follow a train of thought through its subtlest meanders, when no intellectual difficulty had ever stopped or deterred him before the accident. The sense of concordance, which is the essential cord of the investigative faculty, was gradually slackening within him. He perceived, painfully, that his vision, shaped or colored by memory alone, did not possess any direct stimulant, any spark capable of illuminating an entire problem by propagation. He expressed this in three words: "I'm becoming stagnant."

On the morning of the twentieth day, he experienced a false joy. His blindness, his blackness, had become white—a dead white, to be sure, but which gave him the impression of a prison door opening. Was it the dawn of the return of vision, and, in consequence, the conjugal joy of desire and discovery?

At first, he did not mention it, dreading that the opaque blackness might come back, that it might only be an ephemeral remission. Then he confided in Tullie, Dévonet and Bénalep. They decided to take advantage of the amelioration, fragile and aleatory as it seemed, to carry out the German experiment. Just as everything was ready, however, Monseigneur de Blois was announced at Dyonisos. It was impossible not to receive him, after the assurance given to Abbé Parroy.

The bishop was human, highly intelligent and full of good intentions, but not familiar with the veritable psychology of the majority of men of science, save for rare exceptions. For a long time he had numbered among his friends a physician and an engineer of the obsolete variety, men who were chaste, at least in appearance, hard-working and pious, and he had remained committed to the dogma of ever-benevolent science: of good cinema, utilizable for virtue as it was, on the other hand, for vice; of benediction via wireless telegraphy; of eternal peace by virtue of bringing men of good will closer together. He began by taking Ségétan's hand paternally, in the gloom, in order to make consoling but banal speeches—which made the latter's hairs prickle—about the necessity of ordeals and their benefits.

"God knows what He is doing, my son. Trust in divine mercy. Pray with an honest heart, and even if you are far distant from faith, prayer will gradually bring you closer to it. For want of the light of day, you will have the interior light that surpasses it in magnificence. Have you ever tried to pray?"

"When I was young, until my fifteenth year, I recited the prayers that my mother had taught me, half-heartedly and without conviction. One day, I perceived that they no longer meant anything to me, and I stopped...without the slightest hostility, I assure you, against matters of religion."

"What is it that stops you, my dear son?"

"The assurance with which you Princes of the Church, or simple priests, dispose the Unknown, which you claim to know."

"It's no less than the assurance with which you scientists dispose the enigmas of a nature that flees incessantly as you approach it. Are you not impressed by the fact that the foremost among you—Pascal, Pasteur, Branly—have denied the supposed opposition between scientific confidence and religious faith."

"On the contrary—I've been extremely impressed, and I'd like nothing better than to believe, even though the problem of my survival does not excite me and never has; but I have not been witness to a single miracle obtained by prayer, and the argument of the duration and universality of the Roman Church does not convince me. The Orphic mysteries lasted twelve hundred years; Buddhism and Islam are centuries old. Any religion, once implanted, is slow to disappear. I will add that neither Renan, nor any other of the same stripe, has ever persuaded me either of the non-divinity of Jesus Christ, or that the spiritual conquest of the world by twelve poor fishermen from Palestine was effectively a unique event. Each of our lives is also a unique event. I live, and I'm afraid of dying, Monseigneur, under the sign of astonishment."

"Let us place ourselves," said the bishop, "under the sign of fact. Here you are, deprived of light. I know that Abbé Parroy, who is part-saint, prays night and day, without telling you, for vision to be returned to you. He wears a cilice[28] for that purpose. If he obtains the result that we all desire, will you

---

28. A self-mortifying device, such as a "hair shirt."

admit Providence and the action of what we call our *oremus?*"

"I would have no way of knowing whether it was the Abbé's prayers, my friends' treatment or the therapeutic inclination of nature that had acted in my favor."

There, the prelate ran into an unanswerable argument. He knew by way of hearsay about the sensual theories of the Avenillon trio, which had leaked out via the servants to the right-thinking people of the neighborhood, and he briefly considered raising that scabrous subject, but he feared provoking a reaction of revolt in the umbrageous invalid and he held his tongue, making a vague allusion to Lourdes, which fell into the silence. From the summits, the conversation, still amicable, descended to the plains of discovery, notably the research into the waves of duration: "one of the greatest discoveries of the era, my dear child, which will make you a glory of science."

"Oh, Monseigneur, I would gladly give that windfall, along with all the other results of my poor labor, for the return of vision. The darkness in which I now live is a terrible torture, and everything that was once—I can still say recently—a profound joy to me is now hostile."

"Don't worry, my son; you'll be healed, I'm sure of it—for there is in you, I can see, the spirit of humility that permits the great healer, the soul, gradually to act. Permit me before leaving, to give you my blessing."

To his great surprise, after the visit of the prelate—who was no eagle, but had a good heart—Ségétan experienced a genuine relief. He had discovered a true sympathy beneath the arguments, which were rather banal but not as poor as he had feared. Besides which, he had not revealed to the bishop any aspect of his moral—or, rather, amoral—life, and the other had not questioned him about it. Finally, it gave him pleasure to know that Abbé Parroy was praying for him. He had experienced a secret irritation with regard to the religious obsequies that the saintly man had granted to the mortal remains of his assassin, Jean Calvat.

* * * * * * *

"Now, old chap: our project—or, rather, the project of the Boche from Bonn—is ready to start. We're going to search your epidermis, facial and dorsal, in the specified fashion, for a favorable location, a spot or area of metavision, an ersatz retina."

Thus spoke Bénalep to the patient, followed by Dévonet, who was carrying the electrical and undulatory apparatus and immediately began setting it up. Ségétan was still seeing whiteness, with brief periods of redarkening—but the transformation did not change anything, in terms of the weakness of his virile faculties or his intellectual faculties. Every night, a distressing dream now returned the sovereign faculty to him, which awakening snatched away again. After the brief refreshment of the Episcopal visit and speech, the desolation insinuated itself into him mutely once again, and he fell into long and worrying silences.

Ségétan was lying on his bed, face down, his upper body bare and his eyes bandaged. The curtains had been opened. Dévonet marked, with a paintbrush, the area identified by their German colleague as propitious for the experiment, along the vertebral column. Bénalep, seated at a small table, got ready to write. Tullie, in a nurse's smock, passed the requested items of equipment.

"If I see henceforth with my back," said the Master, "like some damned soul in Dante's Inferno, it will complicate my life considerably."

"Less so than an artificial anus," Bénalep retorted.

"Indeed! You're more explicit than Monseigneur de Blois."

The electrification and irradiation began. After a quarter of an hour, in accordance with the inventor's recommendation, the operation was halted and a lamp of a certain intensity was placed on a table near the bed.

"Well?" said Denoet.

"I seem to perceive a luminous dot," the patient replied.

"Of a particular intensity?"

"Comparable to that of a glow-worm."

Without a word, the experimenter signaled to Tullie to double the luminous source.

"And now?"

"There are two glow-worms."

"That's conclusive," said Bénalep.

Both lamps were extinguished.

"And now?"

"Now there's my white blindness again."

Ségétan turned round and sat up on the bed. Tullie threw a pajama jacket over his shoulders, but he kept his eyes bandaged, and said, with the waxen expression that the blind have, but with a certain hope: "There's evidently something. That's also your feeling?"

Bénalep remarked that the fibers of the optical cortex might well be able to form an anastomosis[29] with the threads of the spinal cord, which would explain the result materially. At any rate, in his opinion, there was a certain integrity of the profound visual apparatus, which remains unknown and mysterious to us, and which distributes forms and colors to us. The loss of sight by accident might well be called accidental.

"We'll pass on now to the facial areas, especially the mid-point of the forehead, or 'third eye,'" Bénalep said

They repeated the previous dispositions. Ségétan remained seated into the bed, his eyes blindfolded.

After the application of a few currents, mingled with waves, and when the two lamps had been illuminated simultaneously again, the blind man declared, in a voice trembling with emotion: "I can make out two glow-worms, more distinctly than

---

29. An anastomosis is a connection between elements of the same or different bodily systems. When the novel was written, surgeons had begun to create such linkages artificially with respect to the gut and the circulatory system, in order to relieve various blockages, and there had indeed been some speculation about the possibility of forging novel neural connections, and the possibility that the body might occasionally make such connections spontaneously in response to injury.

in the back."

"And this time?"

"Only one glow-worm."

"And this time?"

"I can make out three of them, of greater intensity."

That first proof was sufficient. Obscurity was reestablished. Tullie wept with joy, covertly. The two experiments did not hide their satisfaction. They estimated that the German method, although it was not yet a powerful therapy, had great value in prognostics. According to the inventor, the rods of the retina, being merely differentiated epidermal cells, could be substituted by the latter, with an appropriate technique.

Dévonet formulated the idea succinctly: "The skin is the organ of ambience, as it is of sensuality and amour, hatred and repulsion. Popular parlance speaks of 'having someone under one's skin.' On the other hand, the eye is the translator of ambience, and, according to your own theories, Ségétan, the stimulant of the mind by desire. There's a circuit there, which takes account of the results, still trivial but significant, that we've obtained."

Turning to the gentle and violent Tullie he added: "Have confidence, my dear friend. Romain will recover sight, and not gradually, but suddenly, as he has passed from the perception of one light to that of two. Is that your opinion, M'sieu Bienallé?"

"Entirely."

Encouraged by this result, as he had been on hearing that Abbé Parroy was devoting special prayers to him, Ségétan asked for the first time to visit his laboratory—or, rather, to grope around his laboratory, under Tullie's guidance. The authorization was given to him. He hoped that his place of work, even unperceived by his gaze, would render him a little of the intellectual and vital zest that blindness had extinguished in him. He had learned, from the waves of the past, to attach importance to locations, which are to the terrestrial surface what particular areas are to the skin.

His cherished mistress took him by the hand and they went

out of the dark room that had become his prison. They went down the stairs, which he had omitted to count while he could see clearly. They went through two doorways, climbed a few steps and arrived on a landing. There was the sound of a key in a lock. They were there.

"Only Abrice has come in here during your absence," said Tullie, "with Dévonet, who came to help him clean the apparatus. Where do you want to start?"

"With the electromagnetic apparatus...then we'll go on to the apparatus for emitting and receiving waves. We'll finish with the Dyonisos."

Tullie took him to the items of apparatus and presented them to him one by one; he palpated them very gently, with subtle gestures of his fingers, as delicate as antennae. He held his head up, as blind people do, overwhelmed by an intense emotion—for he already had gaps in his material memories, even though the design, improvement and simplification of the pieces had originated in his ingenuity and emerged from his meditation. How did they relate to the conjectures that had linked them together?

Never, since the drama had begun, had blindness been so painful—but when they arrived at the Dyonisos he found that the apparatus was not there. Tullie searched the room, opening all the cupboards, but did not find it.

"It's doubtless Dévonet that has taken it away," the Master said. "Nevertheless, it astonishes me. He should have told me."

Having sat her lover down in his usual armchair, where he had known such fecund hours, Tullie was going out of the laboratory to run to the Dévonets' house when she met the tall and stout Abrice, whose clean-shaven face had a Tartuffian expression—that of a servant caught at fault.

"Abrice, we can't find the Dyonisos. Was it Dr. Dévonet who took it away?"

"No, Madame, it was me. The porcelain stand was cracked and I took it to the electrician in Blois to have it replaced. It was him, Monsieur Anselm, who fitted it to the apparatus."

"You should have told Monsieur...."

"I don't want to trouble Monsieur, and I didn't think he'd come to the laboratory so soon, so...well..,."

"When will the stand by replaced?"

"A week from now, Madame. Anselm's very precise."

When these words were reported to the Master, he was keenly irritated, summoned Abrice and gave him a through scolding.

In fact, Abrice, by virtue of hearing talk of the Waves of Time, while "doing" the laboratory, had thought that he too might try to evoke the dead. Knowing that the vibrational systems of the very recent past returned more frequently than those of the remote past, in the same way that short waves sometimes skim the ground, he had set up the Dyonisos in a secluded place on the route from Avenillon to the Loire followed by Jean Calvat during his last dash. Five or six times a day, under some pretext or other, he ran to his hiding place and activated the apparatus, as he had seen his employer and Dévonet do. Thus far, there had beeen no result.

What would happen now that the alarm had been raised and he had lied? He consulted his wife, the cook Caroline.

"Don't fret, my love," she said to him. "Madame and the Master don't go out at present. Tomorrow, or the day after, crack the stand with a hammer and take it to Anselm—and keep your mouth shut, of course, if Dévonet interrogates you."

The next day, on a clear blue morning, Tullie, who had not left Ségétan's side since the drama, went out early to get a little exercise, leaving Mélanie with the Master. She went out of the village and went past the cemetery where Jean Calvat had rested while heading for the railway. It was there that she met Ariana, dressed in an orange silk quilted dress, her hair golden and undulating, slipping out of the abode of the dead at a rapid pace.

Doubtless she had come to pray for the handsome rustic who had pleased her momentarily.

The young women embraced, and the star asked: "How is it going?"

"Still the same, my dear. No improvement yet."

"Dévonet and Bénalep have told my lord and master that they have some hope now."

"Oh yes—the epidermal experiment. I confess that I can hardly believe it. The Germans have a habit of discovering the moon in their imagination."

They walked side by side in silence through the blue-tinted clarity of the atmosphere. In the distance, the silhouettes of large hayricks formed a circle of bright sentinels around the three villages, brightened by a fresh breeze. They were both thinking that the spectacle of their juxtaposed beauties, the brunette and the blonde, would have delighted the Master, if he had been able to see it. They did not communicate their thought to one another, but it brought them closer together nevertheless....

Suddenly, Ariana, uttering a cry of fearful surprise, extended her arm, pointing at a shadow, which Tullie immediately recognized, a few paces away: a transparent runner, who had the slender, unforgettable form of Calvat. The specter, sparkling in the daylight, bounded forward, then crouched down and shrank, gliding from one hayrick to another, like a mannequin of silver-gray silk. Its mannerisms, as if suspended in the breeze but nevertheless unaltered thereby, were those of a hunted man, a runaway. In the distance, toward the little station on the road, the confused silhouette of a gendarme appeared, also translucent, leaning on the real barrier. Cockerels were crowing, whose cock-a-doodle-doos, might have been contemporary, or evoked.

After a minute, it all vanished instantaneously.

Tullie reassured her companion, who had put her trembling arm lightly on her own. "The Dyonisos isn't far from here. It must be hidden in some covert or behind a hayrick...." And she told the shivering Ariana about Abrice's lie.

Now moving stealthily, the two friends searched in all directions for the magical apparatus, but did not find it. They resolved to clarify the matter.

* * * * * *

While these things were happening, Mélanie was keeping the Master company in the dark room. They were sitting next to one another, and she was holding his hand. He was telling her his secrets, doubtless influenced, like everyone else, by the mysterious waves he had discovered, and inclined to spontaneous confession.

"I confess to you, my beautiful friend, that if I had not recovered a little hope as a consequence of Félix's experiments, I had resolved to kill myself on a particular date, exactly a week hence."

"Is that possible? You, kill yourself? You, who could still be the master of so many secrets of nature, of who the world has cultivated the hope of so many prodigies!"

"Oh, they're two different things, you know, what others think of us and what we think of ourselves. There's nothing more ridiculous than considering me as a benefactor of humankind. No one knows whether my inventions will work to its benefit or do it harm. I think they're almost always inclined to harm, these little Pandora's boxes that we open in the secrecy of our laboratories, and from which so much supposed progress—'mechanical and otherwise'—flies out. Technology, deep down, is a kind of dirt. Sometimes it gives people new means of killing their peers, to the extent that the day will come when the masses, which venerate us at present, will massacre us—we inventors. Sometimes it suppresses the arms of workers, thus delivered to idleness or revolution. In sum, for whom do we work? For a pretended elite who think of nothing but gorging themselves on gold, of their commodities, of their vain pleasures. That elite annoys me, to such a degree that its instant disappearance would leave me as indifferent as a stone. Where would that leave the turbulent masses, who don't understand anything, and can't see that the adoption of new ways of doing things is largely compensated by the loss of old ones?"

While he was making this morose speech, the young woman had withdrawn her hand, drawn slightly apart from him, and, with a prompt and silent skill, had taken off her bodice. By way of reply, she moved her soft, plump fully-formed torso toward Ségétan's neck and face—she standing, he still sitting down—and caressed him with her breasts, as perfect as Tullie's, while she applied her mouth to his.

The scientist shivered, but the memory of the light, the hut and the golden straw, of the divine daylight that he had lost, came once again to sink and extinguish the indispensable flame of desire—and she felt, in the darkness, warm tears running over her naked bosom.

She conceived a dark voluptuousness therefrom, which momentarily caused her to collapse upon that massive inert body.

* * * * * * *

As Abrice, having given up on evoking the waves of the past by means of the Master's method, was taking the apparatus to the electrician Anselm in order for the cracked stand to be repaired, he met Ariana, delegated by Tullie under some pretext or other.

The Dyonisos was enclosed in a big box, which the chauffeur was handling with precaution. Confused by the young woman's presence, he stammered a few vague words, whereupon the "star," amused by his lie, went away. She reported the fact to Tullie.

After some deliberation, the two women decided not to say anything to the invalid, in order not to distress him, and to send Dévonet to Anselm's to recover the precious object.

Localized this time to the frontal area, the second session of electro-radiation did not produce any result measurably superior to the first, but the material state of the eyeballs permitted the elimination of the dark room—the prison, as the Master called it—and he affirmed that his imagination experienced a real relief in consequence.

"I can no longer see the light, but I can now feel it, and it can see me."

He asked Tullie to describe it to him: whether it was gilded or silvered—as it often is in the Blésois—masked by clouds or whether they were scattered through the celestial azure. "Put my hand in the angled radiance, so that I can sense the effluvia with my fingertips."

He also asked her to ask Abbé Parroy, who came for news of him twice a week, in the most discreet fashion, whether he was still praying for him. That conversation, which took place in the priest's house, in his bare and meager room, rapidly turned into a confession, for the saintly man could, on occasion be rather rude and plain-speaking.

"Certainly I'm continuing to pray, but the Intervention I'm soliciting, with all the ardor of which I'm capable, collides with the state of complete amorality in which you and the Master live. Besides which, his sensual theories, with which I'm familiar, reek of paganism. They're the cause, by subtle means, of the misfortune you've suffered, and they'll cause others even worse."

"What do you want me to do, Monsieur le Curé? I'm too small a thing compared with him. We love one another, but if I took it into my head to go against what I call his profound ideas—which are also ardent instincts—he'd leave me immediately. He's not a mortal like any other."

"Don't deceive yourself, my child. The greatest of men is a mortal, like the least, subject to the same errors, the same caprices and the same sins. Only saints—and not all of those—rise to certain summits, stripped of desires of the flesh and of pride. But I don't ask that of him, nor of you. I only ask, of both of you, in order for my humble prayers to be efficacious, to mend your ways. There's no need for me to explain further."

They were going round in circles. They both fell silent. Then the Abbé bid farewell to the young woman, assuring her that he would continue to implore Providence fervently for the man who did not believe in it.

In one of the long monologues that now composed the weft of his days, Romain thought: *The source of vision has not been annihilated in me, since I can distinguish, albeit very vaguely, with the skin of my forehead, two distinct sources of light. But that awakening, by means of the method of the physician from Bonn, is from the outside in; it's centripetal. Now, another kind of awakening, centrifugal this time, produces some kind of vision by means of violent emotion, which I could provoke artificially: emotion that would also be evocative, and would procure me, on a larger scale, the shock inflicted on my memory by Donabella's gilded nenuphar.*

This reflection tunneled away in him—unconsciously, it must be said—like a mole in search of a refuge.

"What is the weather like today, my darling?"

"Magnificent. One might think that it were August, although we're in the middle—have even passed the middle—of September.

"What time is it?"

"Quarter to noon. The sun's shining brightly."

"Is the hayrick where it happened still here?"

"Yes, but only for a few more days. The others are being taken in before the October rains, which would cause them to rot."

"This is what we'll do. Dress me. In a quarter of an hour, everyone will be sitting down to lunch. For the first time since the fatal day, you're going to take me outside without telling anyone, unknown to Abrice, Marianne and Caroline. You'll take me directly to the hayrick, a few hundred meters away. We'll make the journey of the fatal evening in the opposite direction. It's an experiment of a different sort that I want to try."

"All right," the young woman replied, simply, accustomed never to raise any objection.

They did as he had said. The streets of Avenillon were virtually deserted. A few old men and women, going home for the midday meal, slightly late because their appetites had declined with age, displayed their astonishment at seeing Tullie with her sorcerer hanging on her arm, "as if they were going to get married," but everyone has his own affairs to attend to, and the crime and drowning of young Calvat were already old.

Enlivened by the honest open air and by hope, the scientist was walking deliberately, as if he could see, leaning on the woman he had conquered and kept. They were not talking, having an understanding, in order not to exhaust the useful virtues of silence.

They arrived at the rick, and that rustic word, in her as in him, evoked a host of various frissons.

"It's really here?"

"It's here."

"Will you place me in the precise spot where I was when you took off your clothes?"

"Wait a moment while I get my bearings. Here it is."

"The sun's shining brightly?"

"It's directly above us. It's scintillating. One can't look at it."

"That's perfect...and now, my beauty, my beloved, sing me the Neapolitan song that is about Him, the globe of fire, Apollo, vivifying and redemptive."

He was excited, and stood here unmoving, massive, holding his head up, his hat in his hand. Then he dropped the hat and remained upright, head high, presenting his forehead to the star, his hands held out in front of him, but not joined, as if he were imploring while threatening. The moment became solemn, and it seemed that a little of the man, his pride and his destiny, so often beaten down, entered into the cruel, perfidious and also immutable aspects of nature.

Tullie's voice rose up, like a appeal, like a plea, on the flutter of a soul that had become a bird. The song rose, a diamond skylark, which seemed to launch itself toward the star in order to be consumed there.

Romain listened, enraptured.

As one draws back a curtain before a marvelous spectacle, long hidden from a moribund individual, by means of which he will revive, the world of forms and colors suddenly sprang forth for the blind man, out of the accursed darkness of his night.

"I can see, Tullie"!" he cried. "I can see!"

His arms still reaching forward, it was as if he quit the earth, following the enchanted voice. In the place where he had almost lost his life, where he had lost the daylight, the latter gave him back the former, and his throbbing arteries carried the redness, miraculously brightened, of a new blood.

Tullie, beside herself, supernaturally beautiful, her white neck swollen with a boundless joy, continued singing, passionately.

CHAPTER SEVEN
HYMN TO LIGHT

September was still shining and burning over the forest of Sombreval. Ségétan and Tullie were walking, at a brisk pace, along those Cartesian paths, which are the image of the French mind. They were talking about the innumerable letters and telegrams of congratulation that had arrived at Dyonisos when the news of the cure had spread. From all parts of France, England, Belgium, Switzerland, America, Germany and Italy, the people who had been desolate on hearing the news of the illustrious physicist's blindness were rejoicing at the return of the light. Scientific societies joined their tributes to those of individuals. In the world press there was a concert of eulogies, comments on the waves of the past, and their physical and philosophical implications.

The Master did not care about any of that, though. What was important to him, what exalted him, was having recovered the faculty of love, of desire, of creation, of enjoying the light of day, the body of a woman, her changing expressions, the odor of flowers, the taste of bread and wine, concordances between sounds and colors, hidden meanders of the mind, the perfumes of roses.

In the heart of the forest, the sight of a giant oak half-blasted by lightning, whose coarse bark had disappeared over an extent of several meters, an image of courage and resistance, moved him so much that he embraced the tree, while Tullie laughed wholeheartedly. Under the giant plants, a quincunx of chanterelle mushrooms appeared—it had rained the day before—mingled with orange-milk mushrooms of a beautiful eggshell color. The young woman, more lively, graceful and beautiful than ever in the joy of that resurrection, wanted to pick them all and carry them away in a basket brought for that purpose.

"No, no, just the chanterelles!" exclaimed Romain. "I've no desire to die. False orange-milks are fatal nourishment."

"Oh, Old Windy! There's no way to make a mistake. The true orange-milk is like an egg."[30]

"So it's said, but mushrooms are like people—one never knows whether they're poisonous or not."

Chatting and laughing, they arrived at a crossroads, where there was a forester's house of cheerful appearance, surrounded by a vegetable garden, with a small pond on one side, covered by aquatic plants—among which were a few belated water-lilies. Ségétan thought about Donabella—who, out there in Naples, was thinking about him. The forester, still young, with a kind and honest face, was holding a small child in his sturdy arms, who was bouncing, wide-mouthed, up to his ears. He recognized Ségétan.

"Hey, wife—come out here a minute!"

A blonde and cheerful stout-waisted peasant woman appeared, smelling of fresh linen and butter, with an expression as open as her husband's. The latter said to her: "Get us a nice little bottle, a cheese and some fresh bread—if the Master and Madame will give us the pleasure of having a snack with us. The raspberries are in the bottom of the dresser."

"We won't say no," said Ségétan. "We've come from the village, and we walked at a good pace."

"How old is he?" Tullie asked, caressing the infant.

"Four, and we're expecting another. It's not like the city here. One can feed three kids without overstretching oneself."

---

30. In French, the poisonous fly-agaric mushroom is known as a *fausse-oronge* [literally, fake orange-milk], although, as Tullie says, its variegated coloring makes it unlikely that it would be mistaken for its innocuous relative, which is sometimes known as the imperial mushroom.

Glasses full of pink fresh gold were clinked, and the man, having wiped his mouth with the back of his hand, said to his guest: "Master, we were direly afraid for you. The shot fired by that bastard Calvat risked burning your eyes permanently, and, well, eyes, I suppose, are as important to you as they are to us. When you bring back the past, you need to be there to recognize it."

"Are you interested in the waves of the past, my friend?"

"Am I interested! I should think so! When will they be improved enough for the parents and grandparents to come to have a little chat with us?"

"It's not quite like that. We'll see them, come the day, chatting among themselves as in the time when they lived, and in the conditions in which they lived."

The forester seemed disappointed. "Then they won't be real specters, like those of my Breton country?"

"What part of Brittany are you from?"

"Scaër, on the black mountain. The dead used to visit our ancestors, so it's said—then among our others and fathers, the custom was lost. I think you've found it again."

"In another form. For example, with my system, in a hundred years' time, the people who live here will be able to see us, sitting at this table, with these raspberries and these bottles, as we are at this moment."

The forester scratched his head and his wife opened her eyes wide.

When they resumed their walk, Romain said to Tullie: "Intelligence consists of representing things that one cannot see, divining the interrelationships of things and discerning he reality of false appearances. Some peasants hereabouts are very intelligent. That forester isn't, but he has a sufficient stock of good sense to exercise his profession and nourish his family."

* * * * * * *

The following Sunday, at the beginning of October, a simple

ceremony designed to celebrate the recovery of the Master of the Waves was due to take place. Maire Tapin had discussed the matter with Ignacio, Abbé Parroy and his colleagues in neighboring towns. The beautiful Adélaide, escorted by young women selected from among the most attractive in the region, was to present Ségétan with a bouquet and a bronze medal engraved in Paris, representing his bold and superb profile, famous throughout the world. Préfet Dugerbier had promised his collaboration. The Monseigneur, after much hesitation, had decided to abstain, in view of the scientist's notorious misconduct, but he had authorized the Curé of Avenillon to take part in the little fête.

Everything went very well, except that the prefect, unable to attend at the last moment, sent a letter of apology. Before an audience of about thirty—many more had been expected—the Maire made a nice little speech. When Ségétan embraced Adélaide, amid the flowers she handed to him, he felt her shiver and the beating of her ingenuous heart; he obtained a double excitement therefrom, sensual and intellectual, which gave him the sensation that all his faculties were securely in place. Then the brass band played an upbeat tune, and everyone went home.

The thinness of the audience had struck the Master's friends, however, and they mentioned it to Tullie. The fact had not escaped her, and she made enquiries of the farm-workers at Les Arges, of Sylvain and the Ignacios, and ended up discovering the fly in the ointment. It was "the good Marianne," Ségétan's housekeeper for twelve years, since his first marriage to the famous Lili Duvoir of the white slave trade, who was gossiping slyly but furiously with the suppliers, the farmers and their workers, with incredible persistence and perversity. Tullie, the "new one," was not spared, of course, but there the tragic old woman ran up against a reputation for benevolence and generosity that rendered slander more difficult. In addition, being ever-alert, she had caught wind of the fact that the sudden deaths in the region were due to an insect that had escaped from Dévonet's jars—the second auxiliary and accomplice of the

Satan of the Dyonisos, Bénalep being the first. Thus, a zone of muted hostility had gradually been created around the three sorcerers, especially the chief sorcerer. Perhaps Calvat had been more excusable than people had thought.

When the young woman had enough evidence and sufficient witnesses, she told her husband what was happening. She expected some resistance on his part, for he was attached to his habits and petty manias, but since he had recovered his sight, he had freed himself from a host of small constraints and preoccupations of existence, and the adventure started out by amusing him.

"Throw her out right away, with a good reference and a five-hundred-franc bill. Do you have another housekeeper in mind?"

"Oh no—my intention is, if you're agreeable, to replace the old shrew with Adélaide, who's very unhappy at home, who isn't unpleasant to look at, whom you admire, and whom I could train for service very rapidly."

Romain immediately glimpsed a series of potential complications, but also the advantages to which that cohabitation with an amorous newcomer, alternately occupied by devotion and jealousy, might lead. Having added everything up, he agreed. The choice of someone local would doubtless mollify the population of the three villages and deaden suspicion. There was nothing more to do than sack Marianne.

At the first words addressed to her by "Madame," however, the underhanded old woman declared flatly that she would not go, and barricaded herself into her room with a supply of food. After a few tragic hours, the comedy began.

They began, reluctantly, by delegating her friend Caroline, with whom she was on good terms, and then Abrice. The former received a series of insults and clear allusions to the depravities in which she indulged, so effectively that she did not persist. The chauffeur tried persuasion, conciliation and polite cordiality, but without success. Then the Master had to get involved himself and, half mockingly and half pleadingly, engaged in a dialogue through the door.

"Come on, Marriane, my girl, this isn't reasonable. You're going to oblige me to send for a locksmith and a gendarme. Open up and pack your bags calmly. Madame will give you an excellent reference and a five-hundre-franc banknote."

"No, I won't go. I haven't done any of what I'm accused of. I don't want to be chased away like a dog. I won't go."

After half an hour of vain palaver, no further resonse emerging, the local locksmith, Monsieur Paul, was sent for. He arrived, jovial and plump, with a bunch of keys.

"Come on, little mother, make a gesture? It's me, Paul, a mate. Open the door so that we can come in."

"Leave me in peace!"

"Once, twice, three times!"

"M* * *!"[31]

"You're not very polite at present, Madame Marianne."

Irritated by so much insolence, Paul examined the lock as a connoisseur and a technician. He perceived that it was an old, complex model to which he could not adapt any of the long, slender skeleton keys that he had brought. His fruitless attempts, underline by diabolical laughter coming from the locked room put him in a sweat and a rage. He gave the door a solid thrust with his shoulder in order to break the lock, but without success. He hurt himself, and the hinges resisted. He went downstairs.

"Well, Monsieur I don't have the necessary tools for that; besides which, the bolt's shot inside. My opinion is that you'll need the gendarmes. They have tricks."

The intervention of the gendarmerie on the occasion of the Calvat affair, had cost the life of a member of the public force, which had had a bad effect and had cost the scientist twenty thousand francs, which he had given to the widow. An appeal was made to Dévonet, the *deus ex machina* of all difficult circumstances.

The latter suggested using an inoffensive tear-gas that would put the old woman at their mercy, but it was necessary to order

31. The expletive *merde*, literally "shit," can be used in a way more closely akin to the English "Fuck off!"

it from Tours. The response to the telephone call, naturally, was that the stock in Tours had run out, necessitating recourse to the Prefecture of Police in Paris, which certainly possessed the necessary implement but needed an authorization from the Ministry of the Interior to release it to a province. Ségétan's name removed the obstacles.

It was then six o'clock in the evening and, the news of Marianne's obstinacy having spread, the local inhabitants were talking about it on their doorsteps. Fortunately, the window of the room in which Marianne was barricaded overlooked the countryside, so curiosity did not lead to any assembly in front of the Villa Dyonisos.

Meanwhile, negotiations continued. Successively, Mélanie, Ariana, who lavished tips on Marianne, and Bénalep, who treated her annual bronchitis and attacks of rheumatism, employed the most pressing arguments, pleas and threats, which obtained no response but growls, insults or silence. It was necessary to prepare for all eventualities. After the employment of the tear-gas, the victim would have to be transported to a quiet place where she could gradually recover her senses. Another telephone call was made to Blois, where a bed would be made ready at the Villa Requiem. Marianne's nephew, who kept a tavern at Lilas, was informed, and her cousins, who operated a removal van in Rambouillet.

Diner at Dyonisos was sullen. Ségétan was beginning to find that the joke had gone too far and that his "housekeeper" was becoming something of an inconvenience. Perhaps it would have been simpler to keep her, and shut her mouth. Tullie explained to him as best she could that that solution was impossible, for nothing closes the mouths of those who have the sadism of speaking ill, and who seek refined enjoyments therein—the joy of doing damage, of the German *schadenfreude*.

After the meal, as nine o'clock was chiming, Caroline, kept up to date, had the idea of going to warn her comrade that the firemen were coming with "the gases" to force her to open up. The illustrated papers had popularized this police procedure, and Marianne, confronted with these frightful images, did not fail to cry "Horror!" The messenger of terror had hardly finished her story than blasts of a klaxon resounded in the street, soon followed by the roar of a powerful automobile. The Prefecture had moved quickly. Three vigorous practitioners got out of the vehicle and began unloading the apparatus, in the midst of twenty gawkers. They asked about "the job to be done."

"Here they are, my old dear, here they are!"

Then a kind of sobbing roar was heard, and Marianne frightened by the racket, drew the bolt, emerged from her refuge and simulated a faint, which did not deceive anyone.

"Thank you gentlemen, we don't need you. Have you had dinner?"

"No, my dear Master," said the inspector of the judiciary police who appeared to be the leader of the detachment. "We were counting on going to the inn."

"It's simpler to stay here, and you'll eat better. Abrice, my chauffeur here, will prepare you a good meal, won't you, Abrice?"

"Leave it to us, Master."

It only remained to take care of the old woman, who was still lying down, but stood up as if on a spring when she heard mention of the Villa Requiem. She declared, in a voice that was back to normal, that she intended to take the bus to Blois station and retire to Lilas, to the establishment of her nephew—who would exact a terrible vengeance for the ill-treatment to which his aunt had been subjected. Her departure, and that of her ancient and solemn trunk, were thus arranged simultaneously.

"Oof!" exclaimed Ségétan. "That was a fine to-do. The attachment of old servants has to be seen to be believed. Fortunately, we still have Abrice and Caroline! Why are you smiling, Tullie?"

In the meantime, in the ample, comfortable kitchen with an appetizing odor, the the chauffeur and hiw wife were feeding "the gentlemen." The inspectors began eating in silence, and then, after a few glasses of local wine, judiciously chosen from the Master's collection by Abrice, the one that seemed to be the leader, who had an intelligent physiognomy, became bold enough to ask a few questions about the Calvat affair—which, he said, had interested everyone, from school to parliament.

"The court?"

"Yes, criminal cases always cause a big stir in the Procureur Générale's office. There was talk of a drama of jealousy."

Abrice gave details in the reticent fashion of a man who knows what there is to know but is not saying everything. The policeman, without persisting, passed lightly over the waves of the past to ask about the disruption of aircraft engines, of which Ségétan was reputed to know the secret.

"The German war's still threatening. Now the Master is cured, he ought to get back to that and finish it. That's all they talk about at the Ministry of War, and when they heard about the accident they cried: 'We won't have the trick in time!' Do you know how that's going, you who are in on the secrets?"

The chauffeur indicated by means of a gesture of his left hand that the matter was still pending, and then made a sign to his wife, who went out. Then the inspector said, in a low voice: "If you keep us up to date, there'll be a generous fee of six hundred francs a month. All we ask is that you send us word every fortnight saying: 'Making progress' ot 'Nothing new.' Signature, a cross."

Abrice took the proffered card and read: *M. Dugard, Quai des Orfèvres, Paris.* The inspector added: "Post it in another village, of course, not here."

A movement of the head was the only response; thus the bait was taken.

Before taking his leave, the inspector said to the faithful servant of the Villa Diionysos: "You understand that the secret mustn't go abroad, to one of the Boches or Americos that you have here, in the season, at your banquet. It surprises you, does it, that we know about that? My poor old chap, we know almost everything."

* * * * * * *

Ségétan awoke with a start an utter a sigh of relief. He had dreamed that he had gone blind. He leapt out of bed with the vivacity of a young man and ran to the window. Dawn was about to break.

"Tullie! Quick, quick—it's dawn. Put on a peignoir. We'll get dressed when we come back."

They had planned to go into the countryside to watch the daybreak, at the hour that the Master called "the major commotion of the mind."

Like all truly beautiful and beloved women, Tullie from Naples was as fresh and supple, on emerging from sleep, as if she were emerging from water. Her hair still tangled, she ran to the dressing-room with the long strides of a slender-kneed huntress and washed her face in two seconds, with economical movements.

The two lovers were ready in five minutes. They went out of Avenillon and, instead of turning toward Brancheville and Quatrebois, took the road to Saint-Zacharie-du-Bois, the sole slight bump in the vast plain, from which they would have an eastward view.

The old village was deserted; a pale purgatorial light bathed its juxtaposed mossy stone walls, dating back two or three centuries. The church, with its magnificent belfry, was still surrounded by a shadowy mist. Suddenly, it dissipated, and ten, twenty, thirty cock-crows saluted the inflamed arrival, the pink nostrils and red manes of the first chargers of Apollo's chariot. The latter was no longer a mythological figure; nothing could be seen but a gigantic wheel, an authentic wheel, with a golden rim, which seemed to be rotating in a furnace.

The entire extent of the inseminated ground, with its farms, its hamlets, its fires, its copses and its scattered bell-towers displayed its incomparable riches, with a resplendence here of fabric, there of metal. It was France, in its familiar and suave majesty, France cleaving the black and emotion-laden water of the centuries, with its wake of enlightenment.

Hugging his ravishing lover in her peignoir, of a different shade of pink, the scientist felt seething within him that desire for ever-increasing beauty, for mysteries unveiled, for secrets revealed, for confidences proclaimed, for justice rising above injustice, which was the only thing that made life worth living.

The father transmitted to the son the strength to bear tribulations and overcome obstacles; the mother transmitted all the rest, and the aptitude for noble enjoyments, in the first rank of which were the sensual, often commanding the intellectual. *The discoveries that I have made*, he thought, *are nothing compared with those swarming in my reignited imagination. I have traversed death and darkness; now I am reborn to the star of fire.*

"Tillie, won't you sing, like the other time, by the hayrick?"

For the first time in her life, she refused him something. "No, it's too beautiful; I can't."

A home an hour later, at table with two cups of milky coffee, they received a visit from Maire Taupin, who said to them, his sincere and tranquil manner: "Excuse me for disturbing you at such an early hour. I've learned that Adélaide is due to enter service with you today, as a replacement for Marianne, and that you intend to employ her. I'm asking you not to do that. In fact, I've been told that her drunkard of a husband, on learning that, had a terrible fit of anger, and that he threatened to kill you— you, my dear Master—if you and Madame Tullie go through with that plan. I thought that after the Calvat affair...."

"Oh, Monsieur le Maire, my dear friend," Romain interrupted, with a sickly smile, "life here will become very difficult if every week brings us a new complication. We've been obliged to sack that old crackpot who was denigrating Madame and myself, slandering us and robbing us in an odious fashion, and now it's forbidden for us to find a replacement here. I'm not intimidated by that drunkard's threats."

"It's just that he's quite capable of carrying them out. He's as excitable as the other, and, with a few glasses of wine under his belt, he could easily be moved to lash out."

"What a bore," murmured Tullie. "And what do we say to Adélaide?"

"The simplest thing is to tell her the truth, and that you don't want to be responsible for another unfortunate incident."

"Yes, but in the meantime, we're devoid of a housekeeper, and the house is a burden."

The Maire reflected, his leathery face contracted by effort. After a long pause, he explained that he knew a robust young woman in Nativelle, on the far side of Châteaudun: an unmarried orphan, very resourceful, by the name of Antoinette, who would do very well.

"In addition, I know that you're a gourmand, and she cooks veal *au jus* like no one else—a veritable caramel."

"Go for Antoinette!" exclaimed the Scientist.

The Maire had not been gone for a quarter of a hour when Adélaide arrived. She had put on her best clothes, but her charming face was disfigured by the blow of a fist, marked in blue and yellow, administered by her churl of a husband. Tullie received her alone and explained, as best she could, that she had forgotten a previous engagement, and that the agreement could no longer be kept. She handed her two hundred francs in compensation.

"I don't want it," said Adélaide, rejecting the bills angrily. "I see what's going on. It's Mother Tapuin who has ruined me with the Master because I know what happened in the grain-loft. I'll get my own back...." Within a second, she had been transformed into a virago, and had become brutal and ugly.

"We've had a narrow escape," Tullie said to her lover, and begged him not to take all that parlor gossip seriously.

The arrival of Antoinette two days later calmed the great man's apprehensions, but at the first mention of her veal *au jus* Caroline's eyebrows furrowed and she indicated clearly that she would not accept the presence of any rival in the kitchen.

"Anyway, veal *au jus* isn't sorcery. It's a dish within everyone's range."

Since the recovery, Dévonet and Bénalep had been collaborating with their friend in getting his apparatus back into working order. Lugging it around had thrown the Dyonisos out of kilter, which remained mute with regard to the waves of the past in no matter what location it was placed.

Ségétan had assumed the absorbed appearance that was symptomatic in him of some major project. Sometimes, leaving his collaborators on the ground floor amid the pieces of the dismantled apparatus, he went up to his study to consult, for hours on end, the famous tables mapping the passage of waves of duration of particular epochs within a given area, between Touraine, Blésois, Beauce and Sologne. Tullie also noticed that he had pinned a large map of the Bay of Naples to the wall, and kept Beulé's book *The Drama of Vesuvius*[32] permanently open on his desk, along with numerous pamphlets devoted to the volcano's eruptions and the excavations at Pompeii and Herculaneum.

She told Mélanie and Ariana, her two confidantes, about it. "Something tells me that it won't be long before we're all taking the road to the city of my birth, as we agreed."

"The Master must be thinking about Donabella," Ariana said to Mélanie, one day.

"He'd better beware of Hatchinson," the latter retorted. "His varnished mug suggests to me that he's capable of anything...."

The days passed peacefully. The Master, absorbed in his research, worked from morning till night, and, pursued by his idea, said very little even at meals. His two confidants, to whom he communicated his observations and calculations, said to Tullie: "He's making progress."

He sometimes spent hours with the Dyonisos, in an atmosphere of meditation—to the extent that one day Abrice became bold enough to ask. "Has Monsieur completely solved the problem of disrupting aircraft engines in mid-flight?"

The scientist raised his head, astonished. "What business can

---

32. Charles-Erenest Beulé, *La Drame de Vesuve* (1872).

that be of yours, old man? Do you have an airplane to crash?"

"Oh no, Monsieur, but as I read in the newspaper, with regard to the rumors of war, that Monsieur had retuned to work on the problem, I permitted myself to ask, in order...."

"Well, since the subject interests you, Abrice, know that I'm pursuing the two problems at the same time: the waves of the past and the disruption of engines, just as you're able to occupy yourself simultaneously with the cellar and the auto. I'm resting from one by moving to the other. When I encounter a difficulty here, I leave my work ticking over and go back to the other. Do you understand?"

"Perfectly, Master."

That same evening, Abrice took the vehicle to Châteaudun, under the pretext of repairs, and put into the post, to the address indicated a note that read: *Two questions being pursued at the same time: waves of past; disruption of engines. Good prospects of conclusion.*

* * * * * *

A short while afterwards, as night fell, the cry of "Fire!" resounded through Avenillon and the tocsin began to ring lugubriously. Romain, absorbed in his work, did not hear it, but Tullie arrived like a gust of wind.

"A fire's just broken out at the Dévonets' house, following some carelessness on the part of the housemaid. The fire engine from Mouquette has been requested. I'm sending Abrice with our two extinguishers, which I've just unhooked. I've alerted Ariana by telephone; she'll send Sylvain with theirs...."

"Oh damn it!" said the Master. "Poor Félix! What will become of his collections? Go and see what's happening. I'm at such a crucial point in my project just now that I can't get away."

He went back to work, perceiving, at a distance, the coming and goings, the appeals of the firemen and the throbbing of their vehicle—but he was so deep in reflection that he soon forgot all about it. The Dévonets' house was too far away for the Villa

Dyonisos to be endangered by the spread of the fire.

The researcher only became conscious again two hours later, when his friend came in person to tell him, with a crease of anxiety on his broad, usually impassive forehead, that the flames had devoured the kitchen and the laboratory, and had caused the wax seals on his jars to melt. All the venomous creatures had escaped.

"We need to warn the Maire and have a public announcement made to the drum."

"You can't do that! There'd be panic. How can people protect themselves against the stings of insects like those? They're surely not as dangerous as Jehovah?"

"Obviously not—but there's a risk, and the region could be evacuated."

"Many of them must have been roasted."

"Undoubtedly. Nevertheless, some can resist high temperatures."

Ségétan reflected for a minute, returned to a sense of reality—as keen in him, in case of need, as the imaginative faculty.

"Where's your wife?"

"At Brancheville, with Bénalep and Tullie, with the Ignacios."

"Is the fire out?"

"Completely. Thanks to your extinguishers, it was under control before the firemen from Mousquette arrived."

"Well, it's necessary that you and Mélanie get away from here within the hour, with a minimum of baggage—either to Tours or Paris. With my auto and the Ignacios', that's easy. By staying here, if a few accidents of the Jehovah kind occur, you'd both be risking being lynched. Go home and get everything ready while I telephone Brancheville and the Mairie, to which I'll also send Abbé Parroy. The people of Blésois are excellent, but I know from numerous signs that our sorceries are beginning to cause anxieties, and if you want to know what I really think, they're not entirely wrong. Moreover, your misdeeds are more visible than mine."

This program was followed exactly. Not one hour, but two

hours after the decision of the sorcerers confronted with an immediate difficulty down here, Ignacio's automobile was on the road to Tours, carrying Dévonet, Mélanie and their maid. Their house would be guarded by their neighbor, a former blacksmith who had passed on to selling gasoline and automobile accessories—which had fortunately been spared by the fire. The fugitives were to stay at the Hôtel de l'Univers, where news would be sent to them by telephone.

The very next day, a suspicious death was observed in Quastrebois, but it was a matter of an infirm, hemiplegic woman whose death might have been attributable to the progress of the paralysis. Bénalep hurried off, with a syringe of serum, to examine the deceased, and discovered on a characteristic puncture-wound on the right hip of the still-warm cadaver.

The following day there were two sudden deaths, both taking place in Brancheville, one near the château and the other on the edge of the village in a barn. Immediately, the local authorities conferred, and drew up a common decree, made public, in which great caution was urged upon the inhabitants, with regard to dangerous insects that had escaped from a collection in the vicinity as a result of a fire. Although it was not specifically identified, everyone for ten leagues around knew what collection it was, and anger begun to rumble.

The lamentable death of a old farm-worker at Les Arges, who perished five minutes after being stung by one of the sorcerer's "accursed insects," unleashed one of those movements of anger that can suddenly be produced in the most seemingly-calm rural areas, comparable to the reawakening of ancient peasant revolts. Twenty sturdy fellows armed with pitchforks came running from all directions to Avenilloln, where they assembled in front of the Dévonets' house—fortunately abandoned—shouting "Death to the murderer!" and other pleasant remarks.

A supplier deserted by Bénalep found an opportunity to avenge himself, by signaling the nationality of the fugitive's friend, and the same people who had broken the windows of the "merchant of death" and almost staved in the entrance door, posted themselves in front of the "bolt-hole" of the inventor of digitalis coffee with cries of "Down with the Jews!" It was said that he manufactured vegetable poisons in the guise of remedies, and cast spells by the light of the full moon.

Thus far, the public fury seemed to have spared the Master of the Waves, by virtue of the dread that he inspired and the solidly-established reputation he had acquired of having cuckolded Dévonet. It was a punishment of sorts—insufficient, to be sure, but one that satisfied jovial natures.

Seeing that things were going badly, Maire Taupin made a new appeal to the gendarmerie at Bois. The brave policemen had not yet got over the death of their comrade during the pursuit of Jean Calvat; nevertheless, duty comes first. Their appearance in the villages brought about a salutary appeasement, which coincided with a respite on the part of Dévonet's escaped boarders.

Then the rumor went around of the death by a sting of the pregnant wife and young child of the forester Germane of Sombreval—the same one that had fed raspberries to Romain and Tullie. It was said that the husband, mad with grief, had taken his rifle and was heading for the turbulent village in order to kill one of the three. The captain of the gendarmerie, alerted to the rumor, came to advise Ségétan and Benalep to seek refuge in Brancheville, which he would be able to defend against any furious attack.

"Against any attack!" said Romain, stupefied. "Do you think we'll be subjected to a siege?"

"Master," said the officer, "I was born here; I know the natives, and I know that they can go from passivity to violence with disconcerting rapidity. I'm responsible for your precious lives, especially yours, so vital to national defense. I shall permit myself to insist with all my might that you take shelter for a few hours—the time I need to reason with the unfortunate forester."

"What about my laboratory, where I have equipment worth several hunred thouand francs, and my house?"

"Don't worry—we'll protect them. For the moment it's people, not property, that we have to think about. Protect yourself, and Madame. The servants have nothing to fear—but I've been told about a certain Marianne, who's been turning people against you for a long time."

"She's no longer in my service."

At that moment, an orderly came in.

"Captain, the man we're looking for—the forester—has disappeared, and none of our men can find him. He's armed and crazy. It's Monsieur Ségétan that he's looking for."

"You see," said the officer, turned to Romain.

Tullie, who had been listening behind the door, intervened. "It's no time to hesitate. Thank you, Captain. The auto's ready. In five minutes, we'll be at the Château de Brancheville."

* * * * * * *

When he found out what was going on, Abbé Parroy did not waste a second. He seized his rusty old bicycle and pedaled in the direction of Sombreval, in order to find the victim of Dr. Dévonet's scientific whims.

It had drizzled during the night; the ground was sticky and the priest could not go quickly for fear of skidding. He knew from the gossip that the unfortunate forester's intention was real, although, in the event, he had not been able to leave his house in the woods the previous evening because of the official formalities and preparations for the funeral. The probability was that he had not taken the road, which was sufficiently guarded, but cut through the thickets and undergrowth, of which he knew every detail, and which would take him to the edge of Avenillon by some path or side-road unknown to the gendarmes.

It was into that tangle that the Curé went, pulling his machine, parting the wet branches that occasionally barred his route. His calculation was accurate. He had not gone five hundred meters through the woods when he found himself face to face with Germane, in a khaki garment, unaccompanied by his dog, with his rifle on his shoulder, who was advancing cautiously, with a fixed stare and a grim and intense expression.

"Oh, my friend, I was just taking a short cut to your house. What a misfortune, what a frightful misfortune! I learned about it last night, from my housekeeper." He went forward to embrace the man, but the latter shoved him away brutally.

"I don't want to be consoled, Monsieur le Curé. It's something else that's necessary now."

"I know. You intend to kill Monsieur Ségétan, who hasn't done anything at all to you, and has nothing to do with the tragic death of your wife and child."

"His friend, his confidant, has run away. I need to take my revenge on someone and that someone will be him."

"Come to your senses, Germane, my penitent. The Good Lord forbids murder. All the more reason when the intended victim is not responsible in any way."

"Let me pass, Monsieur le Curé. I don't believe in the Good Lord. Given that such things are possible, the Good Lord doesn't exist, and you're telling stories."

"Come on, you're not being rational! Imprudence is human, wickedness is human, errors and crimes are human. God permits them, as I've always told you, but sooner or later, he punishes them. He leaves humans the freedom of their conscience, of good and evil. In the same way, he permits venomous insects, corrosive acids, revolutions and wars."

"Then what use is your God?"

"To redeem evil, to forgive, to save souls."

"Yes, to save that which one can't see and let alone that which one can."

This dialogue in the damp wood, rudimentary in its theology, could have been prolonged indefinitely, on such a delicate— and, in the circumstances, emotional—issue. The abbé came back to the ground from which they had strayed.

"How did it happen, my poor child?"

"We'd had dinner. The wife was in our room, putting the boy to bed, when she screamed. I went in. "It's nothing," she told me. "There it is, running away!" And I looked, but I couldn't see, because there wasn't much light. If I'd known! But a minute later, the boy screamed as if he'd been burned with a hot iron. I brought the lamp and I saw some kind of scarab on the ground, with a tail like a scorpion. At the same time as I crushed it with my heel, I realized that it was one of Dévonet's, escaped again from that murderer's collection in Avenillon. Then I did the same as for a viper, and as I learned in foresters' training. I heated my knife, and after having bound my wife's arm and my boy's leg, between the black wound and the body, I put the blade into the blister, deep down. It must have been too late, or else the poison was too terrible; it didn't do anything. Five minutes later, my wife threw up the milk I'd just made her drink, and five minutes after that, she fell on her side. She was dead. Our little one died at almost the same time. You know that my wife was pregnant. That's three people at the same time! Then I went mad. I beat my head against the walls. I wanted to punish the bandit who had caused my loss immediately, but I also wanted to stay. I was shouting all sorts of things when people came, alerted by my comrade from Brancheville, who was passing by at the moment of their death—both of them, all three, although I didn't know the one who was about to be born. Oh, the misery! Oh, the vileness of fate! Oh, the wrath of God! I could have died!"

This tale, told in a staccato voice that became increasingly hoarse, concluded with a great sob, which shook the unfortunate and his precarious carbine. His legs were trembling. The priest understood that he had achieved his objective. Again, he seized the tottering forester in order to embrace him. The latter no longer resisted. At the same time, with a swift gesture, he relieved him of the rifle with the shiny barrel, which he held to one side, pointed toward the ground in case it went off.

"Oh, I knew that was what you were up to, Monsieur l'Abbé. So, since you don't want me to kill Ségétan, I'll kill myself instead."

He extended his arm, but without any veritable resolution, toward the weapon, whose two shots the prudent curé swiftly discharged into the bushes. The double blast echoed for a long time in the foliage, and a rapid expression of deliverance, scarcely covered by feigned disappointment, crossed Germane's bronzed face. His criminal intention had doubtless weighed upon him, but it had become, like any abrupt obsession, a command.

"What am I going to do now, then?"

"You're going to pray, my lad, and thank God for making you abandon your abominable project."

"But it wasn't God, Monsieur le Curé—it was you."

"Imbecile! I'm only His poor and humble representative. Get down on your knees, right away, and thank Him!"

The forester did not obey. He was suspicious. A sudden image, of a kind opposed to the preceding one, presented itself to his troubled and confused mind, as a tenacious illusion. He murmured: "Since that's the way it is, and since it's necessary to compensate for deaths, can you ask him—Ségétan—to bring me back my wife and the little one with his machine, as at the time he came to my house with his lady, and we gave him wine and raspberries?"

That naïve question, which he avoided, was later to come back to the Abbé, who was sometimes a visionary, along with a host of reflections on the moral, placatory and benevolent aspects of his incredulous parishioners's astonishing discovery, once it was perfected.

To materialize the past, to render that force, that effectiveness of presence, which neither our evocative memory, no matter how powerful it might be, nor the fugitive shadows of knowledge gained from books, possess, would bring about a change in the ordinary condition of human life, revive the joys of yesteryear, and revive or appease its dolors.

For the moment, though, the curé only had one idea—to take the poor fellow to the presbytery and keep him there, as well as his carbine, long enough to render him conclusive relief and deliver him entirely from his obsession.

"Give me your gun. People will understand."

"But they'll hold me in derision, Monsieur l'Abbé."

"Not at all. They'll think you're a brave man, and an unfortunate one."

The Maire and the captain of the gendarmerie, when they found out what had happened, uttered a sigh of satisfaction. They had been worried—and the gendarmes too, had been saved from an onerous task. In the village and the region, Abbé Parroy's popularity increased considerably, and was expressed in such terms as: "The Curé is a saint. He saved the life of the chief sorcerer."

No other accident occurred in the days that followed, and it was concluded that the murderous insects, attracted by the forest, had taken the road to Sombreval, where they had perished, away from the thermal conditions necessary to their redoubtable existence and reproduction. The surveillance around Ségétan's laboratory and the Villa Dyonisos could be lifted.

Alerted to the eventuality, the guests at the Château de Bancheville were by no means the last to congratulate the curé on his initiative and the result he had obtained. The joyful Tullie was untiring in singing the praises of his personal and sacerdotal virtue.

"Well," she said to Bénalep, "your 'social parasite' has been had the opportunity nevertheless to render a great service. The *oremus*, as you put it, might have saved your life."

The old Silenus had been particularly wounded by the cry of "Down with the Jews!" proffered by the ungrateful peasants for whom he had so often cared, and who had testified amity until then. He could not get over that sudden turnabout.

Ségétan consoled him with his favorite explanation. "That's nothing, old man. Our descendants will see, in that order of ideas, many things unforeseen by that fool Renan in his *Future of Science*,[33] and his universally-respected aristocrats of the laboratory. When they understand the evils and the catastrophes already emerged, or ready to emerge, from our retorts and our calculations, our fellow human beings, devastated by us and our successors, will hang and burn us in effigy, with a rage worse

---

33. Ernest Renan, *L'Avenir de science* (1890).

than revolutionaries smashing stained-glass windows, setting fire to churches and pulverizing saints. It will be the great submersion of barbarity. From one end of Europe to the other, the ashes of our achievements and our efforts will thrown to the winds. That has surely happened many times already. The Incas, the Egyptians and others before them knew secrets as redoubtable as ours. They confided messages to plants, birds and atmospheric or telluric currents, some of which have reached us by roundabout routes; the others are scattered through the ages, and lost...."

These notions and others of the same sort were discussed in the art gallery at Brancheville, in front of the splendid and Venusiac women of Titian, Goya and Courbet, the carnal glare of whom had put the mathematician Abramson to sleep, and who seemed to be smiling, in their blossoming flesh, at the ephemeral stupidities of scientists.

No one was astonished when the Master of the Waves exclaimed: "What fools they are who want to place and contain us solely beneath the sign of the number, the ruler and the balance, when there is the sign of the desire to which, as Lucretius[34] saw, everything is submissive!"

At that moment, someone knocked on the door.

"Come in," called Ignacio, whose sybaritism was being disturbed by all this talk, of which he had eventually become weary.

Sylvain showed his plaintive face. He had brought a telegram addressed to Tullie, postmarked Naples, which read: *When are you all coming? The weather is superb, and the villa at Pompeii awaits you. Affectionate regards to the Avenillon Six. Donabella.*

"Well, what do you think?" said Ségétan, having taken cognizance of the dispatch. "This place is hostile to us, for the time being. The Dévonets can't come back to Avenillon for months, until irritated imaginations have calmed down. I've no desire to receive another gunshot in the eyes. You, Bénalep, seem some-

---

34. The reference is to *De rerum natura* [On the Nature of Things].

what detached from the clients you cared for *gratis pro deo*, and who thanked you by stoning your house and abusing the Jews. You, Ariana, are expecting to discover a Jehovah in your bed instead of Ignacio at any moment. You, Ignacio, are hoping, as is understandable, for an existence delivered from such frequent dramas. Given these conditions, I propose that all seven of us depart for Naples by car. I say all seven, not one more nor one less. I can promise you a most interesting and most exciting surprise out there. Are you in? Those who accept, raise your hands."

Ariana, Tullie, Ignacio and Bénalep did so with enthusiasm. The Master had just expressed an idea that they had all been thinking about, since Donabella's visit and her kind invitation. It only remained to obtain the acceptance of the Dévonets, holed up in Tours; that was not in doubt. Tullie made sure of that immediately with a telephone call to the Univers.

"Hello. Is that you, darling? It's Tullie."

"No, it's not Mélanie, it's me, Félix."

"We're all leaving in three days, by automobile, for Naples, to which Donabella has summoned us. That's what the Master's decided. Les Arges? Oh, the steward will look after it. Hello? Yes, directly to Naples, without stopping anywhere. A surprise awaits us, it seems. Hello? As far as your house and ours are concerned, have no fear; I'll take charge of everything—the car and upkeep during our absence.... Yes, about three months. We're not taking anyone apart for the chauffeur, nor are the Ignacios. Too much encumbrance. Details tomorrow morning—but start your preparations."

The meal that followed this discussion was particularly animated. All the arrangements were made during the sitting. Abrice, delighted by the adventure, knew an excellent chauffeur in Tours, and a comfortable limousine for the Dévonets. He sent word to him immediately to be ready.

"And what are we going to do about the Dyonisos?" Ségétan asked his lover.

"Aha—you're taking the evocation machine," said Bénalep,

in a sarcastic tone. "Good, good, I couldn't ask for anything better—but Dévonet will take charge of it. It won't take up much room. As for the repairs, we'll have Hatchinson out there—the excellent Hatchinson, not yet convinced that the waves of the past aren't just a mere conjuring trick."

Everyone laughed. It was a silly idea. To be suspicious when there was no need and not to be suspicious when he ought to be, that was the American's motto.

"What about our paintings?" said Ariana to her husband, whose gaiety and good humor had been restored by the escapade.

Ignacio made an undulating gesture with his arms, running from his torso toward infinity: a gesture accompanied by a sort of susurration, which signified. "Not important—arrangements can always be made." He knew a penniless Bohemian in Paris, a failed painter, who would be delighted to keep watch over the gallery and sleep in his own sheets, with a park at his disposal.

"What's this fellow's name?"

"An ominous one—he's called Malitorne."[35]

"That means he'll go to the bad."

"As for my laboratory and my measuring instruments, I'll summon one of the wiliest of Touranians, my old pupil, whose name is more reassuring, for he's called Lebien." The scientist added: "If you want my opinion, we shouldn't stay with the Hatchinsons—he'd soon find us burdensome. We'll go to the Parkers Hotel, which is admirably situated—to which Tullie will send a telegram this evening reserving three apartments and a single room for M'sieu Bienallé. By the way, old man, what about your plants?"

"I don't care—they can perish, and my digitalis coffee with them. I've had enough of botanic combinations, just as Tullie has had enough of Les Arges farm. I'll devote myself to pure science and the telluric currents of volcanoes. My only client

---

35. A *malitorne* is, conventionally, a clumsy individual, although the etymological derivation does indeed suggests, ominously, someone who will turn out badly.

from now on will be Vesuvius."

At dessert, Romain, benevolent and strong, his restored eyes full of sparks, raised his glass of champagne and made a toast: "To Donabella!"

CHAPTER EIGHT
THE VILLA OF THE MYSTERIES

The vehicles stopped in front of the Parkers Hotel in Naples on a divine October morning. The travelers got out, Ségétan, Tullie and Dévonet, carefully carrying in famous Dyonisos, along with Mélanie, Bénalep, Ignacio and Ariana. They all seemed cheerful and happy with life. They had traveled southwards through Fascist Italy, astonishing in its order and patriotism, provided with perfect autodromes and hotels, having conserved a cuisine that was not international and still regional, with traditional dishes and delicate and various vintages that always taste better in their native region.

The old, supposedly picturesque indolence—which made some famous cities celebrated by poets resemble untidy rooms with chamber-pots on the wash-basin and the bed-curtains bundled at the windows by a negligent servant—had disappeared. Known throughout the world for their artfulness in putting toilets out of order in every country they visited, and taking care of their needs on seats, German professors, metaphysicians and diplomats had renounced that habit with regard to the land of Virgil and Dante. For tidiness, Naples could rival The Hague or Edinburgh, and its inhabitants did not idle around, directing their brisk legs, their frosty political expressions, half-rural and half-cameo, sometimes ornamented with a large mocking nose, toward banks, telegraph offices and film studios.

The amiable Swiss hotel manager and the diligent porter

escorted the notable guests to their luxurious apartments, which overlooked the bay, comparable to an antique libation-cup carved from a giant sapphire. In the distance, to the left, Vesuvius was visible, with its well-behaved plume of smoke.

All was joy, calm and light.

Ignacio was the company's treasurer and accountant. With Ségétan, he was meeting the expenses of the voyage, for its entire duration. Their prodigality was similar, and the hotel staff quickly sniffed out their fashion of ordering, without haggling or calculating, as suspicious Englishmen and jovial Americans do, "the best of everything, and right away." Such was the motto of the Master of the Waves. People in pursuit of one or two big ideas do not have the time to waste on the silly details of everyday life. *De minimis non curat praetor.*[36]

Material organization was left to Tullie and, with regard to linen, to Mélanie. Ariana was in charge of gastronomic and ornamental comfort—which is to say, fitting out the bedrooms and reception rooms to everyone's taste. While her two companions came to an understanding with the chambermaids, she demanded a separate dining-room and examined the wine list along with the cellar-master.

As she had promised, Tullie immediately established telephonic communication with Donabella, who lived in a magnificent villa, The Dream, situated on a hill between Castellamare and Naples.

"Hello, my darling—it's Tullie Moneuse here."

"How glad I am! A good journey?"

"Excellent. We're installed at Parkers—all seven of us, with the Ignacios the Dévonets and Bénalep."

"Oh, the villains, who didn't want to come to The Dream! Hello...."

"I'm listening. It's the Master who was opposed to it...."

"He'll pay me back for that! This is what I want to tell you. Bobby left for New York the day before yesterday with

36. "A praetor [a magistrate or military commander] does not concern himself with trivia."

Pietro, having learned of the death of a rich uncle. Because of the inheritance, which is worth the trouble, he'll be absent for two months or so. In the meantime, I'm absolutely free. Come to dinner this evening. In this magnificent weather we can eat outdoors, perhaps as well as at Avenillon, and not badly, at any rate. Eight o'clock, all right? *Au revoir*, darling."

"Agreed, my darling—rely on us. Seven settings."

It was now a matter of sending away the three chauffeurs and returning the vehicle hired in Tours for the Dévonets, which would take all three of them back. The affair, settled by Bénalep, who never allowed himself to be robbed, raised no difficulty. Abrice received the necessary instructions. He would report any incidents of the surveillance once a fortnight to his employer, and send a telegram in case of emergency or mishap.

* * * * * * *

When her guests arrived, Donabella was wearing the same intoxicating dress that she had worn at the banquet in Avenillon. At the low-cut neckline—what classic breasts!—there was a gilded flower resembling a nenuphar. A pallor swept over her face when she saw the Master of the Waves, and over her heart and senses. She never stopped thinking about him, dreaming about him, giving herself to him mentally, convinced, like all women head-over-heels in love, that she would never have her fill of him.

The others, including Tullie, appeared to her as in a mist. As for Hatchinson, he seemed to her, at a distance as when present, like a wooden doll, sometimes lying on top of her, slightly aslant, gesticulating and sighting, sometimes giving off an odor of varnish, sometimes of whisky.

The table, lighted by candles in the fading twilight, was admirably served in the English style, with crystal and silver that sparkled softly beneath the pink shades. Two fans, skilfully disposed, kept the mosquitoes and their tiny menacing bites away, although they were not very numerous. Everything was set for the delights of love and the clarification of ideas.

Ariana, Tulllie and Mélanie, clad in bright fabrics, slightly crumpled by the journey, were like naiads recently embraced. As for the menu, half-Italian and half-English, it comprised a fish soup, in a style other than Marseillaise, but very good. Chianti, red and white, swayed in its sparkling suspensions. Soon, the sun having disappeared behind the Posilippo some time before, the first stars appeared in the sky.

No soothing music came to spoil the ambience of strength and life that had returned to the Italian nation after a long eclipse by the action of a single man. It really was Neapolis, the new city, but also the city of the Oscans, of the distant times of triumphant Hellas.

Inspired by the soft flesh of the women, the moment and the location, Ségétan talked—or, rather improvised—about the universal mind, Erasmism,[37] and the insidious fashion in which the bitter discoveries of science, the source of facilities and ferocities, were insinuating themselves and would continue to insinuate themselves into the inspirations of art, troubling renaissances with reforms.

Everyone listened with delight to that speech, disengaged from all convention, in which there were gulfs and also capes, according to the anfractuosities of ancient meditations. Then, quitting the heights for more moderate hills, the conversation turned to Keats, the son of Shakespeare and the ultimate descendant of Horace and Euphorion, the sublime rainbow of Anglo-Latin poetry.

Donabella recited a few pieces, notably the famous "Sonnet on Blue,"[38] appropriate to the circumstances. Then the butterfly

---

37. The doctrines of the humanist philosopher Desiderius Erasmus (c1466-1536), which include the sarcastically satirical *In Praise of Folly*, in which the self-styled goddess Folly, once nursed by the nymphs Inebriation and Ignorance, who has an appropriately self-deluding entourage, extols her invaluable contribution of human life.

38. The common designation of an untitled Keats sonnet first published in 1816, also known as "Sonnet X" (i.e, ten).

with wings of fire settled on Théodore de Banville, Bénalep's favorite. From that scholarly, expressive, quadrangular head with the sunken eyes and the sardonic mouth, posed over a flared collar, aerial and Anacreontic verses emerged. The heavy voice suited them very well.

> Young man devoid of melancholy,
> Blond as a sun of Italy,
> Be careful of your beautiful folly,
> It is wisdom.... Love wine.
> Beauty, the spring divine,
> That suffices, the rest is vain.
> Smile, even at destiny severe,
> And when the primrose blooms again,
> Throw its flower into your glass.
> Of the body in the grave enclosed,
> What remains? To have loved
> During two or three months of May.[39]

"That program it's necessary to accomplish, and we shall accomplish it!" cried Ségétan, gripped by his intimate daemon and communicating its frisson to everyone. "Tomorrow, all installation being concluded, our beautiful hostess will take us to that Villa of the Mysteries, to which I feel my destiny calling me. It's certainly not for any other end that I've discovered the waves of the past."

"Master, it will be done."

* * * * * * *

The next day, in fact, three powerful vehicles took the travelers to Pompeii, without stopping at Herculaneum. They went

---

39. Unusually, a literal translation of this poem ("À Adolphe Gaïffe," 1856) conserves the rhyme-scheme of the first six lines as perfectly (or, rather, as imperfectly) as the original, but breaks down in the final six; I resisted the temptation to conserve the rhyme-scheme instead of the precise meaning.

down to the main entrance and, guided by Donabella, walked directly through the cheerful countryside, following a little steam toward the incantatory dwelling, half-residence and half-temple, in which the Orphic Mysteries were celebrated four and a half centuries before the advent of the Savior of Humankind.

The visitors paid a minimal entry fee, went over a little bridge, and immediately passed into the Attic splendor of the great era, in which beauty and the desire engendered thereby were considered to be the sources of the omnipotent virtues of the body, the mind and the soul.

One fresco, sublime in its inspiration, its color and freshness, inscribed on the walls, in several episodes, the passionate initiation of a bacchante. A woman with sad eyes and a noble and veiled figure, half-procuress and half-priestess, accompanied the gracious astonished neophyte through the ritual and erotic ordeals, bearing within her the fundamental gravity that one observes in the most upmarket brothels, in Paris as in Marseilles, Hamburg and London, among the administrators of debauchery—the inheritors of long pagan traditions, whose vibrations they feel, issuing from the obscene wells of being, without being aware of their range.

The Orphic drama, which is that of knowledge by way of sensuality and pain, was thus led by two protagonists, one knowledgeable, the other ignorant, the former, charged with destiny, infusing the latter therewith, by means of bodily contact, raw pleasure, brief suffering, and terror. That carnal prevision of a few of the Christian sacraments, included the adoption of the habit, or sacred vestment, given to the neophyte, after the first dart of a winged love, by her Bacchic intermediary; the catechistic rule inculcated by a child-priest; and the Agape, or communion, over which an mysterious aura, an unquiet anxiety, already floated.

The neophyte, half-naked—and her bent knee is truly charming—carries with measured strides a tray of slivers or "licks" of meat, while looking down into the void. She wonders whether her crown of myrtle, a symbol of the possession of the god, which encloses her pure forehead, might be an exacting honor. She will see.

In fact, the next tableau shows a fat, frightful, bosomy, naked Silenus, with a beard in the style of Victor Hugo, playing the lute, while a young boy plays a panpipe and a bacchante with her legs parted suckles a fawn.[40] Another fawn listens delightedly.

In the following panel, the neophyte, coiffed in the Greek style, her legs supply parted in advance, her arms in the air and the wind of mystery floating in her veil, is giving every evidence of terror. She has understood what Dyonisos demands of her, which the naked little priest is reading in his book. She is screaming, in every fiber of her being, in her bewildered gaze, in her petty prickling hand: "No, no and no!" but you are in the round now, my girl, and your "anangke,"[41] which awaits you, is inscribed in the magic mirror.

That mirror, in which returns, in reflection, the story of Orpheus and Dyonisos, is still brandished by the frightful Silenus, beneath a horrible mask held by a young naked creature with wide-apart ears, an elegant satyreau[42] emerged from the darkness, who is also carrying a triangular shield.

And there...there, close by, there he is: him, Dyonisos, asleep and unconscious, enormous, collapsed, satiated, sticking out, one foot ritually unshod, between the legs and arms of Kore the Agricultural. Around the god of wine are poisons, impulses and ecstasies, a confused mass of rolled-up fabrics, the sandal of the

---

40. Images of Dionysus' retinue sometimes showed his "nurses" suckling fawns or kids, and that is the case with one of the frescoes in the Villa of the Mysteries. Although the author uses the word *faon* [fawn] twice here, the animal looking on in the fresco is surely a kid; the text subsequently distinguished the two but gets them the wrong way round on one occasion.

41. Anangke, or Ananke was the Greek goddess of inevitability, the personification of destiny; the word also existed as a common noun meaning necessity or constraint.

42. *Satyreau* is an alternative rendering of *satyre* [satyr], presumably used here as an affectation.

right foot hurled aside, and an oblique thyrsus.

This time, the neophyte is in a light chemise and a wimple. She begs, before a giant sheathed phallus, which she deems impracticable. She extends her slender hands, graciously imploring, at the end of rounded arms. The person she is imploring for mercy is the daughter of Dyonisos, Telete.[43]

Implacable and upright in a tight garment that covers her and molds her pelvis, her perfect legs clad in buskins, Telete is brandishing a stinging whip. She is there at her post, the daughter of steel, harsh and impenetrable, her eyes averted, her palm repellent, accustomed to rejecting human supplications and flagellating mercilessly the tragic beauties offered, in combined sacrifice and enjoyment, to her august father, gorged on wine and the future.

Whether she has succeeded, we shall see. This time, the bacchante is on her knees, her face turned away, her hair scattered and sticky, her breasts supported, her rump rounded and projecting, under the illusory protection—strike, Telete!—of the procuress priestess, who points to that smooth back, those curved hips, that chiseled navel, the triple delicate fold of the breast and the permanently sterile abdomen, with a movement of her outstretched arm. Strike, Telete—but don't lacerate such a skin, the delight of your insatiable Papa! The rosy nipples of the bacchante have clearly hardened under the blows.

O accomplishment! O miracle! O certain result of ordeals, the rarest of which are hidden from us—because the Greeks had a modesty of the impure, which is like the refinement of pleasure—the bacchante is finally realized! She has traversed the accursed regions, the flames, the streaks, surmounted the intimate dislocations, the harsh embraces and the penetrations

---

43. In Nonnus' *Dionysiaca*, from whom the details of the association of Dionysus with the Orphic mysteries is mostly derived. Telete is identified as the daughter of Dionysus and the nymph Nicaea. Her interpretation as an initiatrix into the Bacchic rites is a much later gloss, and her identification as the whip-wielding character depicted in one of the frescos in the Villa of Mysteries is purely speculative.

that cause tears to flow. She is dancing now—yes, dancing—completely naked, seen from behind, with castanets attached to her hands, in the supple, proud, vertebral, gluteal and crural accomplishment that Venus might envy her, and would drive dark Vulcan with the reek of metal mad with desire. Her tapering legs are taut, the soles of her feet arched. Behind a curtain, the sacred procuress darts a somber glance at her young pupil, wearied by all of it, and also disabused, almost pitying. "Dance, my child, we'll talk again."

The four women and the four men spent a long time examining those prodigious images, recently discovered in the soil of Pompeii, which promised others of similar importance. Each of them had made reflections, which they only shared a few hours later, when they had calmed down, and rested their overexcited imaginations.

For Ségétan, there was a message there, almost an order, addressed to him, the revelator of Waves, which he ought to realize, even if it were fatal to him. A chain of circumstances had led him here, as if by the hand—*here*, to Naples and to Pompeii, for some purpose.

Tullie thought the same, with regard to the Orphic encounter of the Greek frescoes and her husband, without perceiving the sign that masked his immense love from her.

Donabella saw herself as the neophyte of a Bacchus who could not be anyone but Romain.

Bénalep sensed that he was Silenus, and envied the lot of the fat, naked old man who held the magic mirror and terrified the "novice," lifting her veil like a hurricane. He had whispered in Mélanie's keen ear: "How good that would be!"

To which she had replied: "Do you think so?"

Ignacio had noticed two things. Nowhere had the divine expressions of sentiments, by means of faces or attitudes, attained reality on such an elevated plane. It seemed, therefore, that there were two natures: one without Bacchus, the other with him and through him. If only Nietzsche, who had scented that duality, had seen the frescoes of the Villa! His pride, thus legitimated, would have driven him mad a little sooner. The second observation was that the fashions of the fifth century B.C.—the clothes and hairstyles—resembled those of the twentieth century, or, more exactly, had no date.

Ariana, thrown into ecstasy by the twenty-four-century-old film—the power of which contained all of Aeschylus and all of Sophocles, and more—would have liked to be Telete. The movements of the hands, so typical, so various and so nuanced moved her to the brink of fainting. The small indicative hands of the child, or Amour,[44] with the darts; convex and meditative hands, then holding the neophyte's ritual veil. The same, carrying the dish of the agapes; the same, in the gesture of terror; the same, in the imploration before the terrible phallus. The rejecting, merciless hands of Telete. The two maternal hands of the procuress, above the humiliated hands of the neophyte after the Dyonisiac flagellation. The triumphant hands, equipped with metallic castanets, after the initiations and during the dance.

What intrigued Dévonet the most was the forms of the plinths, chairs and stools of the Orphic liturgy, with their insulators and roundels of glass, five in number, organized for the reception, multiplication or interruption of electromagnetic currents.

Mélanie had been struck by the virginal suckling of kids, behind which one of the secrets of Orphism was perceptible: the communion of human being with animal nature; a redoubtable and far-reaching principle.

Everyone had understood that the Master was contemplating a living reconstitution of the frescoes, on the very location of the Mysteries, and it was no surprise when, that same evening, after dinner, Romain explained his project to them in private. Donabella was present, and acquiesced enthusiastically.

"That will be you, the neophyte," Romain told her. "The absence of your husband is well-timed, for he's jealous in the American manner; he's a summary individual, a barbarian, and

44. In this sense, an Amour is an image of a winged child, often holding a bow and arrow, common in Madieval art and adapted into the modern images of an infantile "Cupid" featured in St. Valentine's Day kitsch.

he would have rendered the thing impossible. I reserve the role of Bacchus for myself, if you beautiful women see no obstacle or inconvenience to that. You, Tullie, will be the priestess, the one who gives the necessary instructions. To you, Bénalep, the employment of Silenus, which will fit you like a glove."

"Thank you," said the old satyr, stimulated and grateful—and he directed a covert glance at Mélanie, who was passionately interested, for another reason.

"You, Mélanie, will be the Bacchante gluttonously suckling the little fawn. You will also, be, in the preceding tableau, the priestess supervising the Agape. You, Ariana, will of course be Telete, whose mask and severity you have, beneath the arrogant grace."

"Thank you, Master, on behalf of the poor star! But I confess that I'm content with my role."

"You, Ignacio, will ensure the exactitude of the scenery and costumes, and, with Ariana, the choreography of the bacchante's final dance. Ariana will also be the astonished young servant of the Agape. Oh, I forgot—we need someone for the role of the young satyreau holding the frightening mask. We also lack the Amours, the little catechist and the panpipe-player. We can't think of employing childen; present mores wouldn't allow it. We need to trick a young man of seventeen or eighteen, but extremely discreet, very handsome—that's the difficulty—and, by trade, unsurprised by anything.

"I have what you need," Donabella put in. "One of my husband's laboratory assistants, a young Italian of eighteen, extremely well-formed, infatuated with me, who only swears and lives for me. He was a fisherman in Sorrento, then a model for English and American artists. His name is Giuseppe Vanulicci. He's more than discreet, he's secretive. He's neither depraved nor innocent."

"I'll need to see him," said Ségétan, who was thinking, without pleasure, of a second Calvat.

"I'd like to say something," said Ignacio, before the general agreement. The project, indisputably Bacchic, excited and disturbed him simultaneously, as Ségétan had anticipated. The idea of his wife participating in an antique rite of sacred debauchery was, for him, both precious and cruel, like a bracelet with wounding diamonds. With his role as stage-manager, however, he could easily keep watch on her.

"You have the floor, Châtelain de Brancheville."

"In sum, it's a matter of a living tableau in several parts, of an original and particularly daring kind. It's an adventure, the recommencement of a pagan rite with very different souls, over which centuries of Christian reserve and prudence have been laid. How shall we avoid the grossness of sacrilege—not because of the scandal it might cause it were revealed, but with regard to our own consciences, as people of today, even unbelievers, conserving respect for the gospels and what they have brought to the world?"

"An absurd scruple!" muttered Bénalep, in whom the Oriental was revealing itself, and whose admiration for Romain trumped everything.

"No, Silenus, no! My question is reasonable, although the worship of Bacchus rests on the abandonment of common sense by the combined intoxication of all the senses. We're on earth, in the twentieth century. We're all devoid of physical modesty, that's understood, and we understand Master Ségétan's demands—but we must not degrade ourselves forever in our own eyes, with a more-than-troubling memory."

"Oh la la! What a bourgeois, seeking the prohibition of round-dances!" exclaimed Ariana and Tullie, laughing.

Then the Master said, gravely: "I've thought of your objection, Ignacio. From a certain angle, it's legitimate, and from another, absurd, given the conditions of amity between us and the broad views we all have regarding love and beauty. But this living tableau, or, as you might put it, this adventure, will be lyrical and intense to a higher degree than you imagine, because I intended introduce into it the terror appropriate to render the sacred character to Donabella's initiation. Dévonet, will you make sure—in a hotel one can never be too careful—that no one is listening at the door."

Once their privacy had been confirmed he continued: "One point ought to have astonished you: no role in the neo-liturgy of Dyonisos has been reserved for Dévonet. This is the reason. He has undertaken to evoke, according to my directions, during our celebration in the mode of Eleusis, the great eruption of Vesuvius of 79 A.D., during the reign of Titus, as recounted by Pliny the Younger. Our collaborative calculations have given me the assurance that the synthetic beam of that drama, one of the greatest in history, will return to the slopes of the volcano during all but four of the evenings of the month of October this year, and all but ten of the evenings of July next year.

"The returns of the wave-system are more frequent at Naples and in Campania than anywhere else, doubtless by reason of the electromagnetic nature of the soil, one of the most complex in the world, which acts, over a long period of time on the Italian character and temperament, all the way to Rome itself. There is no doubt in my mind that a Mussolini has been brought back here by mysterious combinations of evocations of the times of Sulla and Caesar, which have created a favorable ambience of political genius. Heredity is not the only force of the past acting on the present, and can combine with all the other influences descending from yesterday and the day before toward today, and moving in the opposite direction from tomorrow and the day after to now. Flux and reflux!

"Thus, Dévonet will ensure, during our ceremony—which will obviously be sensual and strewn with numerous intoxications, but serious, even deeply-felt—the functioning of the apparatus that, by virtue of significant foresight, we have justly named Dyonisos. It's a task requiring complete concentration, and that's why no other role could be attributed to him."

These points having been clarified, it was agreed that an approach—certainly welcome—would be made to the municipal authorities for the obtainment and lease, for three months, of the Villa of the Mysteries, for it was appropriate to organize it in the practical and luxurious fashion that it must have had in the time of the cult of Bacchus. The experiment they were to attempt, according to Ségétan, would bring about in its participants a state of general comprehension and exaltation analogous to that from which Aristotle, Plato, the great tragedians and the great sculptors had emerged, along with the greatest architects of ancient Greece, all parts of the same whole.

Apollo was, according to the savant of Avenillon, nothing but Dyonisos sobered up and, as it were, made respectable, while the Muses were Bacchantes returned to calmness: "the decency and good manners, of which Rabelais speaks in a celebrated passage, and which prevents Eros from attacking them, was only a pale residue, a fatigue of their former ardors, when they danced without veils, castanets in their hands, before astonished panthers."

* * * * * * *

It was in broad daylight, in the "studio" of The Dream, that the Master, alone with Donabella, already clad in the ritual veil, or "sindone"[45] of the neophyte made the acquaintance of Giuseppe Vanulicci. The latter, as beautiful as a Sodoma[46] ephebe, half-model and half-mechanic, fashioned by the priests in the hatred of Fascism, seemed to him to be a more disquieting individual than the young woman had implied, but of a completely different stripe from Jean Calvat. Physically, he was quite capable of enduring the commotion of the sensual jealousy that runs like a streak of fire through the Orphic liturgy, which Shakespeare rediscovered in *Othello* and to which Ignacio could testify. By

---

45. *Sindone* [shroud] is familiar in Roman Catholic mythology in the phrase *Sindone di Torino* [Turin Shroud], but some initiation rituals in which nuns are taken into cloistered orders also involve the symbolic doning of a shroud.

46. The Italian painter Giovanni Bazzi (c1477-1549) was known as "Il Sodoma" [the Sodomite], originally applied to him as a slander, but which he adopted and used as a signature, even writing songs about the name (in which he pointed out that "Il Sodoma" was married, with children).

virtue of a repercussion, however, did Giuseppe also experience the figurative, pathetic and detestable additive of pleasure?

In order to demonstrate the contrary, and that there was no risk of carnal anger or hatred, Donabella advanced toward Romain, with a slow stride based on the one who carries the sindone, extended her beautiful lips to him, pursed for a kiss, with an expression of total abandonment; then, as he kept her at a distance—the moment not having come—she fell to her knees before him. They young man had remained impassive, turning his resigned eyes to the floor.

The methodical preparation of the great occasion began.

Method is Greek in origin (*meta odos*). Everything suggests that it was, in the beginning, the rhythmification and precision of the Mysteries, intimately liked to the megalography, or major signification, specified by the genius of Polygnotus.[47] The Orphic liturgy is a syntax, in which each word, represented by a group of mythical or symbolic characters, is composed of letters that are the attitudes and physiognomies of each of them. From that profound analogy between ritual and dance on the one hand and writing and the manuscript scroll on the other—one still says that a drama "unfurls"—dramatic art and literature are born, as well as the methodical division into scenes or chapters.

Ségétan, versed in these things as he was in all latencies, whether of the past or the present, talked about it to his listeners and accomplices, either at Parkers or The Dream. In both places, the servants were banished and everyone served himself, or was served by the ladies. Indiscretions, the lice of social life, were thus avoided.

To the questions he was asked, the Master replied methodically and in terms all the clearer because they were touching the arcane at every moment.

Ariana, struck by the resemblance between the frescos and a film, asked: "How do these static images and figures give an impression of mobility even more powerful than if they were

47. A Greek painter of the fifth century B.C., famous for vast mythological compilations.

moving?"

"Because they're fixed at the most significant point of their gesticulation—which is to say, at the summit of the mental state that regulates them. They're frozen paroxysms, which immediately evoke all the intermediate states for us. They suggest the movement, which is much more powerful that showing it."

"Are we going to remain immobile, then?" the star asked. "Immobile and mute?"

"This is how I see the method—or, if you prefer, the sequence. With the exception of Dévonet, our technician, we shall be both actors and spectators. That is to say, we shall relive the mystery by means of separate tableaux, in the same order as the frescoes, before each of its compartments. During the passage from one episode to another, total darkness will be contrived and light will only return when the following scene is composed. In order to sustain the unexpected and irresolute part of our souls, at its articulation with our minds, appropriate music will be playing in the wings—I mean one of the adjacent rooms.

"I propose, throughout the development of the first parts of the liturgy, Beethoven's symphony in C minor, for all of Beethoven's symphonies are Dyonisiac mysteries of a sort themselves. But from the terror of the neophyte—you, Donabella—and the magic mirror onwards, the 79 eruption will commence, thanks to Dévonet, alternately plunging the following scenes—the drunkenness of Bacchus, the neophyte's supplication of Telete and so on—into the bright flashes of lightning and the darkness of the rain of ash. At that moment, the andante of the symphony in C minor will be succeeded by the allegro of the symphony in A, whose character is more ritually intense.[48]

"Then, according to their momentary affinities, the couples will each retire to the rooms of the first floor, disposed to that

48. Beethoven's Symphony in C minor is his most famous, more commonly known as the Fifth. The other cited is the Seventh, named by Wagner as "The Apotheosis of Dance." The *allegro con brio* is the fourth movement, but the text subsequently refers (probably mistakenly, although I am not certain enough to have corrected it) to the *allegretto*, which is the second.

effect. Afterwards—and this is a essential point—there must never be any question between us of what will have happened in the course of that night. No allusion must ever be made to it.

"There will be a unique instant of felicity mingled with terror, a return to the obscure and confused states of the ancient soul.

"There will be, above all, my dear Ariana, a confrontation of forms and stimulants of comprehension prior to the Christian Era and anterior forms and stimulants. By examining the differences within ourselves, we shall make the calculation of gains and losses. From that intrusion of the waves of the past into our present souls, we might perhaps be able to conjecture a new world and—who can tell?—a new method.

"The interior experiments that monks carry out, in their cloistered meditations, on the faces and the idea of death, we shall carry out on the idea of life and the continuity of life."

Ignacio asked whether, during the phases of darkness, they would have the right to speak.

"What a question, my dear friend! Does one speak during a meditation? Human silence, save for a few exclamations, sighs or songs, was a condition of the unfurling of ancient Mysteries. Ritual gestures substitute for language. It would only require one comical remark, at points of erotic or tragic conjunction, to ruin everything; one does not see the initiate suddenly laughing because Bacchus has one bare foot or because the fawn is sucking at a bacchante's teat. Speech is a liberation; the Mysteries were a concentration, and thus the exact opposite."

"But Pascal assures us that silence is the greatest of persecutions."

"It's also the greatest of energies. The prideful prey to surgeons, who do not cry out during operations, are well aware of that. The child of royal blood, who falls and hurts himself, murmurs to himself alone: 'A prince of our house does not cry out, and does not weep.'"

Once the ordering and purchase of accessories, low beds and costumes had been made—which took the best part of a month—Ignacio organized rehearsals, which took place every day at the villa, at a different time, sometimes in the warm light of midday, sometimes in the October dusk, more moving in Naples than anywhere else, and sometimes at night, with the aid of improved electric lighting.

Guiseppe proved versatile, having at the same time, like many Italians of his generation, both practical and mechanical sense and a sense of the beautiful. He entered into Ségétan's project wholeheartedly, his employer Hatchinson having represented the latter to him as a trickster of genius, and whose face and mind he admired. He said to Donabella: "I understand why you love him, and it is a great dolorous honor for me to participate in the sacrifice—as he calls the Bacchic initiation—even in a very minor role. But how annoying the telegrams from the other must be for you!"

Every day, in fact, Hatchinson cabled his wife from New York, to give her news of the inheritance and Pietro, and to assure her of his desire. The latter was increased by the separation, and Donabella felt it at a distance, repulsively.

Because the neophyte was brunette, with short hair, and, in the first panel, was dressing her hair before a mirror held by an Amour, with the sad initiant beside her, the young woman had to wear a wig—which, moreover, suited her very well. The first tableau, called the taking of the veil, was an immediate complete success.

Ariana, almost nude, with one unflexed leg crossing the other, equipped with symbolic wings and holding the bow with the first arrow in her hand, was slim and ravishing, with a suppleness of movement equal to that of the fresco, as attentive to the flight of her dart as Eros himself. Ségétan was troubled by it, because it was the first time he had seen her thus, but Ariana was no less troubled, having Giuseppe—as the first Amour—directly in front of her, in a costume as scanty as her own. She compared him mentally to Jean Calvat and preferred him; Bacchus was beginning to operate within her.

Tullie, as the sacred procuress, was admirable in sagacious withdrawal, semi-professional and semi-bewildered.

The overall effect was that the first mimed scene was gripping, forming a carnal design that caused the veil of the centuries to quiver.

Ignacio, internally conflicted with regard to the beautiful and the conjugal, feigned indifference.

The second episode was Donabella alone, clad in the neophyte's sindone, sitting and reflecting. Leaning on her overlapping cushions, she duplicated, by means of her folded elbow—her small right hand under her chin and her left arm slightly inclined—the antique model to such a degree that the two might have been confused. Her gaze, in particular, wide-eyed and staring, weighing the adventure, was identical. Among all those who saw her thus, there was but one exclamation: "An overwhelming and certainly mental resemblance."

"My God, yes," she confessed. "I'm thinking about sacrificing my modesty in the same envelope, according to the same rules, as the neophyte—but I don't know yet exactly what will be demanded of me."

Tullie envied her, but strove to banish all jealousy of the one who would revive, however briefly, her lover's genius. They had scarcely imagined, either of them, when they were little girls playing in the streets of Naples, and then sharing their confidences as young women, that such circumstances would bring them together again.

The third day was devoted to the depicted reading of the liturgical commandments by the young priest of Bacchus, which featured Ariana again; this time, as in the fresco, she was devoid of any veil, holding her svelte and smooth legs and booted feet together. She read the precepts to Donabella, gravely standing up under the affectionate hand of the seated Tullie, ritually clutching her fleshy thigh.

This time, Ignacio was visibly suffering from the exhibition of the treasures that he wanted, at that moment, to keep for himself alone, although at other times he had wanted to make them known. Never had desire for his wife bitten him to that degree, and he clenched his fists in order not to drag her away and take her, avidly, in a neighboring room.

Tullie was even more carried away, however, by the metempsychosis of which she gave proof in the worse-than-melancholic gaze that she directed at Donabella, her veil, her stance and her rings...who fell, collapsing smoothly, in an instant.

On the fourth day they rested. They could do no more, drunk as they were on barbarity and beauty, and bitter efforts of self-control. The pagan Psyche entered into them by means of the intensity of the voluptuous imagination, by means of sensual intoxication. When they put their ordinary garments on again, the Orphic artistes fell silent, even avoiding looking at one another, sensing around them the black magic of the impassive god, whose worship had once been celebrated in this very spot. A table had been set up with Neapolitan gateaux and champagne, but they did not touch it. They went back to Pompeii without speaking, the woman and the men on opposite sides of the path bordered by bright bushes. Above their bodies and their shadows, Vesuvius fumed amid a golden vapor.

The fifth day was devoted to setting up the Agape, preparing the initiate for the rudest ordeals and making her communion with Zagreus. For that tableau, Donabella, the debutante, carrying the tray of sacred slivers and crowned in myrtle, becgan to undress, allowing the sight, for Ségétan's delight, of her long legs, flexible in movement and in walking, and her adorable arms. Her head was turned to the right, presenting her delicate visage, reddened by a certain shame.

"My child," said Ignacio, who was playing the impresario, "don't manifest so much anxiety. It isn't painted on the face of your model. With your hands under the tray, your primary care is not to spill the precious foostuffs. Anyway, it's quite obvious that you aren't hungry."

This time, a dispute arose over the matter of whether, of three women participating in the Agape—the president of the table was seen from behind, her face turned to the right—the other two might be the procuress-guide and the novice, the former considered with avid curiosity by the latter. The latter opinion prevailed, and Mélanie became the median priestess of the lustral meal, the one carving the sacred dish, flanked on the right by Donabella and on the left by Tullie.

On the sixth day, Silenus—which is to say, Bénalep—entered the stage, with a satyr, represented by Giuseppe, and the satyress with spread legs suckling a kid, represented by Mélanie. In spite of Ségétan's proscriptons, they expected a comic effect of the display of adipose meat, surmounted by a head in the style of Victor Hugo, represented by the Hebrew physician. In the Bacchic fresco, his sex was only just covered by a triangular piece of hanging cloth, and it was the same for the living copy. The second problem was the resistance of the young kid, which, having no understanding of its role, rubbed its rosy muzzle against Mélanie's no-less-rosy breast, while she was unsteady on her quadrangular plinth. As for the listening fawn, holding up its little straight horns, it proved to be an excellent actor, as if it had been doing it all its life.

On the seventh day, however, the fear began, with Donabella's great surge of terror, standing with her legs apart, introduced to the contemplation of the drunken, half-naked, sprawling Bacchus by means of the vision in the magic mirror, the frightening masque of Silenus and the faun, ready for dalliance behind his elongated shield. Between Silenus and the faun was the nude neophyte, only her carefully made-up and wavy hair visible. Young man and young woman, and then the god.

This time, Bénalep no longer gave rise to laughter, in spite of being adorned with the same comic elements.

Giuseppe, returned to his modeling function, was splendid in form and allure, and Ariana, awaiting her Orphic role, was breathless with desire, as she had been for Calvat, in the same sphere of incandescent voluptuousness as in the gallery at Brancheville. She calculated the number of days that she still had to be patient, envying the situation of Donabella with a liberty of expression that would have informed a husband less clear-sighted than Ignacio.

The latter even wondered whether he ought not to leave them

in the lurch, consigning the Bacchic resurrections, Ségétan and the company to the devil; but human and esthetic respect, and admiration of the Master, prevented him; and that was his last—one cannot say Christian, because he did not believe in anything, but almost moral—rebellion.

It was at the precise moment of the sexual fright of the neophyte, promised to Bacchus and to the faun, and already quartered in thought, that the debut had been fixed, along with the rain of ash, of the despairing allegretto of Beethoven's symphony in A. Dévonet had to watch from the wings and make sure of the release of the Dyonisos, immediately evoking the waves of the major eruption of Vesuvius, as well as switching on the electric gramophone, ordered from the best factory in Naples.

The only possible snag might be the failure of the Dyonisos, but Ségétan had checked the apparatus and his calculations carefully, and he was certain of complete success. From that moment on, a great external turbulence, with lightning, a rain of ash, the flight of phantoms—feigned, of course, but as tragic as if it were real—would trouble the celebration of the mysteries, but without interrupting it, and the representation, whose liturgy nothing could distract, would become uniquely impeccable and conscientious.

One inessential character from the fresco was lacking: Kore, supporting the drunken Bacchus—which is to say, the Master himself—to whom, in the end, the beautiful Donabella was promised, in full Dyonisiac frenzy.

With his regular and plump mask, his eyes open, as if frozen by drunkenness and indifference to the games of pale humans, Ségétan, gleaming and muscular, full of a bleak grandeur, corporeal and spiritual at the same time, seemed indeed to be a earthly prolongation, or a return, of the formidable deity who had only retreated regretfully before Christ, charity and redemption. The orb of time appeared within him, sprawling, with the dial of the centuries and ages, mores and mores—and the rejection of his sandal was that of convention, repetitive things, pagan or Christian, without his having experienced or meditated them.

"Perhaps it's more beautiful without music," Mélanie said, in a low voice.

"The desire you have for Him will be even stronger with the music," Bénalep replied, having got dressed again. "Gratify it, and let's say nothing more about it."

"Consecrated, my old Victor Hugo, consecrated," said Dévonet, mockingly, as he set up his gramophone. He had heard everything, but thought that the Master would be too busy elsewhere to cuckold the "pyrotechnist," as he modestly called himself.

At this point it was agreed to press on, to do the last three episodes together: the imploration, over the covered phallus, of Telete and Telete's refusal; Donabella's flagellation ordeal; and the resurrection of the unchained bacchante. Ariana, as Telete, displayed all the resources of a consummate actress who has melted into her role.

As for Donabella, she offered in action, and no longer merely in depiction, her corporeal profile, facing the spectator, kneeling, prostrate, before the pitiless initiatrix, then upright with her raised arms, her back, her hips, her rump and her legs, entering into the dance, the incomparable marvel of antique beauty, a blossoming flower of skin. Like Tullie, but in another manner, she was faultless in form and line, an amphora of flesh, and in consequence, more than flesh: the One whom Lucretius invokes at the beginning of his poem,[49] and whose Dyonisos himself, once he has tasted her, never lets go.

It was impossible to tell whether the fresco was the copy of her supernatural body, or whether she was the copy of the fresco. That radiant victory of Venus-Aphrodite, in the exercise of her excitatory functions, surpassed twenty battlefields in its capacity to engender twenty or thirty great captains, and as many legislators and diplomats, scientists and artists, at the

---

49. *De rerum natura* begins "O bountiful Venus...."

same time. This was entirely different from occasions when the goddess hides her vagina or her breasts, by virtue of a modesty of which no one can approve, from which results the population of hypocrites, Tartuffes, Academicians and members of the Faculté. If they happen to glimpse raw beauty, transcendent beauty, the beauty that incessantly inseminates races and gives them the strength to continue, they turn away in horror.

That final rehearsal, which went on for a long time because there were a great many little things to rectify in order to obtain the perfect resemblance, had made the Bacchic actors and actresses into a veritable heptameron. Night had fallen. The electric lighting, set up by Ignacio, Dévonet and Giuseppe, poured down upon the frescos and the living tableaux a compound light veiled but a colloidal quality, a combined violet, silver and roseate glaze, of a delicacy almost equal to the faces emerged from the depths of the ages. The moist coloration of the kneeling bacchante and the smooth gleam of the same person standing were rendered exactly, to within a tenth of a nuance, by the chromic syntheses in question, falling upon the delightfully-veined pink skin of Donabella's legs and arms.

Everyone was ecstatic. Giuseppe, occupied with his tableau and the controls he shared with the châtelain of Brancheville, did not say anything, but he had understood perfectly that in the passionate sequel, immediately after the terrible masque and the magic mirror, he cleared a path for the drunken Dyonisos and dropped his long shield. He was the one who opened the immense perspective of the possession of the woman he loved, in the favor of the phantasmal eruption of Vesuvius. He dreamed about it night and day, acting now as if in a trance, but with a superhuman precision of movement.

The bacchante had put on a simple pink silk peignoir and was lying down on a convex bed in the antique form. Tullie was crouched at her feet, in the decent costume of the fresco, and had set aside her sad and savant expression. Ariana had retained the costume—the boots and panther-skin—and nude torso of Telete, and was making her birch whistle. Mélanie was sitting down, her breast entirely uncovered, caressing the kid and the fawn. Bénalep had remained the thickset and bearded Silenus, like Victor Hugo in his later years. Ségétan Bacchus, undressed to the waist, poured himself a large glass of burgundy, more dyonisiac than any other wine.

On the floor there were tiger-skins, black fur carpets and plinths or cairs upholstered in bright colors, mainly reds, all in the ornamental style of sublime paintings. One might have thought that the procession of characters had come to life, or been duplicated; and two huge mirrors, positioned slantwise across two of the corners of the room by Ignacio, multiplied the enchanted poses.

They talked about painting and sculpture in a desultory fashion. Ariana-Telete said that only Courbet and Rodin, in modern times, had approached the lyrical animality that was manifest in the bacchante's two final positions.

"That's entirely my opinion," said her husband. "You have an exquisite and sure taste in art, which, extraordinarily, the cinema hasn't spoiled. That taste is the emanation of form, which might outdo our baccante."

"Many thanks, my lord!" Telete bowed.

"We look like an actors' or photographer's studio," said Dévonet, half in jest and half in earnest, his wife's semi-nudity having put him in a bad mood. "Except that, in the time of the frescos, nothing in the entire painted sequence was artificial. The initiate was genuinely fearful, the initiatrix truly grim, and Dyonisos really was drunk."

"How do you know that he won't really be drunk on the imminent day of our plunge into Dyonisos. By the way, my dear Silenus, you, along with Mélanie, will take charge of the indispensable aphrodisiac, slightly toxic beverages, which your genius will be able to contrive for the occasion. The villa is "set up for it," as Abrice would say. You've seen the big press with its ram's head, the stone conduit for the flow of the septembral purée, the amphoras in which the aforesaid purée is collected.

"This time, the largest room, after the one in which we'll

celebrate the Mystery, will be consecrated to libations, and the bottles of Bénalep's choice beverages will be placed in the ancient sacrificial cupboard. The only sacrifice today will be that of your modesty, beautiful ladies. Don't worry, we've heard talk of a great contemporary poet who, twice a year, at a magical site, gives to his friends, artists almost equal to his lyrical stature, a lunch that is simultaneously Pantagruelesque and Dyonisiac, served by young women chosen for their beauty, entirely naked, who are not whores but admirers. That biannual eroticism was useful to his literary conceptions, just as the Orphic liturgy will lend powerful service to my scientific conceptions, numbed by a few weeks of blindness."

There was a pause. The Master's more-than-indecent attire added a strangeness to his words, in the antique style generated by the scarcely-veiled nudity of the four women promised to the god of drunkenness, the god of all the fulgurations of intelligence and instinct.

"May we know, Master," Donabella asked, in her warm voice, "what these new conceptions are to which our poor bodies are to be useful?"

"That's the least I can do! It's a matter of annihilating bomber aircraft at a distance in time of the war that is threatening. I had abandoned my research in that direction for the waves of the past, which are now complete. If I were to disappear, although Dévonet and Bénalep would continue my work on the latter, my death would deny humankind, at least for a time, the chance of being liberated from the prospective scourge of mass annihilation by toxic gases and the aircraft carrying those gases. Such is the stake, my dear collaborators, of our imminent bacchanal, the foundation of my thought and my hope. Need I say more?"

"Yes, certainly, Master. We're listening passionately."

"The awakening of poetic, philosophical and scientific invention by the accomplished female body is not a new idea. The great tragic Greeks had recourse to the Orphic Mysteries and physical intellectual excitation by bacchantes of flesh and blood. Sight, hearing, touch and possession cooperated in that mental escape from the laws of the city, and sometimes, their transgression. Later, the Romans, invaded by the Greek rites—*Graecia capta ferum victorum cepit*[50]—gave themselves to the celebration of the God of all intoxications, and an imperial edict, *De Bacchanalibus*,[51] forbade them. We—you—are going to reawaken an exceedingly glorious corpse."

These perspectives led to an initial intoxication of the keen intelligence of the four women, visible in the palpitations of their breasts. Donabella, lying down, was as taut as a bowstring, Ariana stretched like the feline whose skin she wore. Tullie got up slowly, her cheeks pink. Mélanie pushed the kid away and stretched, as if to summon someone—Giuseppe—who was not far away at that moment, busy with the adjustment of the lamps.

A surprise awaited the Avenillon colony at the Parkers Hotel: a packet of correspondence.

The first letter, addressed to Ségétan in the handwriting and style of Abrice, seemed at first to be incomprehensible. It read: *Nothing new regarding Naples. They haven't taken any persons in service from here. I only know that they're staying at Parkers, not with their friends the Americos.* It was signed with a cross.

"This note has been sent to the wrong address," Romain concluded. "But who the Devil was it intended for?"

"For the police, of course," said Dévonet, after a momentary examination. Laughing, he added: "When our house caught fire, those fellows from the judiciary police came to yours. They probably made a deal with the faithful Abrice."

Everyone laughed heartily. They imagined the chauffeur mistaking one envelope for another, and sticking the wrong message inside with his plump fingers with the black nails.

---

50. The quotation is from Horace: "Conquered Greece has captured her rude victor [and brought her arts to rustic Rome]"

51. *Senatus consultum de Bacchanalibus* [Senatorial Decree relating to Bacchanilia] is an inscription discovered at Trilio in Souther Italy in 1640, which dates from 186 B.C. The Senatorial edict banned bacchanals throughout Italy, except with special permission; the historian Livy referred to a subsequent persecution in the reign of Augustus.

There was also a letter from Maire Taupin, affirming that everything was quiet and that the forester Germane had recovered his sanity; a letter from Malitorne to Ignacio assuring him that all was well with the château, the gallery and the precious paintings; and one from Lebien, giving the best possible news of the state of the laboratory, unstinting in its praise of Abrice—"in whom one can have every confidence"—Caroline and Antoinette. The two caretakers seemed delighted with their new functions. Les Arges farm was working normally.

"Optimists indeed!" said Tullie, with the most charming moue. "But how far away we are from all that business." She had noticed that, since their arrival in Naples, Romain had been less amorous of her, and thought that perhaps she was playing the melancholy grave procuress of the ritual for real.

That same day, Donabella received a long telegram from Hatchinson giving her a long list of instructions related to The Dream, the maintenance of his instruments and the staff, especially Giuseppe. The matter of the inheritance was making progress; the American expected to return, with or without Pietro, sooner than he had thought. He would be in Naples in a fortnight. He expressed in English, but vividly, in spite of the alleged reserve of that winged language, the keen desire that he had for his beautiful Italian: "I can't wait to eat the velvety fruit." The fruit was her, and the closer prospect procured her a sentiment of horror. She had opened herself up to the man she adored, and to whom she gave herself—with what ardor!—every night in her dreams.

It was decided that the Great Experiment would take place, without fail, a week hence.

That last week was entirely taken up with the final preparations. They were all like actors on the eve of a première performance.

Several costumes and accessories were late, of course, and it was necessary to harass the suppliers, who have been very intrigued by the unusual orders. Ségétan's sojourn in Naples had not gone unnoticed; every day he had to defend himself against some journalist, photographer or mere curiosity-seeker. The well-trained hotel staff assured these pests that he was in Rome, Palermo or somewhere else.

They did not go to the museums, in order not to spoil their new conception of Greek art with works that were beautiful but cold: the lamentable head of Socrates, subtle and oily, and all those cadaverous statues, which chilled the pleasure of looking at them. On the other hand, they often went to the Aquarium to enjoy the bright shades of silver and gold, crystalline fins, pink scales and supple movements of the agitated and inconsistent marine population, as mobile as the element itself. Captive without being aware of it, the dazzling fish came to sniff the transparent walls of their prison, like humans scrutinizing the unknown on the ball that causes them to rotate without perceiving their rotation.

Ségétan and Dévonet had once had a schoolfellow named Marbrebrot who, in every natural history class, had asked in a loud voice with regard to every new animal, quadruped, insect or crustacean: "How does that one have sex?"—to which the irritated professor replied: "Get out, Marbrebrot." The two scientists pointed to the extraordinary hairy, gleaming, polychromatic swimmers in tanks of water filled with silvery bubbles and asked one another naively: "How does that one have sex?"

Then the coarse Silenus whispered: "We'll know next week."

The month of October was as mild and fine as May, except that the days were shorter. Every day, the Parkers seven and Donabella went to watch the sunset, in order to maintain their excitement, from one point or another of the coast, and remained silent before that forge of Vulcan, beside which Venus, before nightfall, weaves in crimson and violet the indefinite fabric of renascent human desire. Complete abstention had been decided and observed by the lovers a fortnight earlier.

* * * * * * *

Finally, the great day, so eagerly awaited, arrived. It was

the end of an extraordinarily arm and calm dusk. When they arrived, the Villa of the Mysteries was plunged in the half-light and silence behind the little gleaming canal. Pompeii was deserted, the caretaker absent by order.

Dévonet took his place to one side with the gramophone and the Dyonisos. Giuseppe, very pale, busied himself with the operation of he lights, which had to be done at a single flick of a switch. On tiptoe, the couples disappeared into the wings or dressing-rooms, in order to drink deep of wines and cocktails or put on their various garments. They also entered, by a hidden door, into the complete and cynical illusion of their respective roles.

Donabella put on her sacred robe. Ariana stripped off as an Amour. Tullie costumed herself as the grave madam of the terrible game. Mélanie fitted wings to her perfect and elastic body. Ségétan, enlivened by several glasses of myrtle-infused champagne, awaiting his turn, which would not come until later, stayed with Ignacio, the stage-director, in the middle of the large room, or stibadium.

The fateful four chords of the symphony in C minor resounded. The fresco and its first living replica were illuminated brightly at a stroke.

The reproduction of the first three tableaux—Donabella doing her hair, meditating on her cushions, coming to a decision, advancing veiled and clad, listening to the catechistic rule—were meticulously and absolutely perfect.

The young initiate had only drunk three cocktails, in order to keep her head at the great turning of her amorous life and to enjoy the gift of herself more profoundly. Ariana, on the contrary, had yielded to the iced alcohol, but nevertheless held the the initiatory regulations straight and steady before her small breasts.

Then, in accordance with a slow and beautiful rhythm that was only to be accentuated in due course, Donabella, half-undressed, still almost decent, advanced, carrying the carved slivers of the Agape. That scene was very successful, the movements of the ensemble calculated by those of the fresco.

Then Bénalep appeared as Silenus, hairy, deformed, hideous and epidermal, completely drunk, lucking the lute. He directed a terrifying gaze toward Mélanie, full of professorial bestiality, by which he was reunited with Germanism: an antique reconstitution of a Hamburg brothel. That was the snag that Ségétan feared, but he had to keep his observation to himself. He renounced it when, sublime with sacred effort, her little bare feet parted at an oblique angle, one little hand clenched in advance, the other sustaining the hurricane of the veil, Donabella appeared, springing forth.

Her presence effaced the rest. Beside herself, terrorized, she was nevertheless utterly animated by the very object of her terror, half-orchid in color, half-woman in exquisite form. The unfurling of the silk sindone caused her to participate in universal gravitation, as if borne away by the solar orb. A green light burst forth violently. Her toes and thumb were distinct, and her little hollow palm, and the eyes of a hunted hind at bay.

The music fell silent momentarily; then, like a sequence of ardent, cruel, upright but soon bowed-down images, the allegretto of the symbohony in A erupted.

The air quivered, strange vapors, accompanied by a dull growling and a crepitation on the roof of the stibadium, came to interpose itself between the fresco and its replica of ardent flesh, like an unstable veil, rent from side to side and top to bottom. It was the moment of the magic mirror. The shoulder and breast, equally round, of Donabella, her eyes chilled with horror, but avid, her black hair undulating, brushed the svelte and muscular body of Guiseppe, who was brandishing above Silenus the grimacing mask of another Silenus.

The music; the noise of the hail of lava; the abrupt flashes of lightning, which did not trouble the regulated elsectric gleams of the ritual; the giant flatulence of Vesuvius in 79 A.D.; those young and glorious bodies, grouped around the quuinquagenarian but athletic torso of the recumbent Ségétan, sleeping off his intoxication: the auditory, visual and chronological ensemble, running from Praxiteles and Pliny over the Beethovian chords, surpassed any scenic and dramatic evocation. The Dyonisian spirit was reborn, and the Master, in his drunkenness mingled with desire, perceived, juxtaposed with his reason, flourishing at the extremity of his instinct, the great principle of the disruption and fall of aircraft, enemy or otherwise, in mid-flight.

There was only one slight hitch; the thyrsis slid along his thigh and fell on top of the sandal of the ritually unshod foot.

The symphony entered the vale of tears, of the weeping damned, at the moment when the kneeling Donabella, her arms outstretched over the phallus hidden in the basket of a liknon,[52] was imploring the ferocious Ariana-Telete, beneath the whip.

That tableau was scarcely accomplished when the shades of the fugitive men and women of 79, evoked by Dévonet's Dyonisos, glided from all the issues and through the walls of the villa, carrying cushions over their heads to shield them from the fall of ash and lava, like stampeding mushrooms, giving signs of spectral terror, jostling one another, knocking one another down, getting up again.

They passed between the arms of the goddess, brandishing her whistling birch. They went through her, and the imploring Donabella, without dissociating—and when, in the following tableau, the latter was prostrate on Tullie's knees, her hair disheveled, her back striped, her torso undulating, her nipples vibrant, with a mixture of dread and pleasure, shivering with overlapping spasms, she was surrounded by a crowd of women, the courtesans and matrons of the tragic Pompeii of Pliny the Younger, carrying away and dropping statuettes and jewels.

Outside, the racket redoubled, and the rattle of the rain, splashed with fire, battered the windows of the villa, without marking them with droplets or trickles. The gathering and summation of a nervous tension, carried to the extreme redoubts of being, was the frenetic turbulence of Donabella, offering her

---

52. A liknon was a basket-shaped winnowing fan, sometimes used as a symbol of Dionysus because he was said to have been borne away in such a cradle as a child.

entire, long, full, magical body, for which the desire of Dyonisos Ségétan was crying out, to the impalpable friction of the panic-stricken shades.

Then, through the lacunary vapors, while the final chords of the desolate symphony resounded over the real volutptuousness and the simulated catastrophe, the figures of the living fresco were seeen to move, their models becoming immobile.

Amid the fading of the antique mirage, like the scattering of a delicate fabric, Silenus, recovering the strength of a bull, carried the kicking Mélanie away in his enormous biceps, her angry voice drowned by the force of the eruption.

Tullie was subjected to the brutal and supple assault of Giuseppe, who, in his confusion, had mistaken her for Ariana—and who then, realizing his error, released Tullie and hurled himself on to the consenting star, already swooning.

The couples came apart, then rejoined, then mingled, disappearing into the depths of the villa.

Donabella, now a bacchante, and Ségétan Bacchus were invisible; but when the music fell silent, appeals in the Italian language, originating from the delirious parts of the sunlit race with the serious expressions, muffled cries of "Mamma, Mamma," traversing profound sighs, contralto stammering and stifled gasps, were audible in the distance, throughout the Villa of the Mysteries.

The obsolete, illuminated stibadium had withdrawn backwards into the ancient time, no longer able to trouble the living.

In the distance, a kid began to bleat.

In the corridor, on the floor, lay a kind of soft cadaver, still twitching slightly; it was Ignacio, blind drunk and snoring.

A man came in, with a distraught expression, as if he had escaped from a fire or a shipwreck, who almost stumbled over the recumbent figure: the pyrotechnist Dévonet. He had the face of a tragic mummy, his eyes sunk into their orbits, his cheeks like two cameo profiles, his tread leaden but not unsteady.

A specter ran to meet him, fluid and transarent: that of a Pompeiian woman of 79. He burst into sinister laugher and ran to search for—and, he honestly believed, to "rescue"—his wife.

CHAPTER NINE
THE BACCHANTES

A week had gone by since the emotional soirée in the Villa of the Mysteries, Ségétan had shut himself up in the hotel and was taking his meals separately, alone in his apartment, uniquely absorbed in the arduous problem of the aircraft, which he now thought, thanks to the physical image of Donabella, to be complete—that he was finally in possession of the solution.

Tullie, the Dévonets, Bénalep and the Ignacios respected that solitude, still shivering from the Dynosiac night. They did not say anything about it to one another. Donabella had not telephoned and gave no sign of life.

On the eighth day, which was a Tuesday, Hatchison returned suddenly to The Dream, without Pietro. He had liquidated his inheritance. He was glad to get back to his wife, his laboratory and his work. He found the first dispirited, with an absent expression, and immediarely conceived the suspicion that something had happened during his absence. He wanted her immediately, there, like a glass of port. She gave the excuse of a terrible headache and locked herself in her room. Not only did the idea of such a contact horrify her, but she still bore on her tender flesh a few apparent traces of Dyonisos, and she was afraid of the conjugal eye.

The American did not ask any questions, but the next morning, when he resumed his calculations and got his redoubtable apparatus under way again, Giuseppe, moved by the irresistible need to confess that the waves of the past sometimes communicated to their adepts, especially to begin with, told him *everything*, in a low voice, and in the most ample detail.

The confession lasted an hour. During the story, heavily illustrated—for the boy had been a model and knew how to describe the movements of the body—Hatchinson did not flinch. His angular and varnished face became impassive. There was no alteration in his gaze or his voice. When it was finished, he simply said: "Well...all right," and gave the narrator a hundred-dollar bill, which was not refused.

Such precision had been furnished to him that there was no possible doubt. He had been cuckolded from head to toe, and in public—and by a man of fifty that he considered to be a charlatan.

Twenty-four hours later, Donabella opened the door, resolved to carry out the frightful conjugal duty that would mask her mental evocation of Ségétan—but her husband, ceremonious and mute—did not make use of the facility. He asked her to invite for dinner, that same evening, "the seven friends in Naples," saying that he had a communication of great importance to make to "Master Ségétan."

Joyfully, Donabella ran to the telephone and asked for Tullie, in a voice that was unrecognizable at first, but gradually became firmer. The response was affirmative. The voluptuous Neapolitan ordered a sumptuous supper beneath the stars on the terrace of the villa, as before, and put on the same sparkling low-cut dress. It did not occur for her for a moment that any indiscretion on Giusepppe's part was possible. In truth, she had almost forgotten him, in the frisson of her veritable ecstasy.

As night fell, Naples lit up behind the cerulean bay and the guests arrived at The Dream in two automobiles. The welcome the American afforded them was polite, and even, in Ségétan's case, quite cordial. No questions were asked on either side, and Donabella showed herself, with regard to her guests, as free, affectionate and innocent as if nothing had happened. Romain, however, could not see anything before him as he kissed her hand ceremoniously, but the neophyte, swooning against his skin, as if melted by foaming passion between his muscular arms.

Dévonet, who was very intuitive, experienced a strange unease, which became sharper when the man he thought of as "the Americo" invited the Master to come to his laboratory to look at a high-precision apparatus he had brought back from America, which could detect the arrival or passing of an aircraft at a very long distance. He joined in the conversation in the hope that he too would be invited to the inspection, but there was no response.

The two men drew away into the darkness, silently.

Ségétan was walking as if in a dream, like a sleepwalker, sometimes haunted by his problem of national defense, sometimes by the warm statue of Donabella. Hatchinson preceding him, they arrived at the lighted laboratory, whose window resembled an enormous phosphoresecent carbuncle.

"Do come in. Oh, I found everything entirely in order. Giuseppe is a precious auxiliary. You wouldn't believe the servives he renders me. The Italian people are extraordinary. I truly have every confidence in him. Ah, here, Master—this is the object."

Donabella's initiator saw, prominently placed on a table, a metal circle terminating in two minuscule elelectric bulbs.

"I put this diadem around my head, like this, and if there's an airplane within a radius of a hundred and fifty kilometers. I know it, and its direction.

That metallic head-dress gave the physiognomy of the cuckold a pleasure superior to the classic horns, and Romain was savoring the irony of it when the other said, in a perfectly natural tone: "Try it for yourself, my dear Master. Permit me to place it....yes, that's it...just right!"

At that moment, Hatchinson, with a rapid gesture, pressed a button on the electrical console, and Ségétan collapsed. A crackle of blue flame, like a striking viper, shone for a second on his occciput.

Phlegmatically, unhurriedly, with the gestues of an attentive nurse, the survivor broke the contact, uncrowned his victim, put the murderous object in a drawer, locking it with a key, and strode out of the room.

When he had rejoined his wife and guests, he recounted laconically that the Master had collapsed, struck by a congestion, while he was explaining the system to him, which was an automatic bell activated by wireless telegraph. All of them rushed, with Tullie in the lead, but Donabella fainted.

Half an hour later, gthe Italian authorities, summoned in all haste, disembarked at The Dream. They could only certify the death of the illustrious French professor, whose demise would put the entire scientific world in mourning. All the desperate efforts of Bénalep and Dévonet to reanimate their friend had been in vain. Responding to the appeal of his employer, Giuseppe seemed astounded, but Dévonet, who was observing him, perceived in his excessively bright gaze a kind of submerged, barbaric and complicit joy. If he had had any doubt, that removed it.

Tullie's distress was that of a form of stone or marble.

Suudenly, Donabella came in, having recovered from her faint. She came to kneel beside the cadaver, next to her childhood friend. Ignacio, who was sobbing, with his head in his hands, and Ariana, compared the funereal image to those of the Villa of the Mysteries, to which it seemed linked by some fatal thread.

It was decided that the body of the deceased would remain in Naples, at the hotel, where it would be placed in a coffin.

Hatchinson organized the macabre transfer by automobile with great delicacy, and helped to place the heavy body on a stretcher. When the cortege had gone, he said to Donabella: "I'm hungry. We'll resume the interrupted supper. Giuseppe will sit down at table with us."

"You're mad!" replied the horrified Italian woman. "What will the servants think! As for me, I admired my dear Tullie's lover; I'm heartbroken. I'm going to bed."

"You're going to eat with me." Her husband seized her arm,

brutally. "Your dear Tullie's lover is also yours. If you don't obey me I'll cause a scandal that will dishonior you publicly. To table, I tell you, and behave appropriately."

Then he called out: "Giuseppe, order the meal to be served, on my behalf, and come and sit beside Madame, facing me. This champagne doesn't please me this evening. Ask the cellar-master for a magnum of Clos-Vougeot of the finest vintage."

When they had taken their places, he said: "Oh, my darling what a beautiful starry night! Ségétan's soul, if he has one— with these Frenchmen, one never knows—will have an excellent celestial journey. My best wishes accompany him...."

He seized a large glass, laughing. "Keep me company, my dear Donabella! And you too, boy. To the Master of the Waves, as they say! Between us, it was probably a farce. Perhaps his death was a farce too, and he'll revive shortly as Zagreus. Is that how it's pronounced?"

Overwhelmed with disgust and hatred, the recent bacchante had the desire to grab a knife with a strong blade and plunged it into the murderer's long throat, where the Adam's apple was dancing like a ludion.[53] But the god advised her to wait, and to savor a colder and better-balanced vengeance. He breathed that rule into her intimate ear, and called upon her, until then, passively to obey her vile spouse.

The news of the sudden death of the foremost physicist of the era, the victim of a banal congestion, immediately spread throughout the world, and brought the post-box of Parkers Hotel a host of telegrams, letters and newspaper-clippings in which the phases of his great career were recalled. The academies of various nations suspended their sessions as a gesture of respect. All the necrological notices made allusion to the new discovery, so impatiently awaited, of the disruption of aircraft engines, which would have liberated humankind from a frightful menace.

---

53. A kind of toy, also known as a Cartesian diver or bottle imp, in which a small figure enclosed in a fluid-filled tube can be made to rise and fall by submerging the tube in water at varying depths, by virtue of differences in pressure.

Condolences came from the Villa Dyonisos, Les Arges farm, the Mairie of Avenillon, Abbé Parroy, the Prefecture of Loir-et-Cher and the Archbishopric of Blois, as well as the Ministry of War and the Undersecretariat of Inventions.

In London, a Society for Physical Research adjourned its sessions for a moment and delared that the next issue of its bulletin would be a memorial to the dead man.

The wireless telegraph service broadcast over the air, in a low, husky voice, a detailed funeral oration that was very nearly exact, with the result that the civil and religious obsequies, celebrated with great pomp, were attended by large numbers of people, including distant relatives of Tullie Moneuse, whom she only knew by name.

Hatchinson, stiff, icy and impenetrable, accompanied the devastated Donabella. The Italian government and the Neapolitan municipality were represented. The English and American consuls were there, as well as the Swedish chargé d'affaires. It was, in everyone's opinion, a beautiful funeral, without a speech, but at which at least eight people were violently agitated beneath calm exteriors by very various sentiments.

Henceforth, the magician with the Dantean facial expression would rest *in aeternum* in Campanian soil, under the plumed guard of Vesuvius.

Meanwhile, the conviction of his friends and his mistressss was firm. He had been murdered, Hatchinson having caught wind of the bacchanal at the mysterious villa. The immediate observations of Dévonet and Mélanie were combined with the measured reflections of Ignacio and Ariana, and the savant intuition of Bénalep. It remained to discover how the American had known—via Giuseppe or some imprudence, perhaps due to the mental influence of the Waves, on Donabella's part.

When the latter came to find Tullie in secret, forty-eight hours after the funeral, all doubts were removed. In fact, the young woman, mad with despair but rendered lucid by a thirst for vengeance, had undertaken a personal investigation and finally obtained a confession from her husband in bed, with a lubricious perfidy that sharpened her pain. He had then shown her the shiny instrument and described the method of the crime. More than that—he had handed her the metal circle and suggested that she adorn herself with it.

Armed with this information, Tulie communicated it to her companions at Parkers Hotel. Then she took Ariana and Mélanie to one side. All three then conferred with Donabella. The four women, two of whom knew every resource of the escarpments of the coast, by virtue of having played all over them in their childhood, adopted a common plan. It would be carried out at the first appropriate opportunity. In the meantime, Donabella, by means of savant caresses, would lull her husband's suspicions.

The opportunity presented itself one bright but moonless evening, when the wind was blowing at the end of a rainy day, while the clifftop was strewn with pools of water and slippery. The agreed signal was given by means of a ringing telephone, without any subsequent communication with The Dream. Shortly thereafter, Donabella affectionately proposed a short walk in the fresh air to the carefree Hatchinson, who was smoking a fat Havana.

"Shall we take Dick?" That was a dog—a magnificent bulldog, devoted to his master and vigorous.

"Oh, no, carissimo. It's necessary to call him back every few minutees."

While her husband put on his overcoat, the inflamed neophyte slipped a sharp and pointed kitchen-knife, in a leather sheath, into the inside pocket of her fur cape.

"Come along, Bobby," she said to the monster, to whom it was now necessary to submit every night. She took him on to the path going along the coast, overlooking the rather choppy sea, between the brightly-lit villa and the outskirts of Naples. She looked back. The laboratory, witness to "the event," was shining like a lighthouse.

Soon, it would be extinct forever.

They walked in the direction of the city and its constellations, sometimes side by side and sometimes one behind the other, according to the varying narrowness of the track, without talking but taking long strides.

The man whistled, then threw away his cigar, which the sea breeze picked up and bore away. In his hand he held one of those Basque canes, or *maquilas*, in which there is a blade. His wife was not unaware of that detail. As they went around the headland preceding the old factory of Fonderia, they perceived the opening of the bay, the water foaming and dancing beneath a sky freed of clouds by the brisk wind. That too was a haunted site, and Donabella recalled what Ségétan had said about the emotional qualification of marine and terrestrial locations.

Three female forms appeared at a turning, in the semi-darkness. The two nocturnal walkers recognized, coming from the direction of Naples, Tullie, dressed entirely in black, Ariana and Mélanie, whose indistinct faces had something solemn about them.

"Bonsoir, darling! Yes, we too had the idea of taking an evening stroll, after so many cruel hours."

Hathinson had bowed ceremoniously, and had dared to kiss Tulie's hand. She did not flinch. It was decided, with common accord, that they would follow the path together back to The Dream, in order to enjoy the full spectacle of the bay and the gulf. The roaring of the water was audible, mingled with the whistling of the breeze.

After a short pause, the American had taken his position at the head of the caravan. The narrow path reached the summit of the cliff. Behind the skeletal silhouette of the guide came Donabella, Tullie, Arians and Mélanie each with one hand under her cape. To their right was the abyss, to the left an uncultivated heath with two ruined and uninhabited houses.

A strident laugh rang out. That was the signal.

Donabella, unsheathing her forbidable knife, delivered a formidable thrust between her husband's shoulders. He collapsed to his left. The blade had entered to the hilt.

Immediately, the other three women launched themselves

forward and, kneeling down, slashed the tall and angular body, which was no longer anything more than a cadaver. The Basque cane lay by his side.

"Quickly, into the water!" commanded an imperious, urgent voice. "Down!"

Each of the four took a limb, but they were not strong enough, even together, to lift the burden. They contented themselves with rolling him over, still groaning, like a marionette—which brought him to the edge of the precipice—and shoving him, from left to right, like a wooden log.

The plunge and the impact were muffled by the noise of the sea and the wind.

Ségétan's murderer had paid his debt.

Of the four daughters of the Styx grouped in the tragic shadows, as if for a fresco in another style, two had hands sticky with blood. The other two only had a few splashes. There was a black pool nearby. They washed themselves in it without speaking, but carefully, taking turns.

Once they were dry, they separated. Donabella returned to The Dream, from which she telephoned, tearfully, news of the terrible accident suffered by her spouse. The others returned to Naples overland, unhurriedly.

Bénalep had gone to bed. Dévonet and Ignacio were striding back and forth in the deserted gardens in front of the Aquarium. They saw the three bacchantes arrive, walking, on their beautiful legs, at a deliberate pace.

"Well?"

"It's done," replied the first, who was Tullie.

"And well done," Ariana added.

Mélanie concluded, in a low voice, although the avenue was empty: "It didn't take five munites, all told."

They went back to the hotel, pausing from time to time. Recognized by a few late strollers, they were greeted, and returned the greetings.

As they arrived at the domicile, Ignacio said to his wife in a calm tone: "I've just received a telegram from Avenillon. The

Maire informs me that the château has been burgled, the galley emptied of all its paintings, and that Malitorne, the faithful guardian, has vanished." He added: "At any other time, the news would have caused me some distress. Today, it leaves me indifferent."

"Of course," replied Ariana, simply.

As they prepared to go to bed, she confided to him between the sheets, in the merest whisper: "What a beautiful film!"

"Can we be pinched?" asked Ignacio, in the same tone.

"Impossible—no witness...."

And she took him in her arms. When her nerves had been adequately calmed, in the most normal fashion, she told him how it had happened, and the dispositions made for the aftermath. He could only approve them. The telegram about the burglary, once divulged, would furnish an adequate excuse for a timely departure, which ought not, at all costs, to seem the least precipitate.

Leaving Mélanie, who was scarcely trembling, inspecting her little hands in bright light, Dévonet knocked on Bénalep's door. The latter was reading, his large head attentive and seemingly bruised beneath a blue-tinted lamp.

"It's over, old man; it didn't take long." And he murmured the details.

The quadrangular face, with its Semitic features, approved. The body of Silenus bulged beneath the bedclothes. By way of conclusion, he proffered: "Ségétan's organic potential attracted women and death."

At that moment, Dévonet remembered that Silenus, in the Villa of the Mysteries, had made use of his wife, much as Ségétan had of Donabella. Nevertheless, he wept for his friend and rejoiced in the murder of Hatchinon. Everything down here is a matter of viewpoint.

Alone in her chamber, a widow before the wedding, Tullie was pensive, slowly taking off her clothes, still damp from the tragic pool.

She reviewed the entire sequence of events, since the automobile accident that had liberated her from Père Calvat and thrown her into the arms of the dead demigod. The extraordinary logic of things struck her. The forces above human beings, which weigh upon them, are inexorable. Their connections are subtle.

Suddenly, she perceived in the full-length mirror, with her meditative silhouette, the grave, inflexible, expert face of the priestess of Dyonisos who presides over the initiation of the neophyte....

ABOUT THE TRANSLATOR

BRIAN STABLEFORD has translated more than a hundred volumes of French prose into English. His principal interests are the French Romantic Movement and its Decadent/Symbolist aftermath, with particular reference to the evolution of the *conte cruel*, and the evolution of the *roman scientifique* from its origins in the eighteen-century *conte philosophique* to the aftermath of the Great War of 1914-18.